T0037344

# Bird Spotting in a Small Town

## Also by Sophie Morton-Thomas

*Travel by Night*

# Bird Spotting in a Small Town

**SOPHIE MORTON-THOMAS**

VERVE BOOKS

First published in 2024 by VERVE Books,
an imprint of The Crime & Mystery Club Ltd,
Harpenden, UK

vervebooks.co.uk
@VERVE_Books

© Sophie Morton-Thomas, 2024

The right of Sophie Morton-Thomas to be identified as the author of
this work has been asserted in accordance with the Copyright,
Designs and Patents Act 1988.

All rights reserved. No part of this book may be reproduced, stored
in or introduced into a retrieval system, or transmitted, in any form
or by any means (electronic, mechanical, photocopying, recording or
otherwise) without the written permission of the publishers.

Any person who does any unauthorised act in relation to this publication
may be liable to criminal prosecution and civil claims for damages.

A CIP catalogue record for this book is available from the British Library.

This is a work of fiction. Names, characters, places, and incidents either are the
product of the author's imagination or are used fictitiously, and any
resemblance to actual persons, living or dead, businesses, companies,
events or locales is entirely coincidental.

ISBN
978-0-85730-853-5 (Paperback)
978-0-85730-854-2 (eBook)

2 4 6 8 10 9 7 5 3 1

Typeset in 11.2 on 13.75pt Garamond MT Pro
by Avocet Typeset, Bideford, Devon, EX39 2BP
Printed and bound in Great Britain by CPI Group (UK) Ltd, Croydon CR0 4YY

MIX
Paper | Supporting
responsible forestry
FSC® C171272

*To Jimbo, Tilly, Felix and Raffy (and Stewart!)*

# PROLOGUE

They'll know soon enough.

Everything was taken care of to ensure the best outcome. At first the idea was crazy, ludicrous, not thought out. I couldn't say it was the most razor-sharp of plans. It happened so quickly. I remember my breath, raggedy, sharp, as if something was trying to burst out of my lungs. I was losing my footing in the fast pace of it all, the almost-running. I couldn't really run with the weight in my hands. The wind from the sea was whipping at my face in a fury, telling me to slow down. But I couldn't. I had to listen to the other sounds; the calls of the gulls, saying it was the only way.

You've always got to listen to the birds.

# FRAN

## 3 January

The black-throated diver takes its chances; the crash and the slam of colour into the waves catches my eye once again, and I am diverted from my thoughts. He surfaces after a few seconds, prize in beak, turning, a flash of silver, worth embracing the ice-cold of the waves for. I recoil into the warmth of my fisherman's all-weather jacket, sleeves rolled due to the length. Dom won't mind that I've borrowed it.

Most of the caravans are empty, save for the bloke who stays now and then to escape his wife and kids. I lock the caravan door behind me, head along the narrow path to the next one. The guests are few and far between at this time of year, only the most hardened of holidaymakers risking their Christmases on the coast here. Most families stay away until at least April, once the ground has thawed a little. The second caravan I check, number thirty-one, has a door that sticks, and I swear as my fingers sear from the pain of trying the handle with too much enthusiasm. I poke my hooded head around the door. Still clean. Stepping into the caravan, I snoop around the living area, notice the carpet is looking a little threadbare. Rugs, we need to purchase rugs. We keep saying we will, and then we don't. Another thing to do. I step out of the unit and close the door behind me, wondering if I should go to check on my sister in number eleven. She's been here six months, now I think of it. It's late afternoon; the sun set a long time ago, leaving only a pinky-red swirl of a ghost in the sky, something that used to be.

*

Dom and Bruno are sitting in front of the television, feet up, shoes on. There are still swathes of tinsel in the highest corners of the room that we have not yet taken down. Christmas came and went in a tangle of doubt. I don't mind that the festivities are over. The occasion is stifling, too much pressure. I like this bit, just after New Year, the bit that many folks seem to wish away. I think of mentioning the bird to Dom but decide not to. We don't see them often around here, and the sighting was a rarity for me. I think about why we moved here, and why we purchased the caravan park when we had barely even talked about the notion before. I know why I wanted to move here. The birds. Of course, the birds. I don't think I've said this to my husband properly before. My ten-year-old shows more interest in my ornithology obsession than Dom does, though this might just be his age. He does tend to follow in whatever his dad thinks, usually, so perhaps it won't be long until his interest dwindles. I walk through to the kitchen, gather up the dirty plates on the side, and my mind slips to Ros again.

Later, we walk to the beach. We follow the trail that leads from the house, past the caravan site and down along the side of the church. The last wisps of pink are long gone from the sky, our journey lit by the streetlamps on the one main road which runs alongside the coast. Dom holds my hand on one side, Bruno on the other. I can feel a rush of warmth inside me, not felt for a while. Bruno is jigging up and down from the cold, or it could be the excitement of a late evening stroll. He is chattering away about his return to school, his keenness making me smile down into the scarf which is double-rolled around my neck. I glance at Dom to see if he is enjoying the moment, but his eyes are further up the road, not looking at either of us, red brows knitted. Sooner or later, I know Bruno will mention Sadie, ask the questions, but he doesn't. I am holding my breath, but he doesn't.

The lights beam from our left-hand side, my child straining to drag me onto the sand.

*

Ellis has been back a few weeks now. I feel for him. I like his obvious interest-bordering-on-obsession for his daughter. I find myself pacing around the door of their caravan in the cold morning mist, debating whether to knock. It's still early. I hear the pigeons in the nearby tree, wonder why we get just as many of these as gulls here. I need to see if Ros is alright. There's no movement in the van even several moments after I've hammered at the door with my fist. Eventually, there is a face poking at me through the yellowed net curtain of the window where the second bedroom is. Sadie. I grin, and she smiles back, slowly at first, sleep still covering her at the edges. The door of the van rattles, and she is standing there, all of her eleven years.

'Mum's not up yet,' she states. I smile again, but she seems to be intent on beginning to close the door.

'Wait, Sadie,' I say, my hand holding the door still. 'Is your dad around?'

She thinks for a moment, looks upwards, shakes her head. 'He went out last night. Don't know if he's back.'

'Can you check?'

She leaves the doorway, heads towards the bedrooms. I hear a door open and close. She is back in front of me, shaking her head again, narrowing her eyes slightly.

'OK,' I say. The doubt is like an itch. 'No worries. Just tell your mum I popped by.'

As I turn to leave, I hear Ros's slight voice in my ear. 'Fran.'

She is pale, and I am almost afraid to look her way. Dark bags surround her slitty eyes. A rush of concern heats up my veins.

'You knocked?'

I make myself look at her. 'I was checking you were OK. That's all.'

She squints at me slightly. 'I'm fine. You know that.' Her face breaks into a smile, cautious at first.

'Yep.' I don't know what else to say. I just need to know that she is alright. 'Ellis around?'

11

Her shoulders hunch up, a casual shrug. 'No. He's out.'

'Dad'll be back soon.' Sadie is still in the doorway. She thinks she is a part of the conversation between me and her mother.

'Late night somewhere?' I try, looking at my sister.

Ros straightens herself up, pushes hair from her eyes. She might have had two hours of sleep. 'Look, Fran, I know you mean well, but you did say you were going to stop worrying.' She pauses. 'He's not a bad guy, you know. And we're very grateful, what with you letting us stay here.'

I am nodding. I'm not looking for appreciation. I know he's not a bad guy. He's one of the good ones.

'I'll leave you be.' Ros closes the door without a proper goodbye, and I wonder if she will be able to get any more sleep this morning. Mum and Dad would have been so sad to see her like this. I try not to consider it further. Sadie's face appears again at the window, not smiling. She pulls the netting across.

I walk back towards our cottage, the sun pushing its way through the clouds, light on dark.

*

Dom is on his way to work, first day back, rushing through the door, mock-surprise on his face when he sees me on our path. He pauses, and I stop walking too. I wonder whether I should plant a kiss on his cheek, but I don't, and continue my walk to the door.

'Bye, Fran,' he says from behind me.

'Yeah, bye,' I say. Again, I think of leaning in for a hug of some sort. Instead, I bend down, untie my shoelaces.

He is close to me, still. I can feel the warmth from his body. 'Bruno doesn't start back at school today, does he?'

I look up from my crouched position on the floor.

'It's tomorrow, isn't it?' he says, before I get a chance to speak. 'He's so excited.'

'Yup,' I agree.

12

Once I am inside the cottage, I check Bruno is alright in the living room and begin the rounds of laundry from my sister's caravan and the man in number thirty-one. It's a thankless task, makes my arms ache, hanging it all out to dry in our spare room. I prefer to fold the dry stuff. Downstairs, I can hear Bruno's game, cars revving. Dom is right, he cannot wait to be back at school. I know why. The children have a new teacher, and besides, Sadie has promised since before Christmas that she will sit next to him in class from now on. I don't think he has a crush on her, that would be a little strange considering their connection. I let myself collapse on the sofa, try to get my breath back. I'm not fit like I used to be. And certainly nothing like Ros, with her sunrise runs. At the same moment, Bruno stands, wanders into the hallway. I pull myself back off the chair and tiptoe behind him, hoping my knees don't click like they usually do. I know he can't hear me. He's staring out of the little window beside the front door. It's like he's waiting for her. Watching, and waiting.

# TAD

They say I'm the most trusting of all of us. I don't know why, seeing as I'm the oldest. Usually, the oldest from our type of family takes the least shit, has seen and known too much to be bothered with hassle. I'm not sure how much of that applies to me. I have one daughter, and a wife buried in the ground over at the Common. Wasn't going to have a council funeral, nope. We did it ourselves. There was grieving for a long time.

My family are my friends, yes, but I tend to make friends with the rest of the world too. If my brother is going to find a bird or two and cook them, he'll offer some to us, or I'm happy to just go and buy one at the local shop. We do use the shops, we have bank cards, bank accounts.

We were up at the Common for almost a year, now we're moving on. You might think we were sent packing because of mess, or noise, or dogs. We've a couple of collies, and a mongrel. Used to have the two horses, the cobs. But it isn't because of any of that. We're in a bit of a rush, see. Plus, there are new job opportunities by the coast; at least one of the younger lot already has a job secured. I would have been happy to stay, but I went along with what most of the others wanted.

So, we're on the move again, from our temporary stop, this family of ours. The land is owned by the great God in the sky, and by nobody else. *Grass, soil, wind and rain, it's all the same.* Well, that's what my folks used to say. Me, I'm just happy to get somewhere to park myself for a few nights, somewhere to lay my head. Anything more than that is just a bonus.

# FRAN

## 5 January

The school is a dark-stoned Victorian building, standing proud, stark against the morning light. Under the grime of the build-up of sea scum on its walls glints a hint of better days. The wind from the sea bears down on us, making us bow our heads, eyes to the ground.

Bruno, young for his age, is hopping around on the balls of his feet, not letting the bitter wind destroy his mood. He stops biting down on his chapped lips to cry, 'She's here! She's here!'

I glance up and nod at my sister, gloves being pulled on, a quick check of her watch. She manages a smile that does not meet her eyes. Sadie is looking beyond me, oblivious to Bruno's excitement.

'Say hi, Sadie,' says my sister.

Sadie looks up at me, blinks. 'Hi.'

Ros laughs, nudges her daughter. 'I did mean say hi to Bruno.'

Bruno rushes over to her side, and her face breaks into a smile for the first time. Sadie's a real beauty when she's happy.

'Everything alright?' My sister's words brush against the side of me.

I glance up, hands stuffed deep into my pockets. The evening walk to the beach flashes into my mind. The lights at the side of the road, their need to not be obvious, my husband's slight interest in whatever my topic of conversation was. Just before Christmas, we had been close. 'Yup.'

Ros is moving closer to me, eyes not so tired now. 'You know, everything is good. He's fine. He seems like a different person now.'

I know I am blinking lots, batting away her words. She is talking about her own partner, not mine. Ros is a tower next to me, tall yet wavering. She's always reminded me of a reed, yielding to the force of the wind. I've always been the stronger one. I've had to be, I'm the eldest. Ros, she's softer. Kinder. Our dad used to describe her as being like *butter*: easy to cut into. I'm still not really looking at her, the wind whisking around my uncovered ears, heat burning. 'Well, we just want you to be happy.'

It seems like she is smiling genuinely now. 'I know. Thank you. And we are absolutely fine. I'll get some work in the next few weeks. I'll give you some money, obviously. You're not my cash cow.'

We watch in unison as the teachers come out of the building to greet their students back. An unknown woman, red hair with substantial grey at the roots, scraped back into a bun, stands at the front of Bruno and Sadie's line. She must be early forties, with spindly pencil legs in high black platform heels, matching black tights. I can see two large and overpowering rings on her fingers but glance away as I realise I am staring. Bruno turns to me, his eyes alight, as he mouths, *This is our new teacher*. Ros risks a look at me and raises an eyebrow. I think the children had all been expecting a young lady, straight from university. It doesn't bother me. I like the fierceness of her face, the drawn expression, like she won't take crap from anyone, although perhaps she is just scowling at the strength of the perishing wind. I find myself looking towards my niece, trying to take in what she may be thinking.

'Bit of a punky old battleaxe, no?' Ros says into my ear. The wind is whipping around us so dramatically that I pretend not to hear her words. I try not to laugh at them either.

'If she takes a dislike to Sadie, I think Ellis will be having words.'

I notice the teacher is now smiling at the class, but there's something else there; fear, nerves, who knows. I feel sorry for the poor woman, thirty pairs of eyes gunning her down in the first few minutes of her appearance. And that's not even the kids. I try not to think of Ellis, quick off the mark, straight through the school gates in an attempt to defend his child. The thought makes me shiver a little, in perhaps an almost delightful way. It's my liking of his protectiveness towards her. Sadie'll be at secondary school in a few months' time, she'll need to be let go of by then. My own child will never seem ready for such a leap.

*

Later, at school pick-up, it is Ellis who appears. I thought he would be at work, but perhaps that particular job ran dry. I don't ask. He nods at me, almost a smile. 'You were asking after me the other day?'

I had forgotten the sound of his gruff voice. *Gravel throat*, that's how Dom had described him when they first encountered each other. Sometimes I struggle to even make out what he is saying. It's not an unpleasant voice, just so deep.

Finding myself faltering, I nod, frantically trying to articulate the words I need to say. 'I was checking that all was well. With the three of you.'

I wish I hadn't got to the school so early. It's only 3.06 pm. School doesn't break until 3.15 pm, and even then, the kids have to be standing behind their chairs in perfect silence before they are allowed out. Bruno is often the last, due to his inability to commit to being deathly quiet.

'Well, we are just fine. And thanks for paying for my programme. You know I'm grateful; we'll pay you back.' He looks sheepish, blinks with his long, dark lashes. My sister used to joke that it always looked as though he was wearing eye makeup. I think again about what a decent man he is, try not to compare him to my husband. My husband whom I want to be with, the man who has stood by me since our early twenties.

I hope my smile looks genuine.

'Ros and me, we just need time alone, with Sadie. You know, as a family.'

It's almost a word-for-word repeat of what my sister had said to me.

He chats to me about his daughter, how bright she has been over the Christmas period, how she has been missing Bruno. I don't mention that Dom and I are beginning to think it would be a good idea for the two children to take a break from each other. I *think* it will be a joint decision between the two of us. Perhaps Dom is pushing this idea a little more than I would like. Sometimes I imagine their little family will appear at our door like they did back in October, November, probably sick of the four walls of their caravan and desperate to enjoy the heat and space of our cottage. Dom was never that bothered, answering the door with a gruff 'hi', leaving the door open for me to speak to them. I suppose he's become friendlier with them of late. He is trying, I know that. Back then, I wanted to invite them in, offer food, and they would have never said no. It's at times like these I wish that Mum and Dad were still around. No time for moping. It's been six years since they passed away, three months apart.

Sadie comes running out and bundles her father; he spins dramatically and is pulling on her plaits.

'Take the plaits out now, Dad!' she squeals, pulling at the elastic bands at the end. The ribbons her mum must have tied are now flapping on the ground of the playground, abandoned. 'I'm too old for plaits!' I wonder why she has only decided this now, and not earlier in the day.

I can't see Bruno, but watch the other kids file out one by one. He is towards the back, shoes dragging, bag dragging. He catches my eye and smiles. It's not a big smile.

# TAD

It's always best to start moving before the sun is up. Miss most of the traffic that way, although it does make the day feel particularly long. It's winter, so that means starting later than we would have to in the summer months. The others seem to mind more than I do. I've been doing it most of my life, moving. Some of the youngsters, they've got more used to staying put for a few months each time. Some of them would like to be properly settled. They like the security, they like the schools. They make other friends at the school gates, other women. Some of them talk about getting houses, staying put. It's up to them; I wouldn't hold a grudge. But within our family, there is a normality, a sense of being settled, as if we aren't people who move around. We are just the same as you.

I like the feeling of adventure, seeing where we end up. I think I'm the only one. Perhaps I am nostalgic about it; following a tip-off from another family, seeing it through. I know my sisters, my cousins, some of them want to be more like the communities of the towns and cities around us. Their arms stretch out further than they used to. They will allow everyone in. It's not a bad thing.

You may be wondering why we're on the move this time. The main thing is, see, someone got himself into a little bit of trouble at the last place. Not just any old trouble; this was big stuff. My brother, Charlie, he did something. We were so disappointed. It made us look cheap, like people who don't care. But we do. Part of me wanted to leave him behind, to drum home to him that this is not how we function. But I couldn't. Not Charlie.

They won't find us where we're settling this time. Other side of the country, for a start. We've not settled on a proper coast before. The sea will be nice. Great for the kids. Some of the birds are beautiful down there, I've heard – not that I'd be one to snatch them, mind. I just like to watch them, marvel at their ripe colours and their movements. I love to watch their sharp little head turns, as if they think someone always has their eye on them. Some people are more into the valuable birds, the rarer ones. Charlie is more into the stuff that I mean, Charlie is into all birds. He especially loves the ones that hunt, hover over their prey, that kind of thing.

# FRAN

## 11 January

I am early to the beach this morning, hood up, the threat of the gulls imminent as they begin to circle above my head. Their screeching unbearable, they eye me as I interrupt their hunting time, although every hour of the day is hunting time for them. They are mostly herring gulls, but I think I can see a great black-backed gull somewhere among the masses. They don't usually hunt alone, or with other breeds of gull, so today is different. My fingers are already red raw under my puny Christmas-present gloves, I can feel it, but it doesn't prevent me wandering closer to the part of the beach that is met by the open fields that seem to be owned by nobody. I'm preparing to locate any of the breeds I have been spending the past few weeks searching for, my Polaroid camera, my binoculars, ready. There's one in particular that I'd like to see. I've heard it's already been spotted in Sheringham, just a couple of miles away.

The sun is barely up, just a muted glow of promise. I can't see the cottage from where I am crouching, nor even the side of the old church, whose yard of concrete crosses and tombstones dominates the hilly area that slopes down towards the beach. I wonder if the macabre view from one side of the caravan park ever puts off our guests, but I'm yet to hear anyone complain. My sight is drawn to movement in the rushes that separate the fields from the dunes of the beach. I can't make it out at first but let myself exhale when I realise it is merely our cat, Fergus. He doesn't usually make his way down here to the sand; the wind plays with his long hair, blows it the wrong way. He's hunting; a mouse, I think, perhaps a crab. A stab of emotion for our elderly cat is soon replaced with frustration that he is succeeding in scaring away the beloved birds of mine. I place the binoculars that my husband lovingly mocks to my eyes, surveying the land around, looking for movement. I am the only person here. You would think there are a hundred eyes on me. A quick glance around tells me there is nobody watching; still, my gut is telling me otherwise. Silhouettes of darkened faces at the windows of the caravans stare at me with disdain, yet when I turn my head towards the park, I see only the glinting glass panes, no faces. Light glows from the reluctant sun, fractured into a thousand pieces.

The gulls are no longer circling above, but there's enough of a heavy feeling within me which insists I put down my binoculars, shove my camera into my rucksack and head back across the beach. It's started spitting with rain anyway. Maybe today is not the day to find the little tern.

*

'And so she said to Ms McConnell that she wished it was still Christmas because she hates being back at school!' Bruno is tripping on his own words, can't get them out quickly enough. 'She says she misses our old teacher!'

I raise my eyebrow at Dom, who is concentrating on his own dinner, but catches my eye, smiles.

'Then Ms McConnell said, "If you don't want to be in my class, it can be arranged that you are moved to another!"' He is laughing, but there is shock stretched over his small eager face, eyes blinking fast as he waits for my response.

'I can't believe Sadie would be so rude so quickly to the new teacher.' It is Dom speaking. I can see the food going around in his mouth. I know Bruno was expecting slightly more of a reaction, but I don't want to add more. She's just a little girl, an unsettled child, my niece. My feet are crossed tightly under the table. I uncross them, try to relax. For some reason, I can't. Sometimes I wish Dom could be a little warmer with how he words things, how he speaks to Bruno.

'She can't keep going around talking to staff like that,' he says, looking at Bruno. He ruffles his hair. I often wonder if Bruno will follow Sadie's lead. Sure, he traipses after her like a lapdog at times, but it's good for him to have a close friend. There don't seem to be any other friends.

'Do you think she's gonna get it when she gets home?'

I shake my head. 'I doubt it. If anything, her dad will be straight up the school. You know how protective he is.' We will have to wait until tomorrow to hear if Ros or Ellis have complained. I could call her, ask how today went. But I know what she'll say. *Everything's fine*. But I worry. I don't want them to get a reputation at the school as being whingers. Perhaps Sadie *is* being hard work in class. Sometimes it feels like she's hiding something, something that her parents don't see. That could just be me. It's often just the way she looks at me with such *knowing* Or something similar to that. Like she can see right through me.

'She never gets told off,' says Bruno, sadly. 'And I get shouted at for nothing.'

I roll my eyes, hoping it looks comical, reach over to pat his leg. 'You're a good boy. And we don't *shout* at you!'

Dom is nodding, bringing his knife and fork together. He has wolfed down the meal. He is looking around for something else.

*

At the school the next morning, both Ros and Ellis are there, having just waved Sadie off into her line. Bruno is already there, at the very front. I can feel the pair of them trudging towards me.

Ellis is first to speak, clearing the gravel from his throat before he opens his mouth. 'New teacher seems to be a complete dragon, then. Already got it in for Sadie.' He stops, eyes not on me. 'She sounded so decent, on the first couple of days back; Sadie took a liking to her.'

I swallow down, not sure what to say. 'Ah, I think you just need to give her a bit more of a chance, perhaps. She'll be back in Sadie's good books in no time.'

My sister is there at my hip, not saying anything, but I can feel the weight of her looking at me. I want to hug her, to turn and ask if I can do anything, but my mouth feels so dry, full of cardboard, sawdust.

They are standing in the way I need to walk; Ellis has his hands on his hips. The position looks so out of place on him, in his tracksuit. Sometimes he will dress up in his special tweed jacket for a complaint to the school. It doesn't suit him. He looks like the second-home owners over in Wells-next-the-Sea, with their red trousers, their slip-on loafers. 'So we're having a word tonight, with the teacher,' says Ellis.

'That's good,' I pipe up. I watch the teacher come out to greet her class, glasses pushed up on top of her head. She's wearing a coat today, a sheepskin. Her hair is more of a dyed pink now. A pink pineapple. The grey has gone. I see the other parents take in the new shade of hair at the same time as her stripy tights. I like them, personally. Pink, white and green stripes. Reminds me of my old Strawberry Shortcake doll. And my days in Brighton, for a split second. You don't usually see such individuality here, in our little coastal village in Norfolk. Everyone is too scared to be different. We are just cardboard cutouts of each other, stiffened, starched, two-dimensional.

I am walking now, curling up my toes in my boots that don't quite fit, trying to hold on to them as I attempt to speed-walk.

'You in a great rush?' asks Ros. She is panting to keep up.

'Kind of,' I say.

She catches up with me. 'Listen, Fran, I know you worry about me and money and everything, but…' She is pausing, catching her breath. 'We are just fine.' She gives a little laugh, and I find myself laughing too. I want to rest my head on her shoulder for a second, but brush the idea away, fearing rejection for some reason.

24

Ellis is further behind, and my sister ceases to chase me, waits for him. He is saying things, calling things out to her, yet the words are tossed and carried away by the squalling wind, useless.

# TAD

The wheels can get stuck in the mud occasionally in these winters, or frozen in, but it doesn't happen a lot. A few shoves and we'll be there. They're hardly the huge wooden wagon wheels that you used to see in the States, back in the day. Our trailers are glorified campervans for a start, and not the traditional ones from the sixties either – those ones with big white flowers plastered to the outsides. Ours are larger, more homely, have proper rooms, proper front doors and windows. The kids stay inside, peering out.

You might expect us to lead a very traditional way of life here, and that there are great divides between the men and the women. It's not true. Every one of us pitches in and does our fair share, it depends on the person. Some of us are lazier than others, but we try to encourage the children to help. It's good to see them learning tricks so young. I don't know if kids in brick-and-mortar houses do enough, by the sounds of things. Some of the couples here were married at sixteen, eighteen. That happens a fair bit for us lot, but then some of us don't marry at all. It doesn't matter. There is no expectation. You don't have to be wed to be of value.

It gets lonely for me sometimes, knowing some of the other men have wives and I'm alone, but to be fair, I'm never *really* alone. There are so many of us I have almost lost count. And that's what you need. I can't imagine living in a proper house all alone, just me and my daughter. Besides, Jade needs different company, not just her old dad. We had her when we thought we could never have kids. The only couple in the group with no children at the time. Still, she was a right surprise when she came along. We didn't even know anything till my wife was over six months gone. A baby born to a *geriatric couple*, they said. We only saw a doctor a few times before the birth; they were concerned that my wife was *too old*, that something would be *wrong* with the baby. I'm still not sure if they were right.

We should be at our new stopping place long before nightfall. Took too long a rest in the middle, kids were wanting to run about a bit. There was a huge car park that could accommodate all of us. Within the hour, we were moving again, some traffic to slow us down, but that's nothing.

# FRAN

## 19 January

The sea is calm today, mirroring my mood. I am walking as the water laps rings around my ankles. I know I look a little crazy, no shoes or socks in January. It's the best way to really wake yourself up, feeling the ice of the sea on your bare skin. Dom often laughs when he sees me doing this, it makes him squirm, his hands pushed down into his jeans pockets. It is mid-morning, Bruno already dropped off at the school. I'm trying to convince myself that I didn't take him ten minutes earlier than usual, just so I could get to the beach earlier for the birds. That would be ridiculous. My binoculars are in my bag, but I'm not sure if I'll be using them today. I did invite Dom to come for a walk; he's not at his office but working from home. He declined the offer. I'm not too surprised. He's not really a man of the outdoors.

I continue to walk for a while, until I can't feel my feet, and wander from the water to sit on the sand, towel ready in my bag. Drying my feet, I cast my eye over to the caravan Ros and Ellis are staying in. I don't mind that they don't pay, not really. I can see the side of the caravan, watch the door, ready to observe whether Ellis is heading off to a job or not. It was strange that he was there for pick-up at the school yesterday. I decide, once I have fumbled about putting my socks and trainers back on, to head towards the caravan park. I just need to know that Ros is OK. And Sadie.

It's uphill towards the dunes which separate the beach from the field the vans are arranged in, and the gradient almost always catches me by surprise. I am quite out of breath by the time I reach the beach entrance to the park; I hold on to the fence, half bent over, trying to catch my breath. I'm a little overweight, but if you saw my sister, you would think she never eats. Now that I think of it, Sadie herself looks a little underweight. There's a stab of concern hitting my insides, pink growing into red. *She's just a little girl.*

I open the gate to the caravan park, wander towards number eleven. For some reason, I am a little nervous. My heart is pounding faster than usual, but I'm putting that down to my stint of exercise across the dunes. I barely walk uphill anywhere. As I knock at the door, again, there is no response. I try hammering harder. I can see the man in caravan thirty-one shift his curtain to one side, getting a good look at me. I feel like telling him to return to his wife and kids, that they probably miss him, that his wife won't know what the hell to tell the children about where their dad is.

There's still no reply at Ros's door so I try the handle. It shifts with ease, and the door swings open with more compliance than I am expecting. There is nobody in the living area, and my first thought is what a complete wreck the place is. Food boxes and packaging on the table, not cleared away. I recognise one of the boxes as something I gave Ros weeks ago, now out of date, and there is a small, undeniable lump in my throat. I try calling her name, rather than walking straight into the biggest bedroom, but again, only silence follows my call. I try the smallest bedroom first – Sadie's. Her bed is empty and unmade, just some scant bedding on top, nothing thick enough to keep a little girl warm in the winter. I pace across the almost non-existent hallway to the other bedroom, also empty, with an unmade double bed. As I wander back to the living and kitchen area, I see a bottle in the bin. I push the flip-top lid inwards. A spirit bottle, glass, upside down on its head. There are beer cans too, crumpled, forced into carrier bags. I gulp down hard, tell myself it doesn't matter. It's too late, though, my niece has already been affected.

An eddy of wind catches at the back of my neck, and I turn to find the source of the cool air, eyes searching at the walls. The chill feels like a rodent travelling up my spine; I sense that something is wrong, pulling my scarf a little tighter around my neck. I try to ignore the heavy, pushing feeling in my gut. It doesn't take me long to find the source of the sharp air: the cardboard taped up to the window frame, covering where half of the glass pane should be. My heart is beginning to speed up as I consider why Ros wouldn't have informed me of the breakage. Light still streams in through the second pane, causing me to scrunch up my eyes a little in the brightness now I am so close. I run my finger around the length of brown tape that holds the cardboard in place, begin peeling it away, my heart not yet slowing down. As I pull down the temporary cover completely, I see the smashed glass, still spiky, serrated at the edges. I shudder at the thought of my fingers being sliced, find myself wondering why Ros didn't get the glass cleared away cleanly. I imagine her fighting with Ellis, perhaps a bottle being thrown at the wall when he'd had one too many. I shrug, can't imagine gentle Ellis losing his shit in this way. He is a drinker, yes, but not a violent one. I think of other reasons for the gaping hole in the glass. Nobody else is staying here at the park, apart from the lonely man, and I know my sister and Sadie acknowledge my rule, that *no ball games are allowed on site*. Perhaps it was not that something was thrown out, in a fit of rage, the climax of a fight between two people. Perhaps something was thrown in. Thrown from the outside. As I stare harder at the jagged outline of the glass, I can see a slight stain of something dark, burgundy, dried around the edges of the forked glass. It doesn't take a genius to work out that it is old blood.

I scuttle back to the cottage, lots of odds and ends to be getting on with. I can see my sister walking towards me, Sadie in tow. I realise with shame that all I can think about is going to look for my tern again.

'Sadie said she just saw you leaving our van. All OK?'

'I was checking you still had heat.'

'We do, thanks. You know I would let you know if we didn't. I'm not too proud to ask.' She gives the little laugh of hers that I like. It makes her sound so young. I wonder whether to ask her about the smashed window, but balk at the idea. *Not yet.*

'No worries.' If I were Dom, I would be asking when she was planning on getting a job. But I'm not my husband. Sometimes I think I should have become a nurse. Or a teacher, something like that. Something in the caring profession. But now I think of it, the last job I would want is having to lead the way for thirty little open hearts and minds. I can barely lead the way for myself or Bruno. Some days I can't find the right pair of socks to go with my boots. Sometimes my head feels so... woolly.

I lift my hand to wave, but they are already gone, walking away up the path, deep in conversation with each other. I tell myself to call the window repair company when I get home.

# TAD

We already knew the police were sniffing about, like I said. That's why we moved as soon as we could. Well, they would have been right to be checking us out. Charlie hasn't half got himself into some scrapes in his lifetime, but killing someone wasn't meant to be one of them. Until now. He's saying it was self-protection, but from a woman brandishing a hammer? Nah, they wouldn't be having that if they had managed to haul him into court. He would have gone down for life. I'm not sure the rest of us believed him either, our sisters especially. They stopped talking to him for a while, kept him away from the kids too. Can't say I blame them. I kept my distance for a while too. He did his disappearing act, came back after a few weeks. He knew we wouldn't move without him. He never did talk about what happened. I think she was some kind of one-night stand; he did it when he was inebriated, or something like that. I didn't really listen to what he had to say.

So, that was the reason we left before light. And the reason I didn't like us stopping halfway. The others don't seem to worry like I do. They were letting the kids run about, being loud. I became paranoid, thought it made our brother's crime seem so obvious. I'm sure I saw people looking over, thinking we were something of a sight. It's true, one or two of our lot think they are above the law, but we're not. Really, we're not.

# FRAN

## 24 January

I don't know how Ellis's complaint to the school went. All I do know is that he is there every morning and afternoon to drop off and pick up his daughter, his face becoming more stretched with concern each day, paper pulled across a trestle table, ready for pasting. I want to comfort him, but from what, I'm not sure.

I watch the new teacher come out to greet her new class each day, a different outfit most mornings, but more often than not sporting the black platform shoes that make her at least four inches taller than anyone else. Bruno tells me she is quite the taskmaster. I know, deep down, that he likes this. He likes routine and he likes boundaries. Sadie, on the other hand, does not. Bruno tells me how she tries to mute Ms McConnell's requests, pretends not to hear her. Fitting with what Ellis said, Bruno tells me Sadie and Ms McConnell had started off on a good footing, were often having a little conversation between themselves, hushed voices at the front of the class. That seems to have petered out now. He tells me Sadie instead chooses to stand by the window, staring out. There's not much to look at, just the expanse of grey concrete that surrounds the school like a moat. You can't see the shore from the school, and you can't see the birds. Ms McConnell turns a blind eye to Sadie's mysteriousness, so it seems. But Bruno says that he gets on well with his new teacher, and she seems to like him. Dom and I are pleased with this news; I can tell my husband is proud as he listens to his son each day at dinner. A lot of the time he too is gazing out of the window, or concentrating on his *Financial Times*, yet I see him take in every word Bruno has said. Sometimes I suspect they may speak a secret language with each other, when I'm in another room folding laundry, ironing sheets, just a little out of earshot.

\*

Today could be the day. There isn't too much wind, the rain has kept away. Spotting a little tern would make my week. It would make my year. I don't always have as much time during the day as others seem to assume. I have to take these snippets of time with open arms. This is my hobby. Dom seems to like to think of me as constantly cleaning and preparing for the summer's guests. He thinks I'm just there to do the caravans, to look after our son, and it's true. But I need a little something for myself too.

I am treading with care down to the rushes. I'm going to have to do the classic twitcher thing: squat behind the reeds and tall grasses. I've yet to see this bird, and the impatience is beginning to gnaw away at my insides. I am looking for a yellow beak, black tip, listening out for its chattering noise; I've read it's a real *chatterer*. I am closing my ears to the sound of the merciless wind, calm only seconds ago, yet now suddenly at its most sharp, blowing in great gusts around my half-covered ears. I even have the proper bird spotter fingerless gloves. I promised Bruno I would wear them. Perhaps, if I catch a glimpse of the tern, Bruno can accompany me to the beach after school today. I've seen the common tern so many times, and occasionally my heart has leapt as I realise, with dismay, that it is not its smaller relative. The little tern. I'm more adept at spotting the common variety; the same beak, the slightly larger body. I have been squatting in these reeds for twenty, thirty minutes now, my knees beginning to sear with heat, my bottom damp.

As the numbness sets in, I am cursing myself. It is January. Of course. Terns usually don't appear until the spring, March at the earliest. They were lucky in Sheringham, spotting one so early. I doubt I will. I'm ahead of myself. Because I have spent so long preparing the vans for the upcoming months, I am already in spring in my mind. Frustrated at myself, I kick out at the sand, then laugh, slightly hysterically, glancing around to make sure nobody has witnessed my previous moments. I am rewarded with the sand blowing back into my face in gusts, sticking to my damp lashes and making blinking impossible. My gloves are pulled off and thrown into the sand, and I kick at them too. Stupid gloves that don't even cover my fingers properly. It's the hope I build up which then crashes into disappointment that I can't cope with. I pull at my hair as it whips about my face, sticks to my lips, not knowing what to do with myself for a moment. Hands freezing, I put them under my bottom and sit for a while, nudging at the sand with my toe. The dampness of my behind only makes my fingers colder. There are other parts of the beach where there is more shingle, and I wish I had decided to base myself on one of them this morning. Different types of birds on different parts of the shoreline. I'm so sick of the gulls, picking their way through the other birds' meals, taking over the beaches. The smaller ones don't stand a chance. I haven't seen a guillemot for weeks, let alone taken the chance to hike up the Norfolk cliffs in the not so far distance to see where they may build their nests. I decide immediately that it's time to leave the beach. For once, I am happy to do so, as tiny droplets of rain begin to attack me, making a frizz appear in the hair I can see wafting around in front of my eyes. As I pace up the dunes and head towards the cottage, a flash of red delivers itself past my eyes; stunning, tiny, a firework flashing by in a horizontal stripe. The bullfinch, a rare visitor to our village coast in the winter months. Perhaps this morning has not been such a waste after all.

*

There is a knocking at our door that afternoon. I pull the door open, praying silently that it's not someone trying to sell me something. It is Sadie, standing there with no smile, mascara glinting precociously on her blonde lashes. She is a child dressing as an adult. It makes my heart stop for a moment. 'Hi Fran… Bruno there?'

I don't know when she dropped the *Auntie* part from my name.

'He is,' I state, but I don't add any more. I kind of just wanted it to be the three of us tonight.

'Can I see him, please?'

One of her trainers is ripped at the toe, and I wonder about the rain and sleet getting in. The strings in my heart tighten. I feel a stab of guilt for perceiving her as anything other than a child who needs a little more love. Perhaps I can buy her some new shoes. 'Sure.'

I turn to call Bruno, but he has already appeared at my hip, coat pulled on, mucky trainers in his hand.

'Mum, we're just going for a walk.'

I don't want him to go, but he is nearly eleven, and there's not much that they can get up to. I bend to give him a kiss, but he is already gone with Sadie, who's stomping her way ahead of him. I think of running after them, but somehow my feet remain stuck to the floor.

*

When they return, Bruno is full of excitement. He babbles for a while to Sadie, who is fixing her eyes on our cat, saying nothing, stroking Fergus over and over along his back. Bruno is talking about caravans, nothing new there, a speed to his chatter which almost alarms me. For a while, I continue with tidying up the living room, plumping deflated cushions and throwing sweet wrappers into the bin. There are sheets to be folded, and I pace to the utility room to locate them. The smell of the clean linen renders me dumb for a moment, then I make my return to the living room. I hear Bruno mention dogs – a collie, a pug, and a man who shoos him away. He has my attention at this, and I turn to look at him on the old armchair in our living room as I fold the sheets. Sadie is spread out on the sofa nearest to me, now not looking in my direction. Her feet in socks appear so tiny.

'A man *shooed* you away? From where?'

My son rolls his eyes. 'Mum! I've just been telling you! The new caravans.'

It takes me a moment to digest. For a split second, I think someone may have gifted us with some new vans, perhaps Dom, in a rare moment of generosity. But then I realise what he must be talking about.

'Sadie, I think your mum will actually want you home by now, if you don't mind. Bruno, stay here while I call your dad down.'

I watch my niece pull on her trainers which she had yanked off by the heel only minutes earlier, the hole at the toe straining under the pressure.

*

There are eleven or twelve of them, placed beautifully at right angles to each other. The people must be huddled inside each van, or elsewhere, because even though it is becoming quite dark now, I cannot see a soul, no lights on anywhere. There are a couple of dogs tied up outside one of the vans. I choose to loosen the lead of one dog from the limp tree it is attached to, leave the other on its tight lead temporarily, pace my way to the door of the caravan beside the tree. The man who answers the door is young, mid-twenties. He looks me up and down briefly. 'Yup?'

I don't know how to respond to this, look to the dog. 'Ah, hello. How are you? Settled in OK? I was just wondering if you were going to be staying here for long?'

The man stares at me, binbag in hand. It looks as though he was going to take it outside. I glance around for a bin.

He straightens in the doorway. 'Always nice to meet the locals.'

I don't say anything, but I look again towards the dogs, then back at him in what I hope is a friendly manner.

'I own the caravan park in the next field.' It is an offering. 'Let me know if you need anything.' I wish I had worn a thicker coat. This gilet has my arms shivering so much it could appear that I am shaking.

He glances to my field, then back at me. 'Thanks. But you were just asking if we were planning on staying here long?'

Embarrassment skitters under my skin; fresh ants burrowing. 'Yes, well, while you're here I want you to feel welcome.' And I do, I really do.

He is laughing, looking around behind him. There's an air of awkwardness. 'Thanks! I don't know if you mean well by that or not!'

A young woman appears by his side, her made-up eyes looking me up and down fleetingly, just like the man had done only moments before. 'Who is it?' There's a baby on her hip, pink dress, pulling at her mother's earrings. For a moment, I want to grab her, squeeze the chubbiness of her legs. I fantasise about taking her back to my home.

He turns his head slightly, is muttering to the woman. She walks away a few steps, baby shifted to her other hip.

I hear them say something to each other, but I can't quite understand the words. The door is closed as the man says, 'Thanks anyway.' I suppose he was talking to me. The caravan windows of Fran's Holiday Vans stare at me, blank and square, as I cross the field and walk up the path towards home.

*

When I get inside, Dom is like a race dog held back behind a gate. 'Did you tell them that you would notify the police?'

I know he can feel my sigh before I've even released it. I don't say anything.

'They are trespassing. They scared our own child away, for God's sake!' His words are like bullets, trying to savage me. I manage to dodge each one.

'And we don't even know if it's legal for them to live there! We need to find out.'

Again, I don't respond. I am waiting for his next comment. Sure enough, it comes.

'You know who persuaded him to go and look at them, don't you?'

I close my mouth firmly. I don't want this conversation.

'She needs to calm down. She's only eleven. Imagine just how bad she'll be by the time she's sixteen. We don't need her having that hold over our son.'

Dom has left his standing position by the kitchen sink, has wandered through to the living room. He knows I would rather talk about something else. And since when did he care so much about what's happening around us? He used to be so laidback about how other people lived their lives.

I follow him, carrying the damp dishcloth I had been holding. It's getting crumpled in my hand the tighter I grip. The damp is numbing my fingers. 'It's going to have an awful effect on Bruno if you try to make Sadie stay away.'

Now it's he who doesn't respond, just lets his body *floomp* down into the nearest armchair, drags his hand down over his face. I'm sure I hear a slight moan escape his body. 'I don't know what else to suggest!'

The conversation has ended. I am up the stairs before he has a chance to try and appease me, and I throw the dishcloth that's still balled in my fist on the bed.

# TAD

Jade would test anyone's patience, but I don't seem to lose it with her very often. You wouldn't know, at first, that she just doesn't speak. Not until you tried to have a conversation with her. I don't really notice it myself anymore. Back in the day, her mum would deal with her just fine. It was difficult when Marge died. I didn't know what to do. True, I sank into the bottle for a while, smoked my cigarettes, stopped working, stopping communicating. It was hard for Jade. Mum dead, dad nearly there. One of the lads, my youngest sister's fella, had to come to me in the night, shake me up a little, make me see sense. The next day, I saw a huge black-and-white bird swoop down next to our trailer, it was picking at pieces of a dead rabbit on the ground with real aggression. It stopped for a moment, stared straight at me. I knew then that everything was going to be OK. Those birds, those magpies, along with the wagtails I see, they mean joy. Charlie told me about the *good luck wagtail* years back, when he was a kid and I was already a man. Means you've landed in a good place. That's when I started noticing birds wherever we went. I like the really tiny ones. They're ornate, delicate. I think I might have said that already. Our kids like to tell the other children at the schools they attend about these birds. They often go to look for them together.

Well, anyway, I sobered up and then came to realise I was all Jade had. I see her in our new place, eyes wide, looking across the boundary of the field where we've parked up, looking towards the girl from the other side, much younger than her. The girl with the almost-white hair. Jade hasn't asked to go and meet the kids;

this blonde girl and her dark-haired male friend, but I know she's curious. We can mix with other people, and we do. It's not that. It's just that Jade wouldn't stand a chance anywhere else.

Today I should be cleaning my trailer, it's something I usually do once we've moved to a new stopping place. I like things to be spick and span, although I can't say the others here enjoy the same sort of standards. I'm glad I don't have a dog of my own; having to keep the thing away from my face, the licking, the kissing. I know the others love their animals, but I have to remind the youngsters *don't let them touch your faces*. Nothing we eat from should be touched by an animal, in my view. Same goes for our beds, our furniture. Charlie never sticks to this. Neither do some of the kids. They don't have to listen to me, anyway. When we had the horses, I had to discourage the kids from kissing them on the mouth. They always wanted to show them how much they loved them, everyone did. I just don't think it's hygienic. Some of the kids would ask why we only had black-and-white horses – they meant the cobs, brown-and-white animals. Charlie would tell them. *It's so they can't be nicked so easily. They're easy to spot this way. Other folk won't want to steal them.* I don't even know if any of this is true, or if he just made it up to keep the kids amused.

# FRAN

## 29 January

This afternoon, the school playground is freezing. Tiny wisps of white are falling, circling around me; not snow, wetter – sleet. I see the teacher is walking towards me, eye contact unwavering. I can feel myself wanting to look away, at the ground, anywhere but towards her. Bruno is lagging at her side, bag dragging.

'Bruno's mum?' she enquires.

She is younger than I had thought she was, now that she is close up. Her foundation is probably a couple of shades paler than it should be, but it suits the look. She is a fifties pin-up, matching twinset and pearls, her hair tucked up. I heard she's only here on a temporary placement, maternity cover. The children's usual teacher has a baby due imminently.

I notice Bruno is looking at me sheepishly.

'Yes,' I confirm. I am trying not to raise my eyebrows at my son. The sleet is making me blink too much.

'Well… we've had a little trouble today at school, haven't we, Bruno?'

He looks at me briefly, doe-eyed, then stares away across the playground. The wind is beginning to pull harder on all of us, attempting to assemble our bodies into some kind of grouping, a huddle.

'What has he done?'

'Bruno was caught trying to take something from my handbag. I don't take to these things too well.'

I am gulping down, pushing my chin into my scarf. I can see the other parents wandering away from the school, children in hand. A couple of them glance over. I can tell they're straining to hear what is being said. I've heard a few of them discussing the new teacher, whispers that I can never quite grip as the truth. One mother says she's from a school that had to be closed down, it was so bad. Another said that she isn't properly qualified, that they just took her on as she was the only one who applied for the job.

'Bruno?' My voice is wobbling a little.

He looks up at me finally. 'I didn't want to do it.'

I know what he is saying, and I glance at Ms McConnell to see if she understands. I am wondering if my son is willing his old teacher to come back.

'So why did you?' I try, returning to the conversation. 'Sadie?' is all I say to the teacher.

She turns her head towards me, almost in slow motion. The sleet is sticking to her eyelashes. The hair coiled up on her head makes me think of Medusa, with her head of snakes. A shudder runs up my arms, an adder's venom making its way to my heart.

Bruno stares down at his shoes, and I can see a slither of a tear begin to mark its way down his face. My maternal instincts kick in, and I gently shift him by his left arm, trying to edge our way towards the school gate. I see a flash of blonde a few yards away from us: Sadie, peering through her hand, shading her eyes from a few sudden sharp blades of sunlight. In this light, it looks like she is grinning at the teacher, teeth bared.

'Mrs Redlock?' tries the teacher, almost to my back as I turn away from her and her accusations. 'This is a serious matter. It's theft, and it's trespassing.'

'But nothing was stolen?'

'No,' she confirms. 'But it would have been, had I not appeared in time.'

'Well, then.' My voice is steady now, firm. 'No harm, no foul.' I sound idiotic, I know I do. But I can't help the protectiveness that's seizing me. I swear for a moment that I see the teacher turn her head and smile at Sadie, yet when I look over, Sadie's back is already turning, as she begins to make her way out of the playground.

The wind whisks us away from the multi-coloured woman and towards our path home, the gulls crying out in earnest to me, dropping accusations around me that I cannot hear.

\*

'You actually said... What?'

Dom is fuming, the vein in the side of his head pronounced. I swear his eyes look even more blue when he's raging. Red hair is stuck to his forehead in ringlets.

'I told her there was no problem. Nothing was actually stolen.'

My husband's eyes are narrowed. 'And that makes it OK?'

I don't bother to answer him. I knew he would be like this. We're standing in the kitchen. The air hangs with tension. I walk away, sit at the table, legs crossed under me, wondering briefly why he is home from work early on a Monday.

He sits down opposite me; his stare bores into me like a laser. Still, he says nothing.

'I suppose you are going to say this is all Sadie's fault now, are you?' My voice has a slight tremor.

Rubber scuffs on the tiled floor, Bruno enters the kitchen, glances up at the pair of us, tries to leave immediately. Dom grabs him gently by the arm.

'Dad! What?'

'You know what,' says Dom, and motions for him to sit with us at the table.

Bruno sighs dramatically, pulls out one of the wooden chairs. He shoves something into the back pocket of his school trousers.

'Tell me what happened today.'

Bruno looks up at me, blinks, waiting for me to take over. I don't. I can hear the sound of the kettle, just about to begin its invasive whistling. I don't know why I don't just buy a more modern one, rather than put up with this wretched sound every few hours.

'Well… you know what happened. Mum has probably told you.'

'Don't be rude.'

'Well, Sadie told me to take the lipstick out of Ms McConnell's bag.'

I am sighing. Dom will be thrilled that Sadie has been blamed here. I try to bat away thoughts of why she might have wanted Bruno to get into trouble. On the way home from school, Bruno had refused to speak. I talked to him about the birds. Bullfinch, chaffinch, same tree. How I saw both breeds this morning just on the walk back from the school. An arrogant-looking jay had made its way towards our cottage, no doubt scavenging for the next bit of discarded sandwich from our outside bin. Usually, Bruno would be excited about such a sighting so close to home, but today his eyes remained on the ground, occasionally looking behind us. I'm wondering if he had been looking out for Sadie. I don't mention the stolen lipstick again.

*

We are at the beach, the two of us. Dom didn't push the Ms McConnell matter too much more, so I left the house with Bruno to show him the surprise in the trees at the edge of the woods, fifty yards along the beach from where we would usually wait for the birds. I gently tread the path to the spot, one hand over Bruno's eyes. He slows his walking, comes to a halt.

'Open them!'

He takes a moment, then his eyes pop open. I can see from his gaze that he is not disappointed.

'You got the hide!'

I am nodding, failing to minimise my joy. 'Come inside!'

I pull open the door, stiff from being unused, and Bruno follows me in. His eyes are everywhere.

'You can see the seabirds on the coast's edge from here. And the other types of birds in the woods, here.'

He says nothing still, but the grin that is wrapped around his face is all I need.

I have been trying to persuade the council to present us with a hide for the short time I have lived in this little village, and they have never been keen. Never saw the need, despite the hundreds of tourists we receive in the area in the summer months, some just there for the birds. So I funded it myself.

'I can hide in here with Sadie!'

My shoulders drop, and I can't seem to halt the words that leak from my mouth. 'No. Not at all. This is a bird hide, for serious watchers. Not for playing.'

Bruno's head bows a little. He still manages to stare out of the open horizontal gap – barely a window – eyes scouring the water's edge in the distance. 'We wouldn't be playing.'

My one word is final. He stands, stares at the gulls we can both see dropping towards the water, great in number, and then he finally sits on the hide's low bench. The wood is so new I can smell it. We could be in a hardware shop, the huge ones where they cut wooden planks for you at the back.

'The smell is like the sawdust you use for rabbits.'

I am nodding, smile that we are thinking similar things. I sit next to him.

'Will other people come in here?'

'Yes, hopefully other spotters. I can lock it in between the night and the day.' I jangle a set of keys dramatically in front of his face.

'You shouldn't do that. What if you get night-time spotters?'

I pause for a moment. I can't think of anyone who would want to come out here in the middle of the night. I hate to think of our new neighbours making their way into my newly purchased building for a place to drink, and all at once feel a rush of cold shame engulfing me. The sudden drop in my body temperature makes me wrap my arms around myself, then I realise I should drape an arm around my young son, only a T-shirt on under his thin raincoat.

'We'll see.'

We don't speak for minutes; we don't need to. A darkness is beginning to descend gently around us like fog, and I enjoy the weight of its oppression for a while. There is only the sound of the waves, becoming heavier with each crash, the sound of the gulls' angry yelps and cries as the day's light drains away. I forget everything – the school, the caravan site, my husband. I forget my sister and my niece. I notice Bruno's eyes are closed, his legs swinging back and forth, not quite touching the floor of the structure.

We both see the snow at the same time, and our eyes are drawn to the delicacy of each flake as they drop like dust before our eyes, no shape exactly the same. There had been no mention of snow on the weather forecast this morning.

Our reverie is rudely interrupted by the rattle and shake of a weight landing on top of the hide with a crunch. We look at each other in shock, then we laugh.

'Sounds like something decided to land on us!'

I step out of the cabin to have a look, craning my neck upwards. My eyes are met with wet sprinkles, sharp. 'Can't see anything.'

Bruno is at the doorway, but instinct tells me to push him back. A flurry of snow is determined to make its way onto the new floor of the hide; I stamp my feet on the new carpet of white.

'Come on, I wanna see!'

But I am back in the hide with him, pulling the door closed after us. I can feel the snow in my hair, in my brows; icy droplets melting in the heat of my skin.

He is looking at me, curious, and then his eyes are on the foam of the sea as it blusters its way over the shingle. 'Probably was just a gull.'

Just as he says this, I push open the door again, and a larger-than-average herring gull swoops from the other side of the hide, over the darkened trees of the woodland and towards the pull of the water.

As we begin to tread the path towards home, heads down most of the way, my eye catches on the bluest feather in the near distance, its tip twisting and becoming entangled in a tree with white skeleton fingers. I think for a split second of racing to catch it, but Bruno is already there. He runs towards the blue flame, is on his tiptoes, catches it quickly, before it gets lifted away by the snow flurry. He glances at me, pockets it, runs on ahead, the snow and the darkness engulfing us hiding his form. I continue the walk alone.

\*

When we get home, Dom has dinner ready: roasted potatoes and chicken, green vegetables and some carrots for Bruno. I resist asking him what the occasion is, and instead tuck in, not realising my hunger until now. Perhaps it's a form of apology, for earlier. Dom has barely spoken, but he looks at me with something that I cannot quite place. I would have thought that Bruno would have mentioned the hide by now, or at least the turquoise-blue feather he discovered, but he is not in the mood for talking and instead shovels down the potatoes at a dangerous speed.

'I spoke to one of the Travellers from the other field today.'

It takes me a split second. 'Oh, the other caravans? How do you know they're Travellers, with a capital *T*? They might be Gypsies… Romany.'

He is shrugging. 'Same difference.'

I add some more gravy to my plate. There are some lumps in it, but I swill these around in the jug before trying to add any to my food. The cat is under the table, twisting his body around my ankles. He warms me today.

'They didn't say anything about you reading them the riot act.'

Now I am looking at him. Still, I say nothing. Bruno is glancing up from his food, eyes on the kitchen window; the snow's descent is slowing a little.

I clear my throat, buying time. 'That's because I didn't. So, what did you say to them?'

Bruno pushes his plate away, doesn't look at me for a minute. 'They only told me to "shoo",' he offers. 'You didn't both need to go talk to them.'

For a minute or two, there is silence. Bruno stabs at some meat with his fork, swirling it in the gravy. I can feel a chill coming from under the kitchen door. Or perhaps it is from our mostly battened-down window. This house was built before the church, I've heard the locals joke. God knows, it might even be true. There are flakes attaching themselves to the glass pane, reflecting glimmers of light from the lamppost outside. I feel like finding some tracing paper and holding it up to the glass to sketch the prettiness of the flakes, a night-time artwork.

Dom stands up suddenly, the dragging noise of his chair against the floor tiles making me start. I know he expected more support from me. He rests his hand briefly on our son's shoulder before leaving the room.

I think, for a moment, about the drawings I used to create. Birds, but other stuff too; nature – trees, landscapes. I sometimes wish I hadn't stopped.

Bruno looks up at the back view of his father, swallows down his mouthful. Fergus has moved over to his feet now, and Bruno reaches his hand down under the table to stroke the cat's chin.

A jolt of anger works its way through my limbs as I imagine what Dom must be thinking about me. I stand and follow him into the next room. 'What are you so pissed off about, Dom? Our new neighbours? Were you rude to them? Did you tell them I was your wife? Did they mention me?' The thought leaves me cold. I had so wanted to come across as friendly, non-judgemental.

I glance back at Bruno in the kitchen, his food going round and round in his twisted-up mouth. Fergus is now making himself comfortable in my husband's warm, empty chair.

'Why do you care, Fran? Why do you care what other people think of you so much? Why don't you consider our son?'

The accusation hits me hard in my stomach. It's like a winding, like I've been thrown forward in a car that's suddenly braking, seatbelt yanking into me. 'What?'

He sits on the sofa, toys with the remote control. He's not even planning on turning the television on. 'You and your worries about outside people. Instead of worrying about those closest to you!'

I am taken aback, no words forming. I think about my sister, about Ellis and, of course, my niece. I tell Dom this. That they are the ones in need of help. *My niece has shoes so old that her toes are poking through. She barely has a proper duvet to cover her at night.*

Dom nods, doesn't argue, yet I can't forget his earlier comment about our child. I don't want to talk about it anyway, what with Bruno sitting only a few feet away in the next room. I take a step back, peer into the kitchen. He's gone, no doubt scuttled away upstairs for a break from his parents' arguing.

# TAD

I ventured out yesterday, while the others were wrapped up in starting a fire. It was a tiny thing, won't leave a print on the ground. Nobody else would have been able to see it, from the other side of our field. Too many vans in the way. Occasionally we'll have a fire in the summer too, for food. I guess you'd call it a barbeque. I'm not sure if the caravan park owners will mind this, if they catch wind of it. I'm sure my nephews will stop if they do. If not, I'll be having a word.

All day it's been looking like it's going to snow. The sky turned a peculiar shade of grey just before sundown, when I set off. There are flakes dropping down now, soggy on my lashes and my lips, making them drier. I took a walk along the coastal path; I was drawn to the water, even though the light was leaving. Takes me a while to walk, but I don't mind. Charlie says I should be using my stick. I never do. A couple of days ago, I was down by the coastal path, nearly bumped into a man. Seemed a decent bloke, we exchanged a few pleasantries. He said his wife runs the caravan park opposite. Mentioned he has nothing much to do with it, really. Said his wife and son had gone for a walk to find some special finches, but when I asked where the best place for finding decent birds was, he didn't know. I didn't catch his name. We chatted a couple of minutes longer, then he headed back past the church, with those graves all sticking out of the ground on the hillside. I'm guessing he lives past there.

I was just lighting my second cigarette, struggling with the wind and the falling snow at the same time, when I saw a woman – well, the back of a woman – leaving a path from the wooded area right near the beach. There was a boy racing ahead of her. Don't think she saw me. I walked towards the path and traced her footprints back into the woods, found a new shed-type structure there, sat inside for a bit. Don't know what it's for, that construction, but it was a bit of shelter for a few moments from the weather. Nice new woody smell. A couple of crows or something landed on the roof – sounded funny, like someone was dropping great snowballs on the top – and then were scratching away at something. I was tempted to stay there for a while, sitting on that narrow wooden bench but I had to leave. There was a weird open part on one side of the shed where all the snow was coming in.

# FRAN

## 15 February

Today I trudge towards the school with my sister and Sadie, Bruno rushing ahead of us with the blue feather in his hand. We've gone the long way, on a path that meanders near the marshland, away from the caravan park and past the church. A glance at my niece tells me she's not going to follow Bruno. She instead stays, ears pricked to the conversation I am trying to hold with her mother. I am talking to Ros about not having a lot of money, wondering if it will encourage her to offer to pay something towards her van. It makes me feel guilty, talking to her in this way. It would keep Dom happy for a while, though, if they were to offer some money. She never did say thank you for the window repair, but just an acknowledgement would have been good, something to say she had noticed. It's just not like her. She's usually so grateful. Ros does not speak; I can see her gazing ahead, her eyes following Bruno as he leaps from side to side, the feather a plane in his hands. He leaves small footprints in the yellowing snow, twigs and grasses from the marshland poking out like thorns from the slush.

'Don't you want to catch him up, Sadie?'

I see the girl give my sister a curious look. Ros mouths at me, *She's too old for that.*

I continue to talk about struggling with the water bill, the electricity, but shame gnaws further at my insides, and I give up. I should be the one helping her out a little more. I toy with the idea of offering to buy her daughter some new shoes, decide against it. They won't want more charity. Instead, I say that, as it's so bitter with the cold at the moment, I will drop off a couple of thicker duvets to their van. Ros smiles. I try not to think of a time when she would have thrown her arms around me, made me feel as though I was her lifesaver. Now, it's just a wan smile.

Sadie has stopped walking. She has seen something in the distance, on the marsh before the bog turns into the sea. She looks back towards us, perhaps not sure whether to point it out or not. Sadie continues to walk, her school bag held up in her right hand like a handbag. The gulf between her and my son continues to grow as he runs back towards us, making a noise like an aeroplane, the turquoise of the feather twisting in his clutch and in the spiralling wind. If Sadie could stop and put both her hands on her hips, she would. I think, sometimes, that she thinks she's too good for this world, for children such as my son. Bruno doesn't catch her disapproval, doesn't even stop for breath, today's new snow scuffing his black leather shoes.

I hold back for a moment, smiling at Bruno before he dashes off again. I want to see what she noticed. The sun isn't out, but the white light from the clouds is so startling it causes me to squint. A form in the marsh, perhaps just a common bird. It's probably a good fifty yards away.

Sadie turns suddenly. 'Come on,' she says. It is out of character for her to want to speak to us like that. She is eyerolling in my direction.

Ros looks at her, then at me, confusion colouring her features.

'I don't want to be late,' my niece offers. I'm not sure I believe her.

*

It's a bit of a task, trying to get access to the marshland, all sorts of bog attempting to swallow me up, and strands of ice clinging to the reeds, determined to stop me with their bitterness. I lingered longer in the schoolyard than I had needed to this morning, still avoiding the eye of Ms McConnell since our last conversation, two weeks ago, loitering by the wall where there was at least a little protection from the biting wind. A couple of parents I used to chat to smiled at me, and I engaged in conversation with one of them. *Yes, isn't it great they've got more maths challenges this term. Yes, it's wonderful that the children are so enthusiastic. Not too sure about the teacher, though.* It was enough conversation to make me want to begin my walk home again, and I pushed my chin down into the oversized scarf wrapped around my neck, hid the giggle that wanted to escape.

I try to focus on what Sadie may have been looking at from such a distance, and it doesn't take me long to find it. It is tiny, beautifully constructed, on a lower boggy area of the marsh. There is no adult bird there at the moment, and the six minuscule beige eggs, speckled chocolate-brown, stare back at me innocently, lonely without a mother. There are flecks of snow on the outer shell of each one that turn into drips of moisture. How Sadie could have noticed these from the path baffles me, but then, like I've thought before, she has always had something different about her. I lean forward to get a good look, feel the warmth of joy circulate around my being like wine when it starts taking hold. There have been little terns here the whole time. Early, just like in the town a little further up the coast. With a flicker of dismay, I realise I've been looking and waiting in the wrong place. I resist the urge to touch the eggs, instead look around for a protective mother to come and question why I am looking at her babies. The nest is barely hidden by the weeds and grasses growing out of the marsh, but I know that youngsters here do survive. The instinct to hide the tiny nest is hard to fight, but I know I must leave it alone, force my feet to walk back across the marsh and to the snowy path. I realise I am shaking with excitement, yet there is nobody here to share this feeling with. Bruno will be thrilled, but I am quickly smacked by the thought that perhaps I shouldn't share this find with my young son, who will no doubt be telling his class all about it. True, Sadie seemed to be the one to glance over at the nest this morning, but perhaps I was imagining this. Perhaps she didn't see a thing.

\*

My husband is friendlier at dinner this evening, his red hair moulded into tighter-than-usual ringlets from the damp as he stands at the hob. I sometimes remember why I liked him so much in the first place at times like this; the feeling warms me.

'Meatballs!' he announces to me as I enter the room. I've been upstairs for a while, mustn't have heard him come in.

He's in a good mood. He only cooks when this is the case.

Bruno appears in the kitchen too, chasing the smell of the meat from the hallway. He didn't speak much on the way home from school, but that never means anything. A lot of the time he doesn't speak.

'How was work?' I ask. I still don't *really* understand what Dom does. Financial work of some sort. He goes to work in Norwich for most of the week, works from home a day or two as well.

'Good, good.' He glances round at me, smiles. 'Same shit, different day.' And that seems to be the end of our conversation.

I am lingering, wanting to tell him about the tern's nest, but I don't want Bruno to catch hold of the conversation.

'I built the damned hide in the wrong place.'

Dom turns and looks at me, oil splattered on his wrists, his arms. He always goes overboard with the cooking oil. 'Huh? Your hide?'

I know he won't really get it. He just thinks I spent a lot of money on something useless. A look at Bruno tells me he's not going to stay in the kitchen very long, and sure enough, he whizzes away through the other door of the room, to the hallway.

I clear my throat. My husband leans over from where he's standing, sensing my disappointment at something to do with *the birds*, puts his free arm around my shoulders.

'I got the hide constructed in the densest area of woodland near the beach, because I thought I would see the most different types of breeds there. And now I realise it's in the wrong place.' Although I am dismayed at my own stupidity, I'm enjoying the feeling of my husband's arm being wrapped around me.

There is a rapping at the door, the sound intrusive. It makes me forget where I was heading with my chatter.

I remember a few moments later, ignoring the door until I've had a chance to speak. 'But it seems there are terns on the *marshland*. Little terns! A nest, even! Do you know how much I've been wanting to see one of these birds?'

Dom takes more than a second to register what I've said. He lifts his red eyebrows to demonstrate that he is impressed, but really, I know he wants to crane his neck towards the front window, to see who is at the door. I don't blame him. He lets his arm flop from my shoulders, steps back towards the hob. He doesn't have to wait long to find out; Sadie wanders through, ahead of Bruno, screws her face up comically when she sees the meatballs frying.

'You don't have to eat them, you know, Sadie!' I can't resist commenting.

She plonks herself onto one of the wooden chairs at the table, Bruno standing awkwardly at her side.

'It's fine,' she says, not taking her eyes off Bruno. 'I've eaten.'

My husband rolls his eyes from where he is frying, mutters something about *gratitude*. I smile at him. Perhaps, now he seems to have found a better mood, he will be less hard on Sadie.

She is whispering to Bruno, who leans forward to catch her every word.

'No!' he laughs, but then he looks serious.

I am dying to know what she has said to him, but I won't ask. 'Hey, Sadie, how's school at the moment?'

She looks at me for the first time, and her shoulders hunch up then drop suddenly as she delivers the most exaggerated sigh. 'Not great.' Then adds, 'Thanks.'

Bruno giggles, not taking his eyes off her. 'Ms McConnell doesn't like Sadie's *attitude*,' he offers.

'Oh, I'm sure that's not true.'

'It is,' says Sadie. 'I loved her so much at first, we were friends.' She

looks from under her eyebrows at Bruno. 'But now she doesn't...'
She stops herself abruptly.

I find myself wondering, not for the first time, if she's just
desperate to be loved, and to love someone back. Perhaps she
doesn't feel any love from her own parents. I try to trample on any
thoughts about whether she does have a bad *attitude*.

'What does the problem seem to be?' Dom can't help himself.

Sadie is motioning for Bruno to go outside, but I pretend not to
notice and gaze at her, awaiting a response.

'She doesn't seem to like me anymore.' She leans forward to
make sure she catches what Bruno is about to whisper in her ear.
He smiles and covers his mouth suddenly, his eyes darting to me,
then away.

'Right, kids, we're just about to eat,' I try. 'Sadie, can you come
back a little later, or wait in the living room, perhaps?'

She stares at me for a second, smiles and lets herself into the
next room, her voice calling through the doorway. 'Bruno, I've got
something to show you after you've eaten!'

He is laughing, but his smile drops slightly when he sees me.

It is still partially light outside. Tonight, I had wanted to give
Bruno the small Nokia phone I've saved for him, one that a punter
from last year had left behind in one of the vans. I've installed a
new sim card in it. I need him to be safe, now he wanders outside
at all hours. Perhaps now is not the right time. I try to think of an
excuse to keep the children in.

*

They return over an hour later, once it is dark, Bruno trying to hide
something as he shuffles his way past me.

His hood is still up, his face darkened by the shade of it. I can
feel the cold rising off him.

'Not so fast!' I am pulling at his hands. Some cuts, old and new.
Dark red stains. Brighter ones, still dribbling from the grazes on
his palms. I glance at Sadie, who is behind him for once; her face

gives nothing away, my eyes see only the new droplets of snow on her lashes.

Bruno pulls his hands behind him, turns to look at her. She half-shrugs.

'Well, why are you bleeding, Bruno?'

Nobody answers. I think of calling Dom, who has disappeared upstairs for a shower or a shave, but, for some reason, I don't.

'He… fell.' Sadie takes her time to mouth the last word.

Bruno looks up at me briefly from under wet lashes, pushing his hands into his coat pockets. Sadie moves her own hands behind her back.

I guide my son through to the kitchen, and he gently nudges me away as he runs his fingers under the cold water tap. Lumps of snow lie on the floor, fallen from his boots, which he hasn't removed. They could be lumps of coal, blackened, or tiny birds.

'Both hands are hurt?'

He looks at me sheepishly. 'I fell over in the snow. Put both hands out to catch myself.'

I am half waiting for a giggle from either child, but there is only silence, as clean and white as the snow that drew my son to the ground.

Sadie is slowly making her way towards the front door. She'd taken her boots off; she is courteous in our house. She's trying to pull them back on again.

'Are you hurt too, Sadie? Are you alright?'

For a moment, I think she is going to let herself cry, as if that feeling had been bubbling away at the back of her throat for many minutes. 'We slipped over on the path near the church. It was black ice. Please don't tell Mum.' And she holds her own hands out in front of me, eyes now not meeting mine. Both hands smeared with blood, dried into burgundy streaks in the heat of the house. Even though our home is warmed in every room, I swear there is a chill travelling up my spine.

# TAD

The others seem to be settling in fine. Jade wants to be sent to the local college, but no, she can't. She's just not ready. I know she won't want to speak. She'll have to be taught by us, as usual, if she wants more of an education. I know she wants to make friends, but she has her cousins here. Maybe sooner rather than later she can hang around with the other kids in the village, like the younger ones here are hoping to. I just don't think she's ready quite yet.

Some of my siblings, their partners, their cousins, are setting off for work today. They use the skills they have to impress the townspeople of wherever we are living. They are self-taught, these days. I don't understand half of the work they can do, half of the gadgets they play with. Some of them like working with phones, that type of thing. A couple of the women like computers, want to find that sort of work again like they did back at the Common. I'm kind of glad I'm too old to work now; been working since I was fourteen, with my hands, my back aching. You grow tired of it. Most of them here have never had to use their backs, their hands. It's so different nowadays. I used to buy and sell horses a few years back, but that became less prosperous over time. Charlie wasn't even grown up when I was doing that. People just run over to Ireland now for the cheap nags.

I see them set off, in three of the transit vans I've cleaned within an inch of their lives. They all laughed at me, bent over double, cleaning the damned things. You've got to have high standards, that's what I try to tell the youngsters. Seldom do they listen. They have their own ways, they know how to make a steady living. They all seem to want permanent jobs, do the youngsters here. None of this quick-cash-for-a-day's-work stuff. My brother persuaded me to get a bank account, a few years back. Got to admit, it's the best thing I've done. I just can't be bothered to update the bank every time we move address.

I'm going out again today, on foot; need to know where the nearest local food shop is, although the others have already bought supplies for themselves to last around another week, from some huge supermarket seven or so miles away. I don't want to drive. Haven't driven for nearly ten years. When we move, Charlie drives my trailer, and one of our cousins drives his. And we don't really share our groceries. We're all independent, and besides, I like to get my own.

The snow has stopped but is still clogging the ground and making walking tough. Again, I think of how I should probably use my stick, as my knees can't seem to take my weight too well, but I don't need things to make me look older. I think again about the past as I'm walking; the days when we were more self-sufficient. I remember my parents growing veggies, shooting and killing birds themselves, even deer. I still shoot my own birds and rabbits now, mind. My childhood memories are made up of such images. We kids would wash and peel the spuds, my sisters doing as little work as possible, cutting corners, leaving the eyes in the potatoes for me to cut out. My mum would give them a little slap around the head. Would never deter them, though. Our dad, he was a softie, never a harsh word to say to any of us. He worked himself into the ground. Was always working, from as soon as he was ten, he used to tell us. Died twelve years back. He had a good innings. I know Charlie is still sad about it. We don't talk about Dad around him much.

I am wandering near the church, my collar pulled up around my neck as the wind battles with me, determined to pull me towards the sea front. The temperature must be zero, and I long for the warmer days to return. I spend some time looking at the gravestones, peeking out of the mound they are protruding from, try to find a date or a name on any of the stones. The most recent

I can find states *Marjory Jane Higgins, 1921-1992, Remembered Forever, with Love.*

I continue to traipse around the snowy graves, brushing the carpet of flakes off a couple of stones with my bare hand. The sharpness of the ice causes me to gasp. I am looking for a common surname or something, anything that might link these graves to each other, but I find nothing. I can't see the engravings on most of them, for a start. There is a bench, hidden in perhaps an inch of snow, and I slide my hand along the surface to clear it. Sitting down, I already feel a dampness seeping into my behind.

The church stands proudly; not huge, but big enough. I can't see a date for the birth of the building, but it's obviously centuries old. There is nobody around, nobody to chat to, so I try to enjoy the silence for as long as I can. Jade is with my brother, she loves to be with him, listen to his chatter. She was meant to be receiving some type of therapy, the authorities said, years back, but we never took them up on it. She's probably a smidge too old now, anyway. I feel for her, of course I do, and she's really not a burden, but sometimes I just need a rest, a little bit of respite. The others help out so much; that's what has been so good for her.

After maybe twenty minutes of resting on the damp bench, I pull myself to my feet and begin the walk down the path that runs parallel alongside the churchyard. I slip suddenly, grasping at thin air, and find myself sliding on ice before collapsing on my bones in a heap on the path. There's not much fat on me these days, and my knees are the first to feel the heat of the pain. As I grapple around for something to hold on to, to help me pull myself to my feet, I see it. Its tiny puffed-up body, almost a tennis ball, wings spread out at its side, half hidden in a holly bush. Red is leaking from the sides of it like spilled paint, danger reflected in the crimson berries of the holly. I don't know every type of bird in the British Isles, but he looks to be a little sparrow or something. His eyes are still open; they stare at me, lifeless. There's something not quite right with his head, seems to be hanging off. Looks like the damned thing's been strangled.

# FRAN

## 21 February

First parents' evening of the year, and Dom is late. Since we've been getting on better these past couple of days, I'm not as cross as I could be. The snow is beginning to drift down again, unwittingly creating a halo on top of my head; I can see myself in the reflection of the school gym doors. If I squint, I look almost holy, the light bouncing from the circle of flakes adorning my hair, and I try to mould my smile to more of a grimace, just on the off chance that anyone is watching me pose.

Ros was happy enough to watch Bruno for us. It's not often I ask her for a favour, and besides, I'm having Sadie for as long as it takes tomorrow after school for the same reason. I try to enjoy the moment, alone in the snow, rather than feel disappointment towards Dom for his tardiness. He seems relieved to be greeted by my warm grin when he eventually shows up. His coat is sodden from the sleet that was coming down earlier, as well as the new snow, and clearly hasn't had a chance to dry.

'Sorry, Fran.'

I wave my hand casually. *Everything's fine.*

He stops walking, looks at me for guidance into the school building.

'Ellis here?' He is shaking off his coat, his scarf. 'And Ros?' he adds.

I am slowly walking through the reception area of the school, finding myself signing us both into the building. The school has a certain smell to it. New carpets? I'm not sure.

'Nope. No Ros either. They're watching Bruno for us, remember?'

He looks a bit sheepish, keeps rubbing the stubble on his face. We are ushered to another part of the corridor by a child no older than nine, and she gestures to the tiny child-sized seats for child-sized bottoms around a group of small tables. There are workbooks arranged, each with different children's names on the front, and different subject headings. I see Dom grab the one with Bruno's name on it – his maths book. He has a quick flick through, face contorting slightly with concentration.

'I don't know how they expect us to fit in these chairs.' My husband says it every time. He even writes it on the little feedback forms they issue us with at every appointment. Seems they take no notice of the suggestions.

'Well, correct; they're not designed for big people.'

He ignores my comment, drops the maths book onto the table, glances around for something else to look at. I reach over to pick up Bruno's art book. There's another set of parents across the group of tables from us, both laughing at the same time as they flick through one of their own child's books. I don't recognise them, then I realise they are waiting by the door of another year group, not Bruno's.

As I turn the pages, I begin to see a common theme. Birds: gulls, crows. The title on one of the pages is 'My Weekend'. I am anticipating drawings of Sadie, but there are none, only the most bright and elongated shapes of seabirds, stretched out over double pages of the book. My heart is ticking a little faster. I don't feel like showing Dom. This is just for me, my eyes. I hold the book so that the pages are closer together, in the hope that nobody else can get a peek inside. As I turn each page, the birds become more and more obscure, so much so that I cannot tell what breed each one is meant to be, or if they are even real breeds at all. Some are all-white, or not coloured in; some are red, black, complete with fancy stripes on their wings. There are a couple of tiny finches, contrasted next to the huge birds. I stop on the very last page. No bird painting, just a weak pencil drawing. A nest, complete with six beige-flecked eggs, laid out on the marshes, motherless.

*

I'm trying not to stare at the teacher as she talks us through Bruno's work, but I can't tear my eyes away from the little plaits she has adorning her hair from the very top of her scalp. Some of the hair has been left out, pink, wavy and flowing onto her shoulders. She senses me looking, glances up from the workbook she's holding.

'We were just hoping that Bruno was behaving well in class now,' Dom stutters, out of nowhere, apparently no longer keen on looking at the workbooks before him.

Ms McConnell takes an intake of breath, not sharp enough for Dom to notice, but clear enough so that I can tell she is going to launch into a speech of some form. I try to focus on her eyes, aware that I am holding my breath.

'Bruno's behaviour...' This is all she says for a moment. It's like she's not sure where to start. 'Is up and down.'

I cast my eyes towards Dom, who isn't looking at me.

'Up and down?'

The teacher leans back a little, crosses then uncrosses her legs, those pink and green stripy tights again. I find myself staring at the neckline of her slightly twee twinset, perfectly matched. I swear I can see the shadow of a mammoth dark tattoo creeping its way up her chest, towards her neck. I blink suddenly, bring myself back to the moment.

'He is a very quiet boy, but he has his moments...' Her voice trails off.

'Sadie.' Dom thinks he has his answer.

Immediately, I try to laugh it off. 'Not Sadie, don't worry about what Dom is saying!'

Now the teacher's head is cocked towards me, like a little robin. I can feel the heat of my cheeks, not least because Dom is staring straight at me.

'Sadie?' It is a question.

Dom leans forward a little, red brows knitted in that way of his. He looks like he's going to whisper some sort of secret into Ms McConnell's ear. For a split second, I imagine him kissing her, then just as quickly, the vision is gone. I wonder where she's come from, this teacher. I can't figure out her accent. I can't even tell if she's just being stern with us or if she's like this with the children too. I realise I have to suddenly turn my thoughts back to what Dom is about to say.

'Sadie, she's a little… domineering. She's Bruno's cousin, you know.'

My shoulders are tightening. *He's really going to do it. He's really going to land my niece in it.*

The look on the teacher's face is still one of surprise, yet her words don't reflect this. A couple of her narrow pink plaits fall onto her shoulders, distracting me. 'Sure, yes, I knew that.' She picks up her cup of tea, probably cold, takes a tiny sip. Dom always comments on how the parents don't get offered anything *in the shape of refreshments* around here. 'But I don't really see how Sadie has anything to do with Bruno's behaviour. They seem to have nothing to do with each other at school.'

I let the words fall gently onto the child-sized tables we are sitting at. *They seem to have nothing to do with each other at school.*

'What do you mean? They're inseparable, usually.'

'Maybe out of school they are. Not in class. They don't sit together, don't play together, from what I've seen. I thought it was deliberate, because they're related.'

Dom raises his wiry red brows at me, and I try to return a quick look. I visualise turning to him when he's asleep and shaving off those eyebrows for good, then almost laugh at the thought.

'But you must admit she's a difficult character to have in class, Sadie?' His words sound desperate. I know he's clutching at hope, that he's willing the teacher to admit how difficult the little girl is. That she is the one who made Bruno take the lipstick, causes his behaviour to be *up and down*. It doesn't seem to matter to Dom that she's our niece.

I'm trying to stop myself from standing up, walking out, my hands gripped around the sharp edges of the tiny plastic chair I'm sitting in.

'I'm not really here to discuss the other children.'

My relief is palpable, and I let my body go as floppy as it can in its seat.

Dom and the teacher continue to discuss how Bruno is doing in all his lessons, but despite my interest, my brain is zoning out, my eyes peering out of the classroom window, onto the playground. There is nobody out there. I can see movement from one of the trees on the edge of the playground, its branches being whipped mercilessly by the wind that has come straight off the sea. Finally, the snow has stopped but given way to icy patches, more dangerous than the snow itself.

I'm picking up my bag from the floor when my husband decides to try one more tactic. 'So, you do know that Sadie was to blame for Bruno helping himself to your handbag and trying to take the lipstick?'

The silence that curls itself around us is like a snake constricting its prey. Neither Dom's nor Ms McConnell's features change. They are each waiting for the other to speak. I wonder if the wind from the sea has blown through the window and frozen their faces, as the childhood warning goes. Suddenly, we are standing, me ushering Dom towards the door of the classroom, barely a goodbye or wave of the hand. I pull the door shut behind us, catch sight of the art book with the nest, and then we are outside on the ice, me slipping and clutching at the air in an attempt to stabilise myself.

# TAD

Those two local kids have been traipsing around on our field again. I don't mind. We see the girl, probably twelve or thirteen, running to each door, knocking, and running away, so that the doors open up to her male accomplice. None of our family are pissed off, yet the boy looks like a rabbit caught in headlights, a shy smile thinly hiding the anxiety that seems to be creeping up from the rest of his body. He follows the girl, runs to keep up with her, jumps at my brother's dog, which is tied up outside and feeling extra friendly towards visitors today. You get used to the dogs, being here. I don't think I could trust Jade with one. Not that the dog would harm her, no. The other kids spend half their time playing with the animals, wrestling them, rolling on the ground, me sticking my head out of the door telling them to keep their spit to themselves.

I watch the flash of platinum of the girl's hair as she shakes off her friend, forever ten or fifteen paces behind her. I see his mouth moving, perhaps shouting at her to stop. She doesn't. Once she has knocked on most of the caravan doors, she holds up her skirt and runs with speed to the edge of the woods. I watch the boy trip, fall. His mouth is throwing words out again, none acknowledged. I see my brother leave his van, begin to walk towards the boy. I whistle, catch his attention, but he keeps on walking until he is spitting distance from the child. Jade creeps up behind me as I stand at the door of my van, her warm hand on my waist, her body impatient as her shoulders try to push their way through. I lean to the side, giving her a gap to see.

'What's this?'

'Just some kids playing silly buggers.'

'Charlie.'

I nod. We both watch my brother throw an arm around the boy, mutter something in his ear, before staggering back to his caravan, face red from the exertion. There are four of us siblings. Charlie is the one I've always been closest to. He listens to me. He's been a parent to Jade half her young life. I had work to take care of, building and the like, and my wife was working too.

Jade's eyes are on the boy now, watching him trace the blonde girl's steps towards the woods. The girl is staring straight at him, leaning almost suggestively against the bulk of an oak trunk. She is too young to know what she's doing. She flicks her wrist at her blonde hair. *It was just a game.* Any facial expression is blurred from this distance. His back is to us, a dot of blue. I know Jade is fascinated by the girl. Minutes later, the boy and girl are walking back through our field, her in front again, head high, him wiping his cheek with the back of his hand. I hear him say he's *going to be in trouble*, he *forgot to bring his phone*.

# FRAN

## 23 February

Dom has decided that Bruno's *up and down* behaviour at school is being caused by seeing Sadie too much in his free time. I'm not sure I'm going along with this idea. The teacher had made it clear, after all, that they kept themselves apart from each other in the classroom. Still, I agree that their contact is becoming too full on – practically every evening. Last night he came home exhausted, and I swear he's not feeling right. Perhaps he just needs to stop seeing anybody after school. It won't be a *Sadie* ban, per se. It will be a *people* ban. It will just mean that Bruno sticks to his schoolwork and prepares for the jump to secondary school in the autumn. It was difficult to read his face at first; his skin flushed a little, and then I'm sure there was a sudden relief, a slackening of the muscles. We haven't told Ros or Ellis. The thought makes me feel a little heavy inside, like I'm keeping a dirty secret. She wouldn't understand. Neither would I, if it were the other way around. Dom just wants to keep our little boy as innocent as he can before secondary school; I can appreciate that. And, if I'm honest, it wasn't just what Ms McConnell said about Bruno at the parents' evening that made me want to keep him away from everyone. It was what we discovered on the church path.

Bruno wanted a funeral for the little bird. He had run back to the house, asked for plastic bags so he could lift it without his bare hands touching its body. I could tell he was slightly nervous, pacing back and forth, his breathing a notch quicker than usual. I didn't like the look of the thing – a nuthatch, neck twisted awkwardly to one side – but mostly, the blood. This was no accidental death. Someone had set out to kill this bird, must have lain in wait to catch it out. If it were a cat or a fox to blame, surely they would have savaged the rest of its body a little more? Maybe someone was watching it in the late evening, waiting. I saw the mangled little thing close up, felt a stab of sympathy for the mother of the fledgling; I could tell it wasn't yet an adult bird. A mother losing her child. It's a horrific thing for any creature. My blood began to bubble a little, I remember, but with nowhere to go. I had to sit down on a nearby bench for rather a long time, while my son gathered the will to pick it up. He kept looking at me with heavy eyes, then glancing away. The funeral consisted of me digging a four- or five-inch ditch at the very end of our back garden and Bruno laying the tiny body in the space. He wanted to lay it on the plastic bag, but I told him it wouldn't decompose properly if he did that. He didn't want it to decompose. He said he wanted it to stay as it was: whole.

There is a drumming at my front door. School let out about an hour and a half ago, although I have only just got home from the beach. I allowed Bruno to walk home alone, without his cousin. I told him to walk the long way. I make my way to the door, am not so surprised to see my sister. She is radiating cold air. 'Can I come in?'

I open the door wider and gesture with my arm to allow her inside. She stamps her boots momentarily on the mat, and I find my pulse racing a little faster. Didn't take long for Sadie to pass on that she's not allowed to see Bruno outside school. My levels of adrenaline are gathering.

'That bloody woman.'

I motion for us to both sit at the kitchen table, not looking at Ros for a moment. I wonder if she is referring to the teacher.

'Huh?'

'The teacher. Can't stand her already.'

'Has she done something?' The relief that my sister's rage is not aimed at me is enormous; my shoulders are no longer weighted. I move over to the kettle. 'Tea?'

Ros doesn't respond to the second question, so I fill the kettle with water anyway and put it on the hob. She is tracing the sides of a placemat on the table with her index finger. I miss the smile that used to always be stretched across her face.

'Ros?'

'We won't be seeing you at the school for a while.'

I spin on my heel to look at her. 'What's happened?'

For a moment, I think she is going to cry; her bottom lip seems to jut out, she is swallowing something down in her throat. 'Sadie's been excluded from school.'

She must register the confused expression on my face, she blinks and adds, 'Temporarily.'

I pull two mugs out of the cupboard and set them next to the hob. The kettle is beginning to heat up. Soon it will begin its penetrating whistle; I might not be able to hear what my sister is saying.

I don't speak, just lift the lid of the teabag container and pop one bag in each of the waiting mugs.

'You're not surprised.'

I'm not expecting the accusation; I move towards the table, pull out a chair for myself. 'Well, yes, I am.'

My sister is looking directly at me.

'What did Sadie actually do?'

Ros is back to running her finger around the placemat, head bowed slightly. Her ponytail makes her appear younger than she really is, thirty-seven. She's always seemed so much younger than me.

'Something to do with *apparently* putting filthy feathers in another girl's bag. And smearing birdshit on her books.'

My hand is halfway up to my mouth. I force myself to drop it down again.

'I knew you would think it was weird. It *is* weird. And she *didn't* do it.'

There's a punch to my gut at my sister's first sentence. She must think me such a monster.

I am shaking my head. *Feathers. Birdshit.* 'Have you asked her?'

'Of course I've asked her! And she said no, it wasn't her. I believe her.'

The kettle's whistle is spiralling up into the air between us, a shrill warning, becoming more and more startling. It is so piercing that Ros seems stunned for a moment.

'You have to find out what's happening.' My words are more of a shout over the noise.

'I know she's not perfect, but why would the teacher think it was her who could do those things to someone?'

My mind is racing. For no reason, I picture the dead nuthatch. *Could she have hurt that bird? If she is guilty of spreading animal shit in another child's schoolbag, surely she could put an end to a little bird's life?* I curse myself, realise I sound no better than my husband. She's just a little girl. A little girl searching for some sort of attention. Someone else is surely to blame for the bird-killing. And perhaps the shit-smearing of another child's books.

I try to change the subject, although it is done a little awkwardly. 'So, how is Ellis?'

'He is angry too, what do you think?'

I shake my head a little, rising to pour the hot water into the mugs. 'I meant generally. How is he?'

There's a pause. 'Not working. Can't find anything. Not drinking either, though.'

I turn to smile, a wan smile. I really don't know if the not-drinking thing has any truth to it, but I just hope he's still bringing some money into their home.

My sister stands, pushes her chair out with the motion. 'Anyway, just thought I would let you know.'

We both walk into the hallway, and she makes a grab for the front door handle before turning to me. 'You know, it's great that Sadie has Bruno outside school for company. I don't know what would become of her if she couldn't see a single other kid. Especially her cousin.'

She is gone, and I stand at the door, watching her back as her form becomes smaller and smaller on the path. That heavy weight, again, pushing its way into my stomach.

Back in the hallway, I linger at the doorway of the kitchen, stare for a moment at her cup of tea sitting untouched on the table, the steam dancing its way towards the dull light of the window.

# TAD

I managed to chat to the girl yesterday. Her little friend wasn't with her. I saw him, though, just an hour or two later, hanging around outside the door of Charlie's caravan. Then he just disappeared the next moment I looked. God knows if he went inside. I didn't see Charlie later to ask. Anyway, the girl swore blind she wasn't bunking lessons, said the school kicked her out. When I asked her what for, she just shrugged and said that *some kids just don't like birds.* A strange comment, but she obviously didn't want to expand. Jade was hovering at the door of the caravan as I struck up conversation with the girl just outside. The morning was unseasonably warm, end of February. Sun out, no coat needed. She told me her name was Sadie but that she prefers to be called *Sahara.* I suppose I'll call her whatever she likes. She asked if she could come into our van, so I thought, *what could be the damage?* Jade sat on the opposite side of the table from Sahara, eyeing her with ill-concealed envy. A girl who can come and go as she pleases, with the appearance of an angel.

'What's wrong with her?' Sahara may look as pure as the driven snow, but she's not the most subtle.

'Jade is mute. She speaks very rarely, and even then, only to me or my brother.'

The girl continued to stare at my daughter, who said nothing but was rubbing her hand against the fabric of my shirt. I could tell she was anxious. Anxiety is where her lack of speaking comes from. We let anyone inside our trailer, I'm an open kind of man, but I could tell Jade didn't feel safe. I could tell she was about to start mouthing words at me. *Dad dad dad who is she?* She feels safer mouthing words rather than letting them spill out into the real world.

'So, where you do you live?' The question sounded a little forced at the time. It would be good to know a little about her, though.

She pointed out of the window she was sitting by, not turning her head in the same direction. There was a silence for a few moments. 'The other caravan site.'

I think I hesitated before saying anything else; I remember watching some of the younger adults on our own field taking advantage of the warmer weather outside, leaving their trailers with baskets of washing, slinging sheets over the newly erected line tied from one trailer to the next. A couple of the younger kids stepped out of the vans too, hot on the heels of their parents. I think Sahara turned to look at them too. Jade's eyes, I remember, remained firmly on the girl with the platinum hair.

'The caravan site next to this?'

Sahara nodded. For a moment, I wondered why she had wanted to come inside.

'I'm lonely. I don't see anyone now. That cow has ruined it for me… I don't know why I liked her so much in the first place.'

I remember nodding. *Doesn't see anyone?*

Jade was alert. 'Cow.' The word seemed to come out of nowhere. It hung in the air for a moment, echoed uncomfortably in my ears.

After that, I didn't know whether to laugh or feel sad. Jade only has a limited vocabulary. She hasn't repeated a new word for months now.

Sahara was giggling, the sound half muted by the hand she clasped over her mouth. 'Sorry.'

Jade repeated the word again.

The blonde girl was doubled over with giggles, her perfect face creased up with the apparent hilarity of the situation.

'Cow cow cow cow.'

'Oh, she's so funny,' said Sahara. She didn't seem to mean it unkindly. She stood to leave. 'I feel a bit better now, thanks.'

I stood too, leaving my daughter at the table-for-four.

Sahara opened the door of the caravan, turned, whispered to me, almost pleadingly, *'Please don't tell anyone I was here.'*

I think I must have nodded, closed the door, felt a temporary sense of relief at her having left.

I remember looking towards Jade, a smile caked onto her round face, her mouth twisting out the word *COW COW COW* long after the girl had gone.

# FRAN

## 27 February

It's definitely getting warmer. Shafts of light let themselves into the bedroom, dancing at the bottom of the curtains where the fabric touches the floor. The birds are louder, are calling at an earlier time in the morning. I can't always tell which bird is singing; I like the mixed cacophony of voices. Sometimes I will nudge Dom from his slumber, get him to listen. I think he tries, feigns interest, yet today he falls back asleep. You'd think he didn't have to work today. The nest is in my mind, has been all night. I think I must have dreamed about the drawing in Bruno's art book. I pull on some clothes and pad downstairs, after a quick check on my still-sleeping child. The sun is up, so no darkness to contend with, although when I pull the front door open the wind that whips at me is unexpected, reminds me it's still late winter.

It doesn't take long to make it to the marshland, and for a moment, I cannot locate the nest. When I do, I see it is occupied by a tern, the mother; she is sitting flat on top of where the eggs must lay. It's a beautiful thing and near takes my breath away. I can almost feel tears pricking at my eyes as I try to manoeuvre myself into a slightly more comfortable squatting position between the reeds. The bird doesn't seem aware of me, and to get a better view, I fumble around in my rucksack for the binoculars I always bring. It strikes me as ironic, not for the first time, that I had the hide constructed in an area that couldn't be further from this scene. There are some marshlands just fifty feet from the hide, yet this little bird chose this area as the home for her young. I try to relax and enjoy the silence, save for the caw-cawing of gulls and the crash of the waves peaking and dropping. The peace only lasts a couple of minutes as I hear heavy footsteps battle through the reeds behind me, and then stop. Turning, I see a man, perhaps late forties, very short gingery-red hair. I haven't seen him before.

'Come to look at the nest too?'

I don't know how to answer, so I just smile, dropping the binoculars a little from my eyes. I am only too aware how valuable these eggs will be.

The man takes a few more steps towards me, his heavy build drawing a loud crunch from the half-dry reeds around him each time. The bird turns and makes a squawking sound, stands, flaps her delicate wings a little.

He smiles at me. I feel like asking where he's come from. He wears no jacket, and I find myself looking at his bared arms for evidence of goosebumps.

'I'm from the other field,' he announces, my look of curiosity obviously prompting explanation.

'Travellers?'

He raises an eyebrow, laughs. 'Call us what you will.' There is only the sound of the surf for a while, then he adds, 'Romany.'

The man squats down in the reeds, not ten feet from me. The bird has settled onto the nest again. I wonder at what time she leaves the nest to go and forage for food, or for more feathers for lining.

'How are you liking it around here?'

The man laughs, I see he is holding out a hand towards me. 'Charlie.' He looks down at my binoculars for a short moment. 'You mean here by the nest, or at our current stopping place?'

Again, I can't think of words to respond to him. I was going to use the excuse of being seated too far away to be able to shake his hand, but he seems a friendly sort, so I kind of shuffle over in my squatting position. His hand is frozen on the outside, but the palm is warm.

'I guess you don't know our family,' says Charlie. It doesn't seem to be a question. 'But we don't bite.'

Saying nothing, I dig my chin deeper into the fleece collar of my coat. I want to shuffle back to my perfect viewing spot, but don't want the awkwardness, the appearance of rudeness.

'We cause no harm. Just everyday people, like you.'

I put on a smile, mutter, 'I know, yes, of course,' then concentrate my gaze on the tern. I'm wondering if this Charlie will leave soon; I'm not so used to spotting birds in company, although he seems like a nice enough man. The tern keeps standing, fussing, circling. I wonder if she is picking up the sound of our voices. I'm trying to keep my voice low when I speak.

'I like the birds too. I see you've found the nest.' He is looking at me expectantly.

A feeling of obscene protectiveness swamps my body; I feel like swooping up the tern and her babies in my arms and running back to the cottage. He knows about the eggs, no doubt. It's easy to see that the nest is not lying empty.

'Oh, yes.'

'Pretty little eggs, aren't they?'

I risk a glance at him. I can't tell if he's being threatening. Instead of considering it further, I find myself in an almost-standing position, trying not to disturb the bird, and beginning to tread my path backwards.

'I'm not meaning any harm.' His eyes look warm, almost inviting. He's innocent, a chatty local. I watch his eyes trace the line of the top of the sea, the horizon, then cast back towards the tern and her nest. 'I'm the only one who gets up at this hour.'

He must be talking about his family.

'Me too,' I laugh, and I hold his gaze for a while, until it becomes uncomfortable.

He doesn't say anything, so I begin to pick my way across the marshes, through the wetland, head turned, my eyes not faltering from the view of the man and the nest. He starts to back away too, heading in the direction he came from, his head turning towards me briefly, eyes flickering.

# TAD

Charlie came back a little out of breath this morning, I heard him through my window; he seemed thrilled about something. He paused outside my door – you can see a lot through these nets at the window, but the beauty is that those outside can't see in. It seemed like he wanted to tell me something, reminded me of a child or a little robin, puffed up with excitement. Perhaps he thought better of it because of the time; it was only just a short while after sunrise. I was relieved when he kept walking. I've got my hands full with Jade today. He's brilliant with my girl, as I've said, but sometimes I think he comes to spend time with us to avoid being in his own trailer.

From my kitchen sink, I watch him make his way back to the front door of his van. He pauses on the front step, rubs his stubble, looks around. I know there is something on his mind, some plan or fancy. I almost don't want to know. Instead, I'll be looking around for the girl to return. It was an unexpected pleasure to have someone not from our own family grace the bench of my small dining table. I know Jade was mesmerised, influenced in a bad way perhaps, but I can't stop my mind from thinking about her. Sahara.

*

I spend the day cleaning and hoovering out my van. Most of these trailers need a good clean, and it's funny how I'm the only one to ever suggest it. My back is sore as I lean over the pile of laundry I've left to linger for days. I tend to use the machine they've got in my sister's van. She's a good egg, my sister. There are a couple of other vans with washing machines too, but it's a tiny bit further to trek to them. I hang out my washing when it's done, my sister's too. I don't mind, it's good for my back. Whenever there is a glimmer of movement at the corner of my eye, I turn, wondering if it is the girl with the near-white hair. It never is. She is not coming today. Jade leaves the van and hovers by my side. I wonder if she is waiting too, or is filled with dread at the thought of the girl's arrival and is acting as my shield. It's hard to tell. When I make eye contact with her she looks away, hand over her eyes in an attempt to look like she's blocking the sun out. I know it's not the sun she's trying to eradicate.

I fold the washing later, think about the woman running the caravan park next door, wonder if she's doing similar tasks.

# FRAN

## 28 February

Today is van-cleaning day, my least favourite day of the week. I always come armed with the vacuum, dragged from one of the empty caravans, along with polish, dusters and black bags. The bathroom-cleaning stuff comes last. At least the empty caravans take no time at all to do; just a bit of dusting and a quick hoover of the carpets and they're done. I always knock in advance at the two occupied vans, today find myself wondering if we will have any new bookings for the spring. It'll be March tomorrow, and that tends to bring on a fluttering of reservations as people begin to look towards Easter and the summer months. More work on my part, what with the cleaning and preparations, but more money for us too. We've learnt to rely on the cash from the summer, although I leave it up to Dom to deal with the finances and spread the money out for the remainder of the year. My mind wanders to my husband and his indifference to me of late. Sure, it was better for a few days, but now it seems like we're just limping along again. He's always there for Bruno, he dotes on the boy, but his interest in me seems to be waning. I know that marriage after fifteen years can become a little dull, but he seems to be spending more and more time at work in the office in Norwich and less time working from home. It crosses my mind that he may be having an affair, but I find myself laughing out loud as I enter the first van I knock at. The man who occupies the caravan has kindly agreed to leave for an hour just so that I can clean up, and I am grateful for the time to myself. So much has started happening lately that I feel like I'm in some kind of whirlwind at times. Perhaps it is me who has not been contributing enough to our marriage. It's probably me at fault.

I find I'm thinking about the teacher as I'm plugging in the vacuum and putting all my effort into running the head of the hoover over the brown wiry carpet. Her words about Bruno were mysterious, didn't lend themselves to the description of a child perhaps being bullied. She didn't want to talk about Sadie, I get that, I get that she can't. And I don't even know if it's Sadie who has been affecting my child.

\*

After I knock at my sister's caravan again, the door is opened by a pallid face with dark bleary eyes.

'Oh, don't worry about cleaning today, Fran.'

The gravelly tone of his voice always gets me. He smells like he's been drinking.

I try not to frown, always want to appear friendly. 'It's been over a week; it really does need a clean.'

I glance over to the repaired window, the cleanliness of the new glass almost making me blink. It looks out of place next to the filthier pane beside it. I momentarily imagine my sister losing her temper when she's been outside the van, perhaps throwing a mug or even a trainer at the window, trying to rouse her alcoholic partner from his slumber, her fingers pricking the glass as she assessed the damage she did afterwards.

My sister's partner sighs, looking out through the door, beyond my head, reminding me that I am there to clean. 'Why don't you offer your services to the scallywags over there?' He nods towards the field with the Romany vans.

I force a laugh. 'Ha. Unfortunately, my income's not made from their caravans being kept clean. Just these ones.'

He is running a hand through his slightly greasy dark hair. My comment wasn't intended to make him feel guilty for his not being able to pay, and I swallow down my embarrassment. Looks like an age since his hair's been cut; I used to go for the floppy-boy hair when I was younger. 'Well, we're the only ones staying here apart from that other bloke, and we might be here for a while yet. Today I don't care if it's clean.' His voice is so deep, I sometimes can't even catch the words. I wonder if that was part of the charm for my sister. She's always liked a *manly* man.

'A quick vacuum is all.' I am making my way up the two steps to the front door.

Ellis steps to the side, letting me pass. 'Ros isn't here. Neither is Sadie.'

'That's fine.' It's a school day, of course, but then I remember that my niece has been excluded from education temporarily.

'They've gone into Norwich,' says Ellis, as if reading my thoughts. 'New clothes for both of them, you know what Ros is like with her shopping.'

I smile in an obligatory fashion, try not to think about how they would have any money for such expeditions. Lowering my head a little, I take in the number of beer cans spread across every surface of the kitchen area. I decide against even glancing towards the rubbish bin under the sink, concentrate on vacuuming up the filth from the floor. I wince from an unanticipated stab of pain for the little girl who is having to live in this environment.

'Sadie said about that bird having its head near pulled off.' He is having to shout over the noise of the hoover.

I am not expecting a comment. I pause, turn the hoover off so I can catch his voice better.

'Yes, horrible,' is all I can think to say.

'Who would do a thing like that? You sure it wasn't just a cat?'

I find myself looking Ellis in the eye. All I see there is an innocence, a naivety.

'We don't know, but we buried it as quickly as we could.'

'Was Bruno upset about it?'

Perhaps he hadn't seemed as upset as a ten-year-old should be on finding a creature that had been deliberately butchered to death.

But then Bruno never was one to get upset about an animal dying, not particularly. 'He was shocked, I suppose.' I remembered that his eyes had seemed so teary.

'Weird sorts around here these days.' Ellis's gaze is reaching over to the Romany field again, his irises a dark blue colour, much darker than I have seen before on anyone else. 'How is Dom?'

For a moment, it seems as though he has lumped my husband in with the *weirdness* of the Romany people, but then I realise he is just changing the subject abruptly. He never used to ask about Dom. Perhaps he is learning to be more polite.

'Well, I'm not seeing much of him these days, to be honest.'

Ellis doesn't look surprised. I find myself wanting to confide in someone, to tell them that I think I am perhaps losing my husband. There's a grey rugby-style hoodie hanging on a hook on the wall that looks just like Dom's, it catches my eye, makes me inhale sharply. Ellis turns, follows my eyeline, sees the hoodie.

'He seemed stressed the other night. The beer helped him to chill a bit, though.' He is smiling, kindness seeming to emanate from him.

*He's been here.* 'You saw him? Had a beer?'

'Don't look so startled! We're brothers-in-law.' He is smiling broadly now. 'Practically.'

I am trying to hide my surprise that Dom has been spending time with my sister and her partner and failing to mention it to me. 'Here?'

Ellis is looking at me intensely, his navy eyes fringed by lashes that are so long they would look more at home on some kind of animal. 'Yes, here. Fran, are you OK?' He grabs at the hoodie, hands it to me.

A lump is forming in my throat, uninvited tears threatening to prick at my eyes.

'He spends time here often?'

Ellis doesn't blink. 'Once. Or twice. I said, are you OK, Fran?'

That's it. The heat of the tears surprises me as they force their way out of my eyes and down my cheeks. I've barely been sleeping lately; the tiredness must be causing this rush of emotion. I hate crying in front of anyone, use the back of my fist to wipe the wetness away. 'I'm fine, I'm fine. Sleep deprivation.'

Ellis tugs at my elbow, encourages me to sit at the table by the window. 'What's going on?'

I let my body crumple onto the bench seat opposite him. It strikes me suddenly that, despite owning the caravans for nearly two years, I have never sat at one of the dining tables. I don't say anything, just allow the tears to work their way down my face.

'It's just Dom, I suppose. He seems so… distant. And then there's Bruno, and the teacher, and…' I don't even mention my sister's coolness towards me.

'And Sadie being excluded?'

I nod, choking a little on my own tears and the lump in my throat. 'I'm sorry, I don't know what's happening with the kids. I just can't work it out.'

For a while, Ellis doesn't say anything, he just puts his arm around me. I can smell beer on him. I let my head fall back for a moment, onto the crook of his arm. I consider asking him for a beer myself, to calm me down. I've never been much of a drinker, let alone a daytime drinker. My thoughts are interrupted by the shriek of the front door being pulled open from its hinges, my sister and niece gazing at me from the steps outside. Both Ellis and I jump up in surprise as Ros steps into the caravan, followed by Sadie.

'Why is Auntie Fran here?'

'No shopping?' tries Ellis.

I don't try to think of anything to say, just stand up, Dom's hoodie over my arm, make to leave the caravan. As I step out of the van and down the steps, I stroke my hand over Sadie's warm head, my sister's eyes burning into my side. I don't want to talk right now. I hear Ros telling Ellis that all the trains were delayed, that they gave up.

# TAD

Charlie's been round, telling me all about this bird he's found down in the marshland. I can't tell if he is now genuinely interested in seabird-spotting. He's had a real interest in birds of prey before – buzzards, kestrels, you name it, but only these birds that live off other animals. I thought he liked the hunting-for-prey aspect of it, was never sure if he was keen on finding their eggs or just thrilled to see them flying overhead, doing that circling thing they do, as though about to make a helicopter-style landing on some poor, unsuspecting small mammal. True, in the past he'd often been in it for the money, these ventures of his, but he seems genuinely pleased to have met a local woman and chatted with her about the bird. It was a *little tern*, he said, as if I should know what that was. *A smallish seabird, making its nest on the flat part of the marsh.* He sounded so proud. Me, well, I'm still only good at making out the magpies and the bigger birds, even though it's the little ones I like. I can tell any type of tit from a mile off, though. Try not laughing at that. I asked about the woman he spoke to; he couldn't tell me much, other than that she seemed a bit quiet. He said she got there before him, at the crack of dawn. I wanted to ask him if he'd let the boy into his van the other day, but for some reason, I just didn't.

# FRAN

## 28 February (continued)

Ros is on the phone the minute I get home from the caravans. For a moment, I think she is about to launch into a tirade, *Why are you spending time curled up on the dining bench with Ellis?* She doesn't, though, of course she doesn't. She's my sister.

'Ellis says you were in tears. You didn't look great. What's wrong?'

I remember my sudden outburst of emotion, feel shame consuming me. I imagine him telling her all about it. *We were just chatting about Dom, then all of a sudden she was in a right state.*

I try to ignore my paranoia and wonder what jobs I can get on with in the house. The thought of battling with more laundry makes me feel weary so I opt to wander upstairs, see what needs to be tidied, perhaps some paperwork of mine needs filed. My sister's words are circling around in my mind. On the phone I made excuses, told her it was just my *time of the month*, that I had been missing Dom while he was working so many extra days on a huge project he's been assigned to. It was bullshit. I wouldn't even know if he'd been assigned a huge project, the way our communication has been these past few weeks.

As I walk into the bedroom I share with him, my eyes are drawn to his tan leather bag with the long strap that he often takes to work with him. I've never considered what he might be keeping inside it, it's never occurred to me to look. We've always had trust, if nothing else, although I would query that statement given the way I am feeling now. I picture him traipsing off to Ros and Ellis's caravan of an evening, telling me he's going for a long walk. Why wouldn't he

have just told me the truth? That he was going to visit his brother-
and sister-in-law? Perhaps he thought I wouldn't have approved of
his drinking, what with us funding Ellis's rehabilitation stint just a
few months ago. I sit on the end of our compact double bed, open
the flap of the bag. Just papers, lots of papers, and as I flick through
these, there are numerous post-it notes in yellows and pinks, some
containing dates and lists, one containing a mobile phone number.
My heart jolts a little. I've never had reason to suspect him of
anything before. I put the post-it back inside the inches-deep pile
of paper, and shove it all back inside the leather bag, closing the
flap down with a slap. Not moving from the bed, I can feel the cogs
in my brain turning. I consider purchasing some form of tracking
device to place inside the lining of his bag. *I can't do that, it's Dom.*
*Dom, my red-headed, straight-down-the-line husband.* I used to call him
'square' when we first got together. I used to laugh at his ways:
'Fran, you have four minutes to finish your drink before the train
leaves.' My friends used to wonder how I could have any fun while
being in his company. 'Four minutes before you can start having
any fun,' I remember one of them laughing.

I grab at the pair of shirts that have been screwed down, with
force, into the laundry basket that sits on our landing; I sniff at
his collars for the sign of another woman. Nothing. Not a note of
perfume, only the slightly sweaty odour of the underarm stains.
I don't have a clue what worries me the most – that he might be
distracted by another woman or that he has chosen to confide in
my sister and her partner.

*

Bruno was late coming out of school, and today is the last day I've
said that I'll collect him. I've promised him he can walk home alone
from now, like most of the other children do in Year Six. A slight
weight is lifted from my mind as I remember that Sadie is still off
school, and then I wonder why I feel like that. It makes me dislike
myself for a moment. I glance around the playground, an ache

of sadness in my stomach at the fact that my child is becoming more independent and this will gradually render me redundant as a mother. Some of the other parents catch my eye, smile or nod, and I find myself wrapped in conversation with one mum about how the children *seem to be so grown up all of a sudden*. I don't tell her the extent of the sadness I feel, that perhaps I now regret sticking with the notion of having only one child. It was Dom's idea, the only-child thing. *Think how much attention he'd receive from us*, that had been his mantra, which I had happily followed. Secretly, though, I had always toyed with the idea of another one, perhaps from a 'surprise' pregnancy. A little girl, maybe, to balance out the level of testosterone in the house. However, I couldn't bring myself to trick Dom in that way, so we stuck with just Bruno, and we've been content, for the most part. I listen to the other mother making her squawks about Ms McConnell, about how her child doesn't like the woman, that perhaps she should be let go. She tells me that *apparently* the teacher was seen in the local pub, propping up the bar in a particularly short skirt. The mother continues to fill me in on all the details of this night: Ms McConnell was downing drink after drink, was outdoing the men. I find myself stepping away, pretending to look in my bag for something. I don't need to be hearing this. The mother eventually stops talking, stares at me for a bit, then straightens up as if she's been caught spreading poison in a play park.

I watch Ms McConnell lead the class out of the main doors of the building, Bruno nowhere in sight. She towers above the other parents as usual; the children trail behind her, a collection of tiny gnomes. They follow in an obedient line, in their identical clothes. I can see my child near the back of the line now, he's flicking and messing around with the boy in front of him. He catches my eye, drops his hand to his side, clutches harder at his bookbag. The boy in front turns to say something, but I can't make out what it is. I glance at the teacher, but she is already in conversation with another parent, tongue wagging, pink hair tied up like a pineapple again. I try to imagine her being a drinker, her body leaning over the bar, asking for another pint. The wind whips at my face with its pointy fingers, brings me back to the present scene. I watch the teacher as she talks to the father of a child who is struggling in earnest with his bag and coat. There is a tattoo on her wrist I've never noticed before: a swallow, curling around her arm as if it's been twisted on with force.

# TAD

She's taken to leaving the caravan for up to twenty minutes at a time. It's great. She hovers at the door, wavering, as if unsure whether to take the plunge. Then, each time, she lurches forward, throws a quick wave over her shoulder. The others all see her leave, and I tell them not to make a big deal of it. Some of the littler kids can't understand why she hasn't really been going out until this point. I am wondering if it has anything to do with the blonde girl. Perhaps she only goes to look at the birds. I just tell her to always let me know where she's going, and she always replies with the same answer, in that almost-whispery way of hers: '*The sea.*'

# FRAN

## 2 March

I am out early again this morning, not so much to see the tern and her nest, but to use the hide, see if it's worth the money I forked out. I've been here twenty minutes now, binoculars in hand. Only the herring gulls are rife this morning, whooping and screeching overhead, no sign of the rarer bird I was hoping to spot. I know I have the tern, over the other side, but I was hoping to see another glimpse of the black-throated diver. I've only managed to see it once, and what a joy it was. Things were just starting to become unsettled with the kids then, and I had welcomed the distraction and excitement of seeing such a bird. Soon, I will come here with Bruno again, especially as the mornings are becoming lighter and bring with them a sense of near-warmth. The bench I sit on is numbing my backside; I wish I hadn't laughed when the hide-makers had suggested a cushioned bench for just a hundred pounds more. The refuge is cleaner than I expected it to be, since I haven't visited for a week or so now. Dom was pretty sure the Romany people would have been trying to camp out in here just for something to do, but there doesn't seem to be any evidence of their visiting. I close my eyes for a moment, mimicking my son's movements from the only time we were both here together. There is a serenity to being here in this shed, alone. I can hear the waves crashing and imagine them pulling back, frothing with their limey fingers. My mind shifts back to the Romany people again. Their quietness is almost unnerving. You expect some noise, perhaps litter, but there's been nothing. I don't think even the kids have bothered them again. As I leave the hide, I see an older man, stretched white skin, walking back towards

94

the church path, perhaps from the Romany field. He doesn't see me, continues his walk with his head down, eyes on the path. He's got a bit of a hobble to his gait.

\*

Ros is waiting for me at the front door of my cottage, her arms hugging herself, no coat.

'Everything alright?'

She gestures for me to open the door, and I try to oblige, jostling around in the too-large pockets of the coat I have once again nicked from Dom for the morning.

We wait until we are seated in the living room, her nestled in the old beige armchair, me on the sofa opposite. Her long legs look even thinner than before. Perhaps she's not looking after herself properly like I had hoped she had been doing. My brain seeking distraction, I notice the piles of washing I have left on the other end of the sofa, wish I had folded it all away before leaving the house earlier.

'I don't think I can cope anymore.'

I turn my gaze to her, waiting for more information. I want to help, I am just running out of ways how.

'Sadie is allowed back at the school soon. What a mess. She should never have been kicked out. That bloody hippy teacher woman.' My sister quickly glances at me, pauses. 'And Ellis is drinking again.'

My mind ignores the last statement, a fact which I am already aware of, and instead I consider whether the school will eventually exclude my niece on a permanent basis, should she keep misbehaving. What would Ellis and Ros do then? They don't even have a car to drive her to another school. Practical thoughts aside, my emotions begin to feel like they are crumbling. The little girl. I wonder if Ros and Ellis have asked her why she did that thing to the other girl's bag. *If* she did it.

'He's drinking, not looking for work. I don't feel like I can look for employment at this time, when I'm in such a mess.'

I go to lean forward, to touch her arm, but I can't quite reach.

'I understand you're going to be pretty pissed off with the money you spent on Ellis's drinking therapy.'

I wasn't even giving any thought to the money. Money means nothing.

'What are you thinking? Fran?'

I am stretching my legs out in front of me like a cat, buying time. 'Do you need food? Cash?'

She seems to relax a little in the chair, seems a little more like the Ros I grew up with – flaky, disorganised, but my kind, fun sister all the same. 'I hope we'll be fine. Sometimes I just want to… oh, I don't know.'

Ros is looking at me, waiting for me to question what she was just about to say.

'What? Leave?'

She looks down towards her lap. I hadn't been expecting this. Ros is the most loyal person I have ever known. I sit up straighter in my chair, tuck my legs beneath me. I realise I am holding my breath.

I watch her tuck a strand of hair behind her ear. She usually does this when she feels embarrassed about something. 'Perhaps Sadie and I could stay with you a little while? Just an idea.'

I nod, exhaling, a slight sense of embarrassment flickering in me that I hadn't thought of this option before.

'Not for very long. Perhaps a few weeks. You've got a four-bed house sitting here with empty bedrooms.'

It feels like an accusation. *You don't care about us enough.*

'I think maybe you should try to make things work with Ellis a little while longer. He really cares about you two.' It is Dom, appearing in the doorway.

I freeze. I hadn't heard a sound.

She huffs only very slightly, folds her arms. 'Hi, Dom. Didn't realise you were here.'

She looks at me; I make my eyes go larger in a hopefully comical fashion. She smiles approvingly back at me. The atmosphere lifts slightly. For a moment, we are teenage sisters again.

I stand, decide to go and make coffee to dilute the situation. 'Drink, anyone?'

Ros is now frowning, unfolding then refolding her arms. Dom doesn't move from the doorway.

I force a smile to my face, try to nudge my way past my unyielding husband. 'Coffee makes everything better.'

'I'll make them,' says Dom, gesturing for me to sit down again.

I reluctantly turn, walk back to the sofa, mouthing at my sister, *I'm sorry, I didn't know he was coming home.*

Ros is suddenly dabbing at her eyes with a manky tissue. 'Should I go?' It's a whisper.

I shake my head no, feel the shame of my husband's uninvited words simmering over me. Dom returns to the living room, hands us our coffees. I watch Ros lower her mug onto the side table next to the armchair she is sitting in, not even looking at it. It reminds me of the other day, when she left our kitchen abruptly, her tea untouched.

Dom clears his throat. 'I had a think, when I was in the kitchen.'

My sister and I both raise our heads.

'Why doesn't Ellis come and live here for a while? We've been getting on so well lately. Not that we didn't before.'

There is a silence as my sister absorbs the idea, looks like she's chewing something in her mouth. I lean back, take a sip of my coffee, curse myself for burning my tongue. All at once, I think of Dom's hoodie hanging on the door inside my sister and her partner's caravan. *We've been getting on so well lately.*

Ros stares straight ahead for a while. 'It *could* work!'

I try to hide the sigh of relief that is attempting to release itself from my flesh, smile broadly at her. I don't want her to think of Dom as an overbearing person. He's not. I think he just likes the idea of having Ellis around, rather than two more females. Correction: he probably doesn't want Sadie in our home.

'I can talk it over with Ellis. The great thing is that he might feel too uncomfortable to be drinking in your home, unlike ours. I'll see what he says.' She sounds genuinely excited, and I feel a tingle of thrill warm me from the inside.

We talk for a little longer, and it almost feels like old times, before Ros became the mother of Sadie, before her life was mapped out around the unemployment and drinking habits of her partner. She is smiling more as we speak; I think I am too.

As she is fiddling with the lock of my front door, she turns, as if she's just remembered something she needed to say. 'We don't see much of Bruno, now that Sadie's not at school. He must come over soon!'

I smile, open the latch for her, nod. 'Of course. He'd love that.'

She disappears up the end of our front path, and I close the door quietly, straighten out my clothes with my free hand.

# TAD

Today Charlie is assembling and drilling some shelves into the back of his van, the one he drives to jobs. My sisters, they've offered to go buy some wood from the hardware store, but he won't hear of it. I worry about where he's getting the wood from. Probably helped himself from the woodland just beyond here. I watch him, sweat glittering around the folds of his neck, his back bent over the load of wooden planks in front of him. He doesn't stop for air. He is kneeling now, drilling. I half expect him to look, feel my eyes burning into him, but he doesn't, just keeps drilling. There are five or six shelves he's putting in there. I can see some sort of cabinet he's already made. Always looks professional.

There is movement from the eastern side of our field, a small person, not the girl. I stand, mug of coffee in my hand, its warmth bringing my mind slowly awake as I try to focus as much as I can. I should probably wear glasses – I'm able to see less and less these days – but I can't face the idea of heading to a high street in town and being assessed under a shiny microscope like an insect.

Mumbling from the smaller bedroom of the caravan catches me; Jade has not long returned from her morning walk, is having another half hour in bed. She has the ability to just zonk out wherever she lands, it seems. She'll be snoring in a minute.

I look on as the child walks timidly across the field, eyes seemingly not knowing which way to look. He stares up at my trailer, the only one painted blue, then moves his face away. I recognise him now he's closer. The boy who follows Sahara about. He probably knows her as *Sadie*. I make a mental note of this, should I try to speak to him.

99

I'm not sure if I will. He seems lost, yet slightly unapproachable. I grab at my front door handle, yank the door towards me. These bloody doors are always getting stuck; it's the damp. The sudden noise makes the boy turn his head in my direction, and I plaster my best smile onto my face. 'Lost?'

He stops walking, is toying with something in his hands. I can't see what.

He doesn't say anything to begin with, just looks to and from his own hands and what looks like the detached wing of a large bird.

'I found it.'

'It's alright. Whatchu got there?'

He takes a step towards me, cautious-like, then halts way before he is anywhere near my van door. It looks like his little hands are shaking.

'Hello again?' The voice is from just a little further away. Charlie is mopping at the moisture on his neck with his oversized baseball cap, clutched in his red hand. He steps closer to us.

The boy looks at me.

'Charlie, the boy has just come to see me, I shouldn't wonder.'

I step down from my trailer, coat wrapped around my shoulders.

'She said you were a good person to talk to.' The boy is holding out the wing towards me. Looks like part of a pigeon. He looks over his shoulder briefly at my brother.

'She?'

'Sadie.'

He *is* the boy who hangs around with Sahara.

'Oh, is that right?' I realise I sound a little unfriendly, so add a bit of a laugh after my comment.

Charlie wanders back to the spot by his van, watches the younger men move the cuttings away to the furthest part of the field, against the remains of an old brick wall that is barely standing. He cranes his neck towards me, calls out. 'Takin' in all waifs and strays now, eh?' But then I see he is laughing.

I don't respond but usher the boy into my caravan. He obliges swiftly, as if he'd been waiting for me to ask him inside for the past minute.

'No Sadie today, then?'

He shakes his head, eyes taking in everything in my caravan. I feel a stab of embarrassment at the mess I've left on the side of the sink: cuttings of vegetables, meats, not cleared away. Jade brought a dead pheasant back to the van just minutes ago, thinking her generosity would provide us with a meal. I don't take to eating roadkill per se, but I won't tell her that. I'll just let her think I'm cooking her mutilated pheasant later on, and enjoying every morsel.

I gesture for the boy to sit down, notice his eyes are still taking everything in. 'Not been inside a trailer before, eh?'

He finally looks at me, the bird wing still lying flat in his hand. 'Well, yes, actually. The caravan park next door. But we don't call them "trailers".'

He breaks eye contact with me. For a moment, a strange look passes over his face.

I think of the woman I saw leaving the wooded area that snowy day, boy running behind. I wonder if she was the same woman who came and spoke to one of the lads a few weeks ago, when we first arrived. If it was this boy who had been following her.

'Yes, we've been here two years now. My dad doesn't have much to do with the caravans. He works in Norwich. My auntie, sort-of uncle and Sadie live in one of our caravans. They don't pay for it because my auntie doesn't work and is sad, and my uncle is trying not to be an alcoholic. I'm not allowed to be near Sadie at the moment. But we meet up in secret.'

It's such a splurge of information that my brain is slow in processing it all. I sit on the padded bench next to him, realising it is Saturday, that's why the boy is not at school.

My eyes are drawn again to the wing he's cradling in his hand. 'You want to put that thing in the bin.'

He doesn't move. 'You don't think we can find the bird it came from?'

I get the feeling he doesn't want to throw away the bird part.

'This is the second dead-bird-thing I've seen in a week,' he continues. 'We buried a nuthatch the other day. It was pretty. Before it got its head snatched off.' I realise his eyes are filling with tears, so I consider placing an arm around him. It strikes me that he is sitting in exactly the same space where his little friend Sahara sat just days ago. They couldn't be more different.

'Things happen in the wild all the time.'

He is letting the detached grey wing drop gently from one hand to the other. 'Doesn't mean it's right.'

I pause for a moment. 'Why can't you see Sahara anymore?' I forgot I was meant to call her *Sadie*.

He eyes me, saying nothing.

'Sadie.'

'Oh. She's a *bad influence*.' He lets the pigeon wing drop onto the table with a dull thud. It doesn't seem to be missing any feathers. 'My dad reckons, anyway.' He gives a little chuckle.

I find myself nodding. I remember the girl's confidence, her laughter at Jade. I should have felt resentment towards her, or at least a sense of indifference, but now the boy has only piqued my interest further.

'What's your name, anyway?'

'Bruno. Charlie knows my name. You can keep the wing.'

He stands, yanks the heavy door handle, almost trips down the two steps outside. Charlie has gone from where he had been arranging the kindling for the fire; I see his form in the distance, the sun reflecting off the metal side of the axe blade that rests on his shoulder.

# FRAN

## 5 March

We've been mentally preparing for Ellis to move in. Dom's already dashed up to the biggest of our two spare rooms to have a look about, see what he can do to make his almost-brother-in-law comfortable. We don't even know if Ellis has agreed to this yet. He's popping around this evening to discuss it. I guess Ros will stay behind in the van with Sadie. We haven't talked about Ellis's potential contribution to bills, or if he'll be making any. I for one don't need him to. Dom is emptying some drawers of the desk we have kept stashed in the room, never used for anything except storage. There are receipts, papers, and some feathers floating around in the first two drawers. Bruno. Must have taken a liking to the feathers that coat the shoreline where we live. He never had any of this before, back where we were in Surrey. No coastline, anyhow. As I watch my husband become more red-faced as he turns the room upside down, I consider that we have rushed into this decision. I like Ellis, but they say you don't really know someone until you live with them. Perhaps we will discover his drinking is unbearable; Ros has never said it, but maybe he is one of those people whose personality just flips into something else once they have a drink inside them.

'Perhaps we should draw up some kind of contract.' Dom's blue eyes are turning towards me. I can feel my mouth twisting into a laugh. Of course, it would be him who suggests such a thing. I'm embarrassed for him, for Ellis, who isn't even here. There is so much paperwork on the floor that I can't remember what the carpet underneath looks like.

He doesn't say anything else, just carries on emptying drawers, stands up, goes to do the same to the pine wardrobe in the corner.

'We don't even know if he wants to stay here with us.' I sound like I'm having second thoughts. Perhaps I am.

My husband turns, his red brows fold into one as they always do. His hands are moving the pieces of artwork I had forgotten I had stored in the wardrobe. 'If you didn't want him here, perhaps you should have said at the time.' He clears his throat, his hands picking up, rearranging and putting down my sketches from our old home.

I don't know how long it will be for. I don't know if Ros is planning on kicking him out permanently. I still can't believe she's found the strength to tell him to go.

After several hours of messing up and then eventually emptying the room, I leave Dom to continue alone. I'm dying for some food, run down the stairs to make some pasta. Bruno is late home from school; the sky already darkened an hour or two ago. I don't know how I just seem to lose track of time. When he arrives home, he lets himself out into the back garden, and the sounds of him kicking the football against the shed reverberate in my ears. He's barely said two words, didn't seem bothered that both of his parents were otherwise occupied as he came through the front door. I watch him from the living room, through the patio doors, the light from the faux-Victorian torch on the house's outside wall illuminating his small figure. He kicks, turns, yells a cheer to himself. His dark hair is getting thicker, longer, and if I squint for a moment I swear his eyes are tiny, puffy, like a finch fallen from its own nest.

\*

Ellis is bang on time: 8 pm, as we suggested. He is by himself. Dom had seen him making his way up the electronic torchlit path towards our front door, had turned away from the window, mouthing the words *no beers* at me and giving a stupid thumbs-up sign.

We sit in the living room, Ellis taking the armchair that Ros had picked just the other day. He seems so different without her here, and without his daughter hanging off him. 'So,' he says, rubbing his hands together. His manner is kind of awkward. 'It's so kind of you to offer to take me.' I think of when I was crying in his caravan, my head rested against his arm. It makes me squirm with embarrassment a little. There, it was his kingdom. Here, he is cap in hand.

I am smiling, I want to help him. Dom is standing in the corner of the room, hands in pockets. It makes Ellis appear small.

'I promise I won't be any trouble, and it'll only be for a few weeks.' Again, his voice is so deep that my ears are straining to pick up the sounds.

I feel my husband glance briefly at me from where he's standing. I know what he's thinking: *a few weeks.*

'Take as long as you need.'

Ellis smiles back at me. 'You two,' is all he says. For a moment, I think he is going to crumple, but he just straightens up in his chair, sits further forward. 'You've been a lifeline for us.'

Dom paces towards me, takes the seat next to me on the sofa. 'We're just always happy to help, you know that. We've discussed this before.' I notice he doesn't look directly at Ellis, perhaps because of his own discomfort at the situation.

My stomach flips a little as I suddenly remember the nights that my husband has spent at Ellis and Ros's caravan, looking for someone to talk to. I wonder what they have talked about, if Ros was privy to their conversations, if she kept her distance.

Ellis looks at Dom now. It's as if I'm not there for a moment. 'Mate, I know, and I am so grateful. I was so relieved those times you popped around in the evenings. Gave me a break from the Mrs.'

There's a snippet of silence. Ellis quickly turns his head to me. 'No offence to your sister, obviously, Fran.' His voice again. I try not to think of the term Dom came up with for him, but it repeats over and over in my mind. *Gravel throat, gravel throat.* It helps to push away the visions of Dom at my sister and Ellis's place, chatting, having fun, excluding me.

I wave his words away with my hand and a laugh. 'None taken.'

We begin to discuss bills, food, and the fact that I'm happy to cook for him most nights of the week, that he can just join in on our mealtimes. The conversation inevitably turns to Sadie as the evening draws on, how he will miss her, how he will meet up with her for walks.

'So, what's happening with the teacher? She been in touch?'

'Nope. Don't want to hear from her, either. She's difficult, that one.'

Dom is quick off the mark. 'How so? Seems OK to me. I mean, I know she hasn't gelled with Sadie, but…' His voice tails off as he looks at me.

'What, apart from getting her excluded? She's just bonkers. Have you seen her pink hair? In plaits? At her age. She's not normal.'

I am jumping to her defence. 'You don't approve because of her hair?' I don't know if he's heard the same rumours that I was subjected to in the school playground.

He bites his lower lip, like he's not sure whether to say more. 'I've had more conversations with her than either of you two have. She's not right. It's like she's from another planet. I… could say more.'

'More? Like what?' My heart is beginning to thump harder in my chest.

He lowers his eyes to the floor. 'She shouldn't be a teacher. She's been seen out and about.'

'You mean drinking? In the pub? God, isn't she allowed a life of her own?'

'She shouldn't be out behaving like that in a public place. She's a primary school teacher, for Christ's sake. Folk say she's covered head-to-toe in tattoos and piercings, gets lairy in town. She tried it on with a mate of one of the dads at the school. He had to fend her off. Apparently.'

That word again. *Apparently.* I wonder if the word would stand up in a court of law.

The atmosphere in the room causes me to stand, lift the empty teacups from the table, left over from earlier.

'When do you think you'd like to move in?'

Dom is the one to ask the question. I don't feel comfortable asking, don't want to look like I am poking and prodding at my almost-brother-in-law.

'This week any good?' He looks sheepish, then his face drops into something like shame. 'You know, I won't be drinking. If you were worried about that.'

'It's fine, it's fine,' I find myself saying. I don't even think he will drink here. Anyway, everyone is entitled to a drink or two. Even a teacher.

We make plans for him to move into our spare room the day after tomorrow. I can't remember if we've even told Bruno what's happening. I listen to his football hit the side of the house over and over: *bam, bam, bam.*

# TAD

Charlie's different today. He's fixing a laptop for a customer, slamming on the keys. I came to his van for a coffee. He didn't offer to make me one. I can understand. Mum used to call him *a closed book*. He's anxious – still sore from the police being on his tracks, always looking over his shoulder. I get it. He treads down the steps of his van, leaving me alone inside. He's not really talking, so the others leave him to it.

Nearly forgot to mention; I saw a bloke leaving the caravan site next door – messy dark hair, looked as though he could have been wearing some kind of mascara or something weird like that. He didn't look up at me or the others. Was in a world of his own. Carrier bag full of things. It struck me that it was an older carrier bag, not straight from the shop, too dishevelled. My eyes tried to follow the man – don't know his name – but he was gone onto the path beyond the woodland long before I could catch his eye.

# FRAN

## 6 March

When we arrive at the school, I sense that something is different. We are late today; I had expected to have to sign Bruno in at reception, come up with some plausible excuse. But his line is still standing in the playground, the last class there, the wind whipping and fidgeting with parents' coats and scarves. The colder weather is making an unwelcome return. I try to catch the attention of another mother close by me, but she doesn't look in my direction. The teacher hasn't come out yet. After what feels like eternity, the deputy head blusters out of reception from the left-hand side of the building, short and stumpy, rushing towards the line of children. Her tight skirt makes it difficult for her little legs to gain any speed.

'Sorry, so sorry for the delay!' she warbles.

She stands at the front of the line, pulling at the second outside door along the long strip of classrooms. 'Children, you may come in!'

The children obediently follow her in, and a couple of the mums who work as teaching assistants appear from the inside classroom. I know one of them from Bruno being in the same football team as her son, hiss at her, feel immediately embarrassed as she almost gasps in my direction.

'Where's their teacher?'

She steps closer, keeps her voice down. 'She hasn't shown up for work. Didn't tell us. We've not got a replacement yet, so the deputy is taking over this morning.'

I smile with gratitude and wave goodbye to Bruno, who has been straining to catch my eye for the past few moments. The door closes behind him, and I see the other parents group together more where they were previously standing waiting in the playground. The mum I spoke to last week raises her eyebrows at me. *We knew she was no good.* There seems to be no surprise on the faces of the other parents.

\*

My sister calls my phone the minute I get back to the cottage. 'Did you say Ellis could move in with you today?'

'No, tomorrow is what we agreed.'

I can hear a buzzing down the end of the line; my sister's voice drifts in and out of my hearing range. 'Ros, I can't hear you, the line is shit.'

She shouts this time. 'I said, oh, no worries, just wondered where Ellis had got to. Probably gone to buy more beers.' Her voice sounds disappointed, but not surprised.

'Maybe he's gone to buy a few bits for the move to ours,' I suggest. I don't feel hopeful. Perhaps he's got an interview he's not told her about, wanting to surprise her with good news.

'The school just rang, by the way,' my sister continues in a loud voice. 'Can you still hear me?' The line is crackling, but I can grasp what she's telling me.

'Yes! What did they say?'

She is clearing her throat. 'Sadie can return to school in two days' time. A couple of days earlier than they originally said. I'm pretty chuffed. So is Sadie.'

'That's great.' I imagine Ros and Sadie dancing around the caravan. I want to join in with their elation.

'The receptionist said the teacher wasn't in. I wonder if she's bunking off 'cos they made the decision about Sadie's return against her will. Or maybe you just can't trust these supply teachers they end up with. God knows where she came from.'

Her first suggestion could work: the school determined that Sadie could return to the school, the teacher is making a stand, not showing up. 'Irresponsible,' I agree. I consider the rest of what my sister said, the apparent mystery around where the teacher hailed from originally. Her accent is not from around this area; nor is mine. Still, in my mind, I can't place where she may have appeared from, with her overstretched vowel sounds, her guttural wordings.

*

When I turn up in the afternoon, the children have already been let out of the classroom door, a different teacher with them. Another supply. I can hear the children calling to their parents. *We had a new teacher today!*

The teaching assistant from earlier avoids my eye, helps lead the children to their respective parent or carer.

'There was no Ms McConnell today,' announces Bruno, as if I didn't know.

'No? Why was that?' Perhaps he will know if she's not coming back. If the school has let her go.

He reaches into his schoolbag, pulls out the blue feather he's kept hold of all this time. He is stroking the very end of it. It is starting to look a little worn away.

'Bruno?'

'Oh. Nobody knows. We all hope she comes back tomorrow.'

He is echoing the words of whichever staff member spoke to the class, no doubt the deputy head. *We all hope she comes back tomorrow.*

I put my arm around his shoulder and guide him towards the path. 'Bruno. Some news for you. Sadie is being allowed back to school the day after tomorrow.'

I am hoping the fact will cheer him up a little.

He doesn't say anything for a moment, bites down hard on his bottom lip. 'Do you know, Sadie and I don't even play together or sit together at school anymore?'

I am nodding. 'Yes, the teacher did mention that at your parents' evening. Any reason why?'

He walks ahead a little, runs back with the feather between his fingers. He is so young compared to the other children. 'Didn't want to get into trouble.'

\*

Ros is waiting by our front door. She's pretty much hopping from foot to foot. 'He's not back yet.'

I try to look concerned but am in a twist with all the things being held in my hands – a bookbag that Bruno has thrust at me, lunchboxes, drinks bottles. 'Give me a sec.'

We are finally in through the front door, Bruno racing off to the kitchen, me dumping his bags by the hall table.

'Fran, he's not back!'

My sister has followed us into the house, is standing too close. I can smell toothpaste on her breath.

'Are you sure he's not just getting ready to move in with us tomorrow?'

Ros sighs, lets her arms drop to her sides. 'No, Fran, I don't think so.' There's a slight pause. 'Why would he not tell me where he was going?'

I look at her for a moment. She seems so weakened, so frail. It's hard not to feel pity for her. I want to wrap her up in my arms for a moment, like I did when we were small.

Bruno appears back in the hallway. 'Who is moving in with us tomorrow?'

Ros looks at me. 'You haven't told Bruno?'

'Told me what?' Bruno is on his tiptoes, peering, his school coat hanging from one arm.

'Your Uncle Ellis was meant to be moving into your house tomorrow, Bruno.'

A wave of heat powers through the skin on my face. I had been meaning to tell him tonight.

My son looks at me, confusion clouding his round face. 'Mum?'

'Yes, it's true. We were going to be helping Ellis out.'

'So, are we or aren't we?'

I cringe a little at his rudeness, say nothing. Ros squats down a little, so she is level with Bruno's face. 'He's not around at the moment. We don't know where he's gone.'

'He's vanished?'

I am shaking my head, but my son's eyes remain firmly on his aunt.

I raise my voice to try to get his attention back. 'Bruno, he'll come back. And yes, he'll be staying with us from tomorrow.'

My sister stands, pulls me by the arm into my own kitchen, motions for me to sit in one of my own dining chairs. 'I've got a feeling something is wrong with Ellis. Maybe you shouldn't just go telling Bruno that everything is OK.'

'But it hopefully is!' I watch Bruno move away from the hall towards the back door. Once outside, he is kicking his football against the wall of the house again. Gently at first, then the kicks get harder. I wince

'I bet you anything you like that he's not back by tomorrow morning,' Ros says.

I am trying not to think too much, but then a realisation jolts in my mind. The teacher. Ellis. Disappearing on the same day.

# TAD

Sahara is here again. She doesn't speak of her parents, how they don't seem to mind her walking around by herself. There was a knock at my door this morning, around 9 am. I had wondered if it was Charlie or one of the other men, keen to get me to help them lug some of their stuff around again. They've been dealing with more computers lately, fixing them for new customers. It's not great for my back, lifting and moving these damned things, so I was relieved to see the girl at the door.

'You know, your little friend came to see me.' It's one way for me to greet her.

She smiles, walks towards the benches at my table, where we sat last time.

The warmth of the sun is stretching in through the door she's left wide open, and I don't sit down with her immediately. 'Want to go outside?'

My question is answered with a quick shake of her head. 'Where's Jade?'

It sounds like a demand. I'm sure she didn't mean it to be.

I close the door, sit down gently opposite her at the table, stabbing pains in both my knees as I try to shuffle myself along the bench to face her directly. 'You like coming here?'

She smiles again; I'm not sure if it's a genuine smile. It doesn't quite reach her eyes. 'Of course I do.'

She fiddles with the salt and pepper pots I left on the table from last night. Salt is spilling onto the table. She lets it sift through her fingers.

'How come you choose to visit me?'

'Not much else to do. I'm not at school. We had a different teacher yesterday anyway, my mum said. You're a nice person to hang out with. My mum is nice, but… she's away with the fairies right now. She's always pissed off at my aunt. And now my dad's left.'

That's it, it's all she says. A lot of information in a few short sentences. I don't ask about her father, decide not to ask why her mum is angry at her own sister. Instead, I try to keep one eye on her as her gaze continues around my trailer. I wonder if she's looking for Jade. Charlie came over earlier, took her out for one of his walks, despite his mood. Maybe he'll show her the nest he was talking about or pick her up at the water's edge, pretend to throw her in. She still screams with delight at this, despite her age, and her size.

'I've found some eggs.'

Her words catch me unawares. She's talking about the same nest that my brother might be taking Jade to see right now.

'Really?'

She nods, and, for a moment, I think this new line of conversation is suddenly closed too.

'They're special ones.'

'How do you know?'

She pulls her legs up underneath her, so she is kneeling on the padded bench. 'My auntie knows they are. Bruno heard her telling his dad.'

I find myself silent, not knowing what to say. 'You both into birds, are you?'

The girl shrugs. 'I just know that my auntie likes them. She goes to stare at them, sometimes.'

I just sit, glancing out of my own window – notice that the glass needs a damned good clean. 'It's called *bird spotting*.'

'Oh. OK. Whatever.'

I am smiling. She really is on the defensive.

'Where is Bruno today?'

She wriggles slightly, straightening out her clothes. 'School.'

I think of asking her if she knows her friend spends time with Charlie now, at his van, or messing around outside it. Decide against it.

'What did you do wrong, again?' She didn't really elaborate last time. Perhaps I shouldn't ask.

She picks up the pepper pot now and attempts to slide the lid open sideways. I grab it from her hand, move it away like she is a naughty toddler.

She glances up at me. 'I put bird poo in a girl's bag.' She giggles, looks up at me, stops laughing. 'I told mum and dad that I didn't do it, though.'

I pause, try not to think of how she would have got hold of some birdshit and moved it into someone else's bag without them noticing, wonder why she felt the need to keep the truth from her parents. 'Was that it?'

'No. Teacher hates me. Doesn't like me asking questions about her. I only wanted to know where she lived.'

My breath catches in the back of my throat for a moment. 'Which teacher is that?'

She rests her head down sideways on the table in front of us; I can't see her face anymore. I realise with embarrassment that I can't remember the last time I wiped the table.

'Oh, you won't know her. You don't go to the school. She's meant to be teaching us instead of our normal teacher, who's having a baby, but I heard she wasn't there.'

I drop my line of enquiry, cross one leg over the other, as painful as it is.

The subject is changed quickly enough. 'My dad was going to be moving in with Bruno and his mum and dad.'

'Oh?'

'Yes. He can't stop drinking so he was going to live there. Mum hopes it'll help stop him. But it seems he might've gone on one of his *benders*.'

She must mean drinking episodes. Sounds funny, coming from a kid. 'Right.'

She stands, perhaps she has said enough. And then the door is left hanging on its hinges as she marches with intent back over our field. I remember the grey wing that is sitting inside my kitchen bin, lift the bag out, tie its tops, stick it in the makeshift skip outside.

# FRAN

## 7 March

I slept fine last night, but something tells me my sister won't have. The only thing keeping her slightly buoyant will be knowing that Sadie is allowed to return to school today. The pair of them appear at the front door this morning, knocking at it with urgency. I can feel the walls reverberating with the force.

'He's not back. I'll give him one more hour.' Then she bends closer to me, uncomfortably close, and whispers, 'I'm going to have to call the police.'

She hasn't even asked for my advice, like she might usually do. I glance down at her reed-thin legs, enveloped in Lycra.

She sees me looking. 'Had to run. Couldn't sleep.'

I find myself wondering if she left Sadie alone in the caravan while she ran. She must have done. I don't know when my sister became so thoughtless. I think of going over there, sometimes, to see Sadie, but never want to undermine Ros.

'My dad's gone.' Sadie is looking at me. There's a slight wobble to her voice.

'I'm sure it's going to be OK, Sadie.'

'I don't think it will be.'

I look at Ros, who clearly hasn't picked up on her daughter's sadness. Something on the frame around the doorway has suddenly caught her interest; she puts out a finger, strokes at the wood, looks like she's pretending to be somewhere else. 'What if he's gone for good?'

I have nothing to say, other than to invite them both in for tea. They reluctantly step through the door, Sadie looking down towards her feet, as if they might hold the answer to where her father has gone.

*

It's evening now, the sun leaking its last light between the clouds, and the air around us becoming more inky blue, rather than grey. Dom has taken Bruno for a bout of football in the nearest park, around half a mile from here. I take the time to wander down to the marshland, my thoughts spinning. I haven't heard from Ros again. I had thought she might have been on the end of the phone after a couple of hours, explaining away how difficult Sadie has been finding this time away from school, and now the fear that her father has left. My mind slips again to the absent Ms McConnell. She wasn't there again today. I heard one of the other teachers telling another staff member that they can't *get hold of her. No answer on her phone.* They are *thinking of calling the police.* My sister's near-identical words from only hours earlier echo in my head. As I take my steps slowly down to the coastline, I can see the outline of the nest between the reeds, and my heart speeds up a little. My head is still thinking the same thoughts. Ms McConnell doesn't seem the type to just abandon a job without any thought to the children she would be leaving behind, but what would I know? People put on a façade all the time. These days, I don't know what is going on in my husband's head, yet I've known him all these years.

As I get closer to the nest, I see the mother has gone away again. The eggs are still their speckled beige and brown colour, nestling next to each other, touching like the siblings they will be. I notice that other birds keep away, not going within a few feet of the nest. Some of them poke their heads in my direction, calling out a sign of danger to those of their own breed, but I ignore their cries. I can't see any other terns; some of these birds look like common crows, among huge gulls. Crows aren't often seen on these parts of land. All will forage for and eat the same food, though the gulls arrogantly edge more towards human delicacies such as bread and the occasional chip. I perch myself among the reeds, noticing the darkness is pulling the birds closer to the shore, and I take in the cacophony of the creatures. Sooner or later, the mother tern will return to her nest, and I will feel obliged to leave. I try to quieten the thoughts of Ellis and the missing teacher, the waves crashing around me making thinking impossible right now, anyway. If I close my eyes, I could be anywhere.

My eyes open to the realisation that perhaps the teacher won't be coming back. Perhaps Ellis has left for good, too. I had blocked it out of my head last night. I am in my infamous squatting position again, trying to shift myself closer to the nest. It is pretty much dark now. I stand carefully, not wanting to disturb the other birds, yet wanting to stick around just a little longer, should the mother tern come back. She can't leave her eggs for too long, they will perish. I brush off the dead reeds and sand from my backside and turn to pick my way across the marshland again, wishing I had brought along a torch to help guide the way back. Instead, I'm caught by a muted ringing from within my rucksack. Perhaps my sister, phoning with her delayed apology. As I get closer to the path, the ringing stops. My heart catches in my mouth as I can just about make out the form of a man standing a short distance from me, hands in pockets. He's barely there against the darkness. My heart flutters with relief a little as I think I recognise the outline of my almost-brother-in-law. I can't see his dark eyes, though, in this light. The figure doesn't move, just remains still, like a drawing.

'Hello?' I call out, but I am fifteen, twenty feet away. The man doesn't say a word in reply, and for a moment, I am blinking hard, trying not to doubt what is in front of my eyes. My sight is strained, but it doesn't take long for the realisation that it is not Ellis to sink in.

The man begins to step away, advancing further along the path, until he disappears into the night, the trees greedily gobbling him up with their branches and their allegiance to the night-time.

*

Dom isn't too interested in my tale about the vanishing man on the path, but Bruno appears to be. I had thought that he would be having his bath, ready for bed, but it seems his father has let him stay up, perhaps not noticing that it is now long past 9 pm.

'Why do you think he was there?'

I am not keen to discuss this with Bruno. He is hanging the top part of his body over the banister, his feet stuck firmly halfway up the staircase.

'Mum?'

Frowning into my mug of soup, I am willing him to go to bed, so I can at least talk about this at leisure with Dom. The cold has worked its way into my bones, and I pull my feet underneath me on the armchair. The air feels oddly cold around us.

'Bruno, no reason. Now go up to bed!'

He glances at Dom, whose eyes are fixed on the TV screen, ears pretending not to hear.

'Dom,' I cough, waiting for my husband to turn his head to look at me, at least. He doesn't.

'Seems Dad can't hear us. You need to go up now, Bruno.'

'Was he there to take the eggs, Mum? That man, was that why he was there?'

A cold sweat streaks its way from my neck down the rest of my spine, creating a chill that makes the room feel even colder.

My son is frowning at me – his getting-longer hair covers half his eyes, but I can still tell it's a frown. He sighs dramatically and stomps up the stairs, letting his bedroom door slam behind him.

'Any news of Ellis?' I am asking, although surely Dom would have told me the moment I walked through the door.

He is shaking his head, red curls bouncing from the movement. I swear, for a second, there are tears in his eyes, mirroring the faces on the TV screen.

# TAD

There's been talk of moving on. One of the girls saw the cops. Apparently, they came knocking one morning, earlyish, were seen walking around our trailers. Some of us aren't sure we believe her. I'm not ready to move. And anyway, I kind of like it here. I like the sea, the woodland. I even like to hear the birds overhead. The others aren't all so keen, they don't really say why. It usually takes a visit from the authorities to make them think of setting off again, but I don't want to leave just yet. I am waiting for the girl. I don't know why.

He had seemed so cheerful of late, but now Charlie has disappeared. Don't know where to, but he'll be back. He's known for his vanishing acts. I'm not too worried.

Neither of us mentions Sahara to the other. Jade finds it difficult to articulate her thoughts at the best of times, but I can tell when my girl is preoccupied with something. Sahara, she's only come to see us twice, and now it's been a week since she's shown her face. I wonder what is happening in her home life, to make her want to come and visit me, an old man in a van. Jade is often pacing in the caravan, her neck arched to the window, just looking, waiting.

I have taken to walking around the village more than I usually would, and it's still cold out, being only early March. I see the woman who owns the caravan park one day a week, fumbling and dragging that damned vacuum cleaner around with her. There haven't been many punters in her vans, not that I have seen, yet she sticks to her cleaning routine like her life depends on it. I've seen her look over at us; I've smiled, but she probably couldn't see it from where she was.

# FRAN

## 10 March

I am awoken not by my alarm but by the smell of burning from a faraway place. It catches in my throat, makes me think of bonfire night, hotdogs, fireworks. I cough a little. Dom is already up when I pull myself out of the bed. I'm searching the floor for my slippers. The small window on the right-hand wall of our room is open slightly.

'How long have you been up?'

He shrugs. His hair is wet from the shower, his clothes already pressed. God knows how I slept so late. 'You smell burning?'

'Yeah.' I'm trying to ignore the tiny sense of doubt that is niggling at me. 'Bonfire over on the other field. Don't overreact.'

'Why would you say that?' He is already looking for shoes.

I grab his arm as he tries to make his way to the door. 'Dom, what's going on with us?' My heart starts to speed up; it's the first time I've queried him.

'With us?'

I nod.

'I don't know, Fran, you tell me.'

I let go of his arm, see the red hand print I have left there. He looks at it too, then glances back up at me.

'I don't know what you mean.' At least I am being honest.

'Well. You seem to be elsewhere most of the time.'

*Elsewhere.* I could say exactly the same about him, but I choose to refrain. He leaves the room, and I let myself sit back on the edge of the bed, not looking at anything. Once I am sure he is downstairs, I go to his bedside table, open the two drawers, turn them upside down. The contents drop to the floor: pieces of paper which are mainly receipts, more post-it notes. Nothing to incriminate him.

Raindrops are starting to splatter on my forehead and my frizzy hair as I almost chase my husband across our front garden. He's on a mission. The smoke in the sky is near-black, and the smell stronger than I could have imagined from such a distance away. He takes the quickest route, right through our own caravan park, before letting himself into their field. I am ten, fifteen paces behind him. I want to stop him, tell him to turn around. He thinks we'll have complaints from our tiny number of residents. *Not a very relaxing holiday. Couldn't breathe as well as I would have liked.*

The weight on my stomach and thighs from my recent lack of exercise is slowing me down, and I am out of breath while Dom is in spitting distance of their caravans. I have to stop, catch hold of the fence, bend over slightly in the hope of being able to breathe more clearly. Particles of wood and ash are flying around the plumes of dark grey smoke circling into the sky. There are no people about, and for a moment, as Dom's form disappears out of view, I don't know what to do. Two minutes later, and I have made my way into the Romany field and towards the fire. I avoid looking directly into it, it burns too angrily and the size of it terrifies me. It must be ten foot high with wood, pallets and crates. I see Dom, beyond the fire, heading towards a blue caravan. I call to him, but my words are lost in the thick smoke. I see a couple of children retreating into one of the vans slightly further away. The rain continues to spit in my eyes, making it difficult to see anything else, and the smoke is dense, black, heavy, the rain doing nothing to lessen its ascent. Squinting, I try to decide whether to follow Dom towards the blue van, but before I do, I see an older man, perhaps mid-sixties, almost stagger out of its front door. Dom is in his face.

'Do you realise how dangerous a fire of this size is?' I can hear my husband shouting.

The man stops, cocks his head to one side. I can't hear what he says to Dom; my legs force themselves forward, uphill, towards where the men stand.

As I approach them, a piece of material whips up into the air in front of my face and I squeal, step backwards and almost lose my footing. My nostrils are coated with the smell of chemicals or the burnt remains of something dreadful.

'You can't go burning all that sort of stuff around here. It's dangerous. And you've got kids just over there!' Dom points. I call at him to calm down, still not close enough to him. My words are whipped away and silenced by the black force billowing between us.

The old man laughs; I can just catch what he has said. 'You shouldn't be here,' he offers simply. 'Not if you don't like fires.'

His words make me feel a sense of calm, that the fire is nothing to worry about.

'You should never have come here,' Dom is saying to him. I am close up to the two men now, dragging on my husband's arm, pulling him away.

'I'm sorry!' I say to the man, shame creeping up and over me. I'm still trying to pull Dom away, but he is ignoring me, yanking his arm back.

The old man ignores Dom too, offers me his hand. 'I'm Tad. I don't believe we've met properly.'

'Fran,' I try to say, but I am coughing, lungs struggling with the bout of exercise and the invasive plumes of smoke.

'You run the caravan site the other side of ours?' Tad coughs too.

I wonder if he's seen me, doing the cleaning in the vans, going about my daily chores. In reply, I simply nod, still trying to get my husband's attention. He has left us, is walking towards the fire. I don't know what he plans to do.

Tad notices Dom hovering in anguish around the fire, desperately looking for something to put it out with, and we both rush towards him, pulling him away from the flames. 'Dom, you need to go home! Leave everything well alone!'

Dom stops walking, looks at me. His glasses are steamed up, he pulls them off and I see his eyes, red and watery. The smoke, it's got to his eyes, they're streaming. He stares at me a second, shakes his head, then begins to walk away in the direction of our home.

I don't let my eyes follow him for long, instead fix them on the charcoal-black plumes that snake their way around us and into the sky. The smell is starting to make me feel sick; I can feel the saliva gathering in my mouth. I don't tell the old man that Sadie is my niece, but I want to know if Bruno was accompanying her – she's clearly been here. A gull flies stupidly close to the fire, lands beside me, picks at the bread or whatever it is that's been thrown like confetti to the ground. The man stamps his foot, seemingly in an attempt to make the bird disappear. 'You're the boy's mother, aren't you?'

I nod with vigour. 'Bruno. And can I just apologise about my husband? He's just so protective of our land, and our son, in particular. I didn't realise he was coming over here to give you a hard time.'

'He's a nice kid.' He ignores the apology.

'He came over with the girl?'

The man is turning to walk away now, and I see his van door is ajar. I wonder about the smell of the fire working its way inside, suffocating whoever else might be there. I picture his wife on the bed, perhaps mid-sixties, grabbing at her own throat as she struggles for breath. I close my eyes to alleviate the image, try to focus on the man in front of me. He seems familiar. Perhaps I have seen him before, I don't know.

'He didn't come with the girl?' I try again, following him towards the van.

'You should ask him yourself. He comes and goes. Has taken something of a liking to my brother.' Before he reaches the door, he looks right at me again. 'Doesn't seem to like school.'

My mind stops dead. Distractions race around in my head. School. The teacher. Ellis.

The walk home takes little time, and once I get back to the house, I find that Dom isn't there. I do not know what to do with myself. I take out the paints that have been stashed under the kitchen sink for the two years that we've lived here and grab some of the sugar paper we used to keep for Bruno's scrapbook. I paint raging colours – blacks, reds, oranges. There are tiny sparks of yellow at the top of the page.

# TAD

Imet the woman from the other field the other day, seemed nice enough. She had followed her husband over to us – the bloke who had chatted to me on the path that time I had asked where to find the birds. He was in a rage about our fire. Seemed so different this time around. Something had really rattled his cage. He came across as quite an angst-ridden kind of a person, face all twisted and scowly. I didn't go into details with the woman, Fran, about her little boy spending time with my brother – that they light miniature barbeques together, cook all sorts of food over the tiny flames. Well, they were doing that, before Charlie took off. The boy is often here. Bruno. We see more of him than Sahara now, don't know why. Sometimes he comes into my van for a chat, but mostly, it's Charlie he's after. Charlie's always wanted a son.

# FRAN

## 12 March

I'm in Norwich, have decided to take a day out; it is a relief, for once, to be away from the claustrophobia of the little village in which I spend most of my time. I could do with some new clothes; my current ones make me appear more dowdy than any sane woman would want to be. I never have the chance to dress up, or go anywhere decent. The older-style buildings and the cathedral are a breath of fresh air to me, and I consider making my way to the office where Dom works, to surprise him. Perhaps I will catch him on a desk with his secretary, her pencil skirt hoisted up as far as it can go, her lipstick smudged crudely across her cheek. As I get to the front door of his office, my heart is pumping and I realise I am more anxious than I had anticipated. A quick glance at my phone shows a text message from my sister. I pause before deciding to open it.

*Still no Ellis! Have you seen the news?!*

Already I am stepping back from the office, eyes fixed on the screen. I can see I have a missed call and a voicemail message, no doubt from my sister too. *Have you seen the news?!*

I find an unoccupied bench by an antiques shop on the corner and look up the BBC website. It's there, the second story down. *Norfolk teacher missing, presumed dead. Search for mid-thirties man who may be connected.*

I can't read the rest of the article for a moment. My eyes are transfixed on the woman in the photo: pink hair, conservative smile, hand holding up a glass of what might be Prosecco, wrist displaying her miniature tattoo of the swallow. Thankfully, I am sitting down.

129

The adrenaline is beginning to power its way through my veins, up my neck, to my face. Wires of heat are spiralling through me; I can feel sweat bubble on my back. I bite down on my lower lip. It's beginning to feel too real.

*

I can't remember much of the drive home, or maybe any of it. I park up in record time, just to see my husband get out of his own VW Golf and make his way to the front door. *We were both driving home from the same city at the same time.*

I shout his name, slam my car door shut, hurry up the pathway.

He stops in his tracks, turns to look at me. His shirt and work trousers are crumpled, sweaty-looking, even. 'Fran? What is it?'

'I've been in Norwich.' The first words to come tumbling out, as meaningless as random scrabble pieces thrown across a board.

He pulls at his tie, doesn't say anything for a moment, just yanks the tie looser around his neck. 'I wasn't at the office because I've been checking on your sister,' he announces. Now his key is in the lock, his hand turning. 'Perhaps you should be checking in on her more often, rather than chasing me.'

I am blinking away what he's said. I can't even take in the meaning of his words right now. 'The teacher from school. Bruno's teacher… They think she's dead. It could be intentional, an intentional killing! They're looking for a man in his thirties!'

I had expected him to turn around, look at me, tell me I am being silly. But he pulls the key out of the lock, pushes the door open. 'Really?' I can hear the back of his red head say. My mind isn't even registering whatever else he has said to me since I got home.

'Dom! They think it's murder, are you listening? They reckon she's dead!'

Finally, he turns, looks straight at me. The sweat on his face has made his red hair curl up all the more. I used to love playing with his ringlets. He always said he hated them, they made him feel less masculine. *Girls' hair*, he used to say.

'Murder? Just 'cos they think she may be dead doesn't mean it's murder.'

I push him into the house, see that he's struggling to move now, or at least pretending that he is. 'Dom, go inside!'

He takes a moment to shift his feet, not entertaining the idea of removing his shoes. I guide him into the kitchen, pull out two of the wooden chairs for us to sit on. He looks like he is short of breath, blotchy-faced, not able to concentrate.

For a minute or two, neither of us speaks. Then he lifts his head from its bowed position, begins looking for his phone in his pocket. 'They're going to blame Ellis.' He stops. 'Is that who they're searching for?'

I can't think of anything to say. My mind is fuzzy.

'What's going to happen? I was just looking for your sister! Does she know?'

'What?' I stare at him. 'Yes, she knows. About the murder. *Potential murder*. She tried calling me when I was in Norwich. That's how I found out. She left a voicemail, in the end.' I look around the room; there's not enough air. It's being sucked away by something. 'You were looking for Ros? Why? And why aren't you at work?'

Dom stands up, makes his way to the cupboard where the glasses live, grabs one. He lets out a bit of a sigh. 'I knew this was coming. I've been worried for a few days.'

I try to butt in, but he continues.

'The school phoned on Friday when you were out, they wanted to see if we had any inkling where Ms McConnell might be. The Head said the teacher's family is *unconventional*, aren't helping much with enquiries. What does *unconventional* even mean? Nuns? Travellers? Anyway, that's meant to be kept hush-hush.'

It sounds like a lie. 'And you didn't think to tell me about the school asking that? Did you know the police and the papers were involved?

'I didn't. I swear it's the truth. They were just asking if any of the parents knew anything about her disappearance.'

'So…' My words drop away, the last drips of water on a draining board. 'Do we know where Ellis is yet?'

Dom looks at me, his eyes screwed up slightly. 'You're asking me that question? You're not trying your sister? Or the police, for fuck's sake?'

I can feel my shoulders sag. I wish I had listened more to Ros when she said she was worried about Ellis disappearing.

I step outside the front door, wander up the path and onto the walkway that leads to the church, no shoes, no socks. I had been hoping for fresh air, some clarity, before attempting to go and see Ros. Instead, the ripped-off head of a song thrush greets me, its body thrown to the side of it a couple of feet away, barely covered by shrubs and bushes.

# TAD

I saw Fran running to one of the caravans on her site, the one where Sahara lives with her mum and dad. I saw her, and Sahara's mum, the tall one, at the door of the caravan, in tears. It was late afternoon, but they made so much noise, not that I could make out the words. I saw Fran gesturing something with her hands, showing the action or the size of something. I could see the other woman repeatedly bringing her fingers up to her face, her eyes, seemingly not saying much. Fran stayed at the van for a while; I couldn't tell if she was angry or not. There seemed to be a lot of tears.

Bruno, he's been here again. It seems to be helping, what with everything that's been going on lately. He still comes round after school some afternoons, has told his mum he's got art or music classes or something. He told me that he loves to draw birds, any birds, but mostly the ones he sees on the beach. I had a vision of the bird's wing he brought to me the other day, the wing I had to dispose of. Today, Sahara came too. She walked straight to my trailer. Bruno left her, walked away when she came up my steps, went to look for Charlie, as usual. Didn't find him. I don't know where he's got to. Seems these kids would rather hang out here than with their real parents, though. Sahara tells me, again, that her dad has disappeared. I didn't know how seriously to take this comment, I let it become buried under the ravel of stories she was telling me about school. I didn't bother telling her that my brother disappears from time to time too, but only when he's particularly upset about something, usually. She'd probably think it was normal for Romany men to travel away.

133

# FRAN

## 12 March (continued)

Ros is at her wits' end. The police came to her before I got there, told her that Ellis is the only person they are interested in talking to about the teacher's disappearance. We both cried, then Sadie came home from school by herself because we were too caught up in ourselves to remember to collect our children from the playground. Sadie didn't stick around long, not after seeing her mother in such a state. Out of the window on the door of Ros's caravan, I could see Bruno waiting for his cousin, kicking at some rocks on the ground. His head was down, probably didn't even know I was in there, or if he did, he did a good job of not looking out for me. I wanted to go outside, to tell Bruno to go straight home and not to play out on the streets, the shore, in the hide, but I didn't want Ros to think I was being unreasonable.

When I ask what happens when she tries calling Ellis, my sister just says *his phone is dead*. They've had no contact for five days now, the same amount of time as the teacher has been missing. I asked Ros why the police say she's *presumed dead*, why Ellis is the suspect, but she just keeps sobbing and wringing some kind of matted old teddy bear in her hands. I wonder if it's Sadie's teddy, perhaps the only thing to bring her comfort now that her father has gone.

It fleetingly occurs to me that Ros knows more than she is letting on, then I curse myself for such thoughts. She lets her tears flow a little while longer, and so do I. Once the tears have begun to dry up, I see her glancing around out of the windows of the caravan, more alert than she had been while crying to me.

'Sadie went out. With Bruno,' I explain.

134

She sighs, with relief or annoyance, I don't know, and closes her eyes. She sits upright against the wall, the chair she's sitting in having no back to it. 'They just think it's more than a coincidence. Him being gone at exactly the same time as the teacher.'

She's talking about the police. I process what she's said for a little bit, take my time in choosing my next words. 'So, they know that Sadie was suspended from school?'

At first my sister doesn't respond, but after a few moments, she turns to look at me. 'What are you saying?'

It's painful, the way she's staring at me, and I have to divert my gaze. I can see across to the Romany field with real clarity from here, can see that man, Tad, helping move some computers into one of the vans with a couple of younger men. If I squint, I'm sure I can see the face of the Charlie person I met down at the marsh, wearing the same red top. I realise that they probably know each other well, he and Tad.

'Fran!'

I glance back towards my sister, see a new set of pearly tears threatening to spill onto her ruddy cheeks. I wish I knew how to take away her fear.

'It's just, if the police know that Sadie was suspended, then they might come to the conclusion that you and Ellis were angry at the teacher and that you wanted to get back at her.'

'Then why aren't I a suspect too?'

It's a fair question, and one that I can't answer. Perhaps Ellis will be cleared, and then they will try Ros. I suddenly feel tired, so tired, from the panic and all the emotional conversation. I can feel my eyes becoming heavy, fight the urge to rest my own head back against the wall. Next time I get these caravans looked at, I'm going to put proper seats in all of them, seats where you can rest your head.

'It's because he's a drinker, isn't it?'

Her words seem to have materialised from nowhere, and I consider them, before deciding that perhaps she is right. 'How would they know?'

She tips her head to one side, in a *come on, Fran* kind of way. My sister knows that, from a very young age, I would be the one to try to play the angel on the shoulder, the reassuring sister. She was always the one to jump to conclusions, to fear the worst. To be honest, that's what I thought she had been doing in the days since Ellis's disappearance. I don't think that now.

'They'll know he has a drinking problem, they'll have done the research, found he went to rehab. They all think alcohol equals violence.'

I jump to my protective-sister stance. 'But there's no body. There's not even the hint of a body. How do we even know they've spoken to the teacher's family? She might have just gone AWOL to clear her mind. Must be hell having to be a teacher and deal with pissed-off parents all the time.' I realise my words after they have left my lips, and I blush, a red haze no doubt treading its way across my face, my cheeks becoming flooded with not-wanting-to-be-there.

'It's OK, Fran, don't worry about it. But I'm sure they must have their reasons for thinking she might be a goner. They don't just claim every missing person is dead within a few days. Or maybe they do. I don't know how it all works.'

I give in to my weary head, let it drop back against the wall. I find myself wondering about Bruno, whether he's gone down to the beach with Sadie, whether they are looking out for the terns. Perhaps Sadie is showing him the eggs, the nest. The thought makes me sit up straight for a moment, and Ros jumps a little.

'What?'

'Nothing. Well, something. Nobody is keeping an eye on the kids. They could be doing anything right now.'

My sister wafts her hand freely. 'What could they possibly get up to?'

I feel like telling her about the tern's nest, the value of the eggs inside, but it feels like small fry when her partner is missing, and the local teacher is missing, presumed dead.

136

# TAD

The girl is running towards me — well, jogging — as I help Charlie move some parts around. He's been back a few hours now, barely said a word. She has a dark trickle of blood, burgundy, like wine, dribbling through her fingers and beneath the thing she is holding. She is sniffing. No real tears just yet. *Bravado*, my dear, sweet mother would have suggested. Bruno jumps out of Charlie's caravan to see what the commotion is. He stands on the concrete steps, not moving at first, then edging closer to see what is cradled in his friend's hands. When he sees it is a bird, he stops.

'Guilty as charged,' Charlie whispers into my ear, laughing. 'They're great kids, aren't they?' It is the first time he has spoken since his return. He genuinely looks happy to see the kids again.

'Grim findings,' is all I can think to say. I edge towards the two kids as Charlie heads back towards the water tap on the side of his trailer.

The girl, Sadie, she dumps the body of the bird to the ground. There's a little thud that makes me feel sad, just like the bird wing from before. I've decided not to call the girl by her made-up name anymore. It feels like a bit of a pretence, too theatrical, though I suppose that was the whole intention. A bit of attention. Sahara is the name of an actress, perhaps from a far-off land, not this blonde child who seems to be practically parentless and perhaps in need of a little more love. A movement catches the corner of my eye; Jade has returned from somewhere, a walk around who-knows-where, and she picks her feet over the body of the little white bird on the grass as she gets closer to our caravan. I heard her give a bit of a gasp, look over at Sadie. Jade's been gone over an hour this time. I can hear her breathing, unsteady, almost wheezing. She's been exerting herself, and I try to swallow down the concern I feel for my adult child. She should be able to cope without me worrying. I see Sadie and Bruno's eyes follow her, taking in her graceless body, her lumpy way of moving. Her legs have never seemed to move in time with her arms. When the boy says a rather-too-loud 'hello', Jade covers her ears and almost hops through the front door, making her body appear even more uncoordinated. Bruno, though, he doesn't smile. He is staring at the tiny body of the little white bird, moving closer to it. Its head has been nearly pulled off, is hanging from a delicate and sinewy red string.

'Lift it up again.'

The girl looks at me, and I look back at her. Neither one of us knows who Bruno is talking to.

'I said lift it up again.'

Sadie frowns. 'No. I don't want its head to come rolling off. I've been trying to save it. I told you.'

I'll admit, I am taken aback at Bruno's forwardness, though he now looks at me for help. I don't want to touch the damned thing either, but I don't want an upset boy on my hands. I crouch, hear my old knees click, pass the bird from my right hand into the palm of my left. 'There,' I say. 'And who on earth would kill such a creature?'

The kids don't say anything, nor do they look at each other. The boy doesn't make a move to touch it, nor to move any closer. 'She just looks like she's asleep,' is all he says, and then he moves away, turns his back and begins to walk out of our field. The girl is picking at the blood on her hand, already dried. She makes her way over to the tap where she's seen Charlie washing his hands.

# FRAN

## 14 March

The woodland this morning is desolate, as it often is, and there are no sounds from the gulls who are normally swooping and screeching overhead. I suppose it's still too early for anyone, including the birds. I decide against spending time in the hide; there's been a distinct lack of interesting breeds whenever I have frequented it, and again, I curse myself for having it built in an area I hadn't researched properly. I should check in there from time to time, and occasionally I do, but the floor has become something of a wasteland for leaves and twigs, and whatever else the wind has carried in. I had expected cider bottles from local teenagers, or the odd passer-by, but there is nothing like that. I think, perhaps, that only my little family knows about the structure. I pick my feet up as I leave the woodland and begin to stroll along the shore. There are herring gulls in front of me, peck-pecking at some dead creature they've found in the reeds, some unlucky mouse or such like. When they see me, they gnaw faster, with more aggression, as if I am a threat, come to take their meal. I find myself laughing, continue to walk past them, noting the other birds that are taking their time to land gracefully on the water, some floating, a sense of serenity about them. I haven't felt this calm in days. The last two nights I haven't slept, though I doubt anyone else has much, either. Ellis has not been in touch, let alone returned, and the police have been to interview some of the teachers and the Head at the school, so I've heard. They have pretty much admitted that they are looking for Ellis mainly because he took the great decision to up and leave at such a wonderful time.

I am teaching myself today that *none of it involves me*, and this mantra is helping me to feel calmer. I am training myself not to be in Ros's pockets at this time. That's why the birds help me. The beaches, the woodland. That's why we moved here. To escape the chaos of living in outer London (*Surrey, actually*, Dom would say.) The calmness of this place; seeing things grow; the wildlife; the sea never changing.

\*

A smile is stretching across my face as I draw nearer to the marsh and can just about make out the shape of the little tern, sitting on her nest. It's slightly further towards the sea than I remember, but as the tide is out half of the time I am here, it is difficult to always place the nest's location immediately. I haven't seen the mother tern here for more than a few minutes before, and the sight creates little bubbles of joy that seem to be popping up inside me. It's a private joy, it's all mine. Days have passed, and she has no doubt been returning to her nest, her eggs thriving. I take my binoculars out of my little rucksack to get a clearer look. She is beautiful – her striking black head and grey wings, her warm white throat. It's such a risk for her, building her nest here on the marsh, where predators are always near, and even an unexpected high tide could take her eggs and the nest away in a matter of moments. She's been here a couple of weeks now, as far as I can tell. I do tend to lose track of time these days. Nevertheless, the eggs should be ready to hatch in a matter of days. I feel the need to protect them, to wrap myself around the bird and the nest, yet I know that this would make the process fail. I realise an hour or two has passed, and I remember with guilt that I promised earlier to go and watch Bruno playing football at his school this afternoon. I feel like calling *goodbye* to the bird, realise my stupidity and refrain. As I walk away from the marshland and towards the church path that leads to our cottage, I am reminded of the man who had been standing there in the darkness, watching. I hadn't thought about him since that night. I guess he could have been anyone; a dog walker, anything. I remember now there was no dog.

*

Just as I arrive at the front door to my house, I am aware of the sound of footsteps on the path leading around the perimeter of the front garden. A person passes by the rose bushes, yet to bloom, and I can see it's the older man, Tad, from the Romany field. He nods at me, and I notice he is balding, grey around the edges of his hair. It makes me wonder if one day soon my husband's auburn ringlets will turn to snow and ice too. I nod back.

As he gets closer to me on the garden path, I see he is holding something. It's a white bird. On closer inspection, I can see it's not a small gull or anything similar, but a young dove, a fledgling, its head dangling off, barely attached to its body. I swear, a pretty nasty word, and then let my shoulders drop with relief once I can see it's not a little tern in his hands.

'The children were holding this.'

'OK?'

He steps a little closer. I hadn't noticed quite how tall he was the last time. The plumes of smoke from the field, nearly making me choke, must have been a distraction that one time we met, just days ago.

I wonder why he is really here, with the carcass of this bird. Perhaps he's come to lay blame at my door.

'Do what you will with it,' says Tad. He is offering the little body out towards me.

I find my eyes turn to the driveway, to see if Dom's car is at home. I could do with some back-up right now. Not that he's been great at that lately. His usual parking space is empty.

I hold my hands out, but then pull them away, a reflex as my body realises it doesn't want to be involved in this. The dove lands on the ground, neatly rolls. I don't want to glance up at the man, but I know he is looking straight at me. I notice that the bird's head has now come away completely from its body. Its lifeless eyes gaze past me.

'Someone around here is doing this to innocent creatures.'

His forwardness has caught me slightly off-guard. I had been too busy staring at the ping-pong-ball head of the bird. I fight the temptation to push it closer to the rest of its body with the toe of my shoe, and instead force myself to look up at the man. The sun is bright, directly behind him, and I can't make out the features of his face. 'Horrendous, isn't it?'

He doesn't say anything, doesn't really move.

'You know my son wouldn't do this.' I am pre-empting what he might be about to say. 'Neither would Sadie.'

The man steps a little closer. 'She's not your niece, then? You said she was.'

I swallow down the extra saliva that is gathering in my mouth. 'She is, yes.'

He steps back a little, his body at last blocking the sun from my eyes. 'And how do you know she didn't do this? That neither of them did?'

'I just do.'

I realise I don't need to justify my reasons to this stranger, as friendly as he had seemed before.

He is chuckling now, rubbing the grey stubble on his chin. 'Tough little cookie, ain't she?'

I know he's trying to be amicable. The scratching sound of his stubble feels like sandpaper on my own skin.

'How so?'

'I get the feeling… she's just needing a little more attention in life. Something like that. Seems like a lost soul.' He steps back. 'Sorry if I've spoken out of turn.'

I am frowning as hard as I can at him, the sun's glare back in my eyes. I don't like the insinuation that my niece is not cared for properly, yet I can see where he's coming from.

'Well, I'll let you know if I hear or discover anything about these birds,' is all I manage to say.

He nods, walks away, backwards for a few steps, then turns and lets himself out of the gate.

# TAD

I *think* she took on board what I was suggesting. I didn't pick up the bird carcass after she had closed the door, decided to leave it there. Today, I feel a bit alone in my own camp; Charlie has taken off again, and some of the others are keeping to themselves a bit more than usual. The atmosphere hangs like a dank sheet over us. Part of me longs to be elsewhere, but I stick around in case I'm needed – although there's not an awful lot to do once you're my age and past doing most of the work. It's not like I can reprogramme a computer or a mobile phone. The younger adults are out, a few of them work in shops in the next town. Sometimes I'll have a play with the kids as they run around on the field, but despite the warm weather that seems to be reaching us now, most are either at school or locked up in their caravans. They've all got those devices, those tablets or whatever you call them, to keep them busy. Some of the couples here decided that their kids should go to school now, after having kept them away since we arrived here nearly two months ago. We're often told by the teachers that they are the *sweetest things*.

I begin to stroll down to the shore; I crave the feel of the salty breeze on my face, the calmness of it all. I can pretend I am anyone when I am alone down here. Where I live, there's not a huge amount of privacy. And not much space to move, really. I wonder why the others don't all argue more. Perhaps they argue in whispered tones. I find myself laughing out loud, imagining a full-blown fight taking place in only the tiniest of voices. My feet are taking me towards the water, not far from the woodland, and decide to rest on the shingle there. I let my body fall down into a cross-legged position, sighing with purpose as I do. It's a strange piece of shore: mostly shingle by the woods, then turning gradually into sand. This is where the beach appears its most beautiful, where I can imagine families excitedly dragging their picnic blankets and windbreakers to find the best spot. It's still early spring here, and no sign of holidaymakers, although I'm sure it won't be long.

# FRAN

## 16 March

It feels strange to be collecting my niece from school; recently the two kids have been making their own way home, seeing as they are not far from secondary age. But today, the parents are all there, waiting eagerly for their children to leave the classroom, keen to hold them tightly. The school hasn't spoken too much about the case; they issued an email saying that *Ms McConnell is in everyone's prayers*, and that they are working with the police as best they can. I try to imagine her family, her husband if she has one, and what they must be going through. We haven't heard any details about her family, or whereabouts she was living, merely that she was at the school on a maternity placement. I heard the deputy telling another parent *what a surprise it was* that she upped and left – *she had such brilliant references*. Seems the opposite of what Ellis was making out, and the gossips of the playground.

I picture the family lying awake at night, trying to piece things together, wondering why she went away. I personally still don't think it's a murder case. I think she must have chosen to leave. According to the press, her cousin says she was quiet. *Is* quiet. Sounds like she just wanted to get on with the job of teaching the kids. Ellis is still missing too, and the police are even more keen to speak to him. They have his phone tracked; some young policewoman told Ros it hasn't been used since the day he vanished. I was with her when they announced this, saw her grab her stomach, bend over double, scream out loud. It was a stab in my own stomach, seeing my Ros in such pain, made an immediate lump come to my throat, tears prick at my eyes. Occasionally, over the past few days, I have been wondering if Ellis has committed the worst to himself. I would never admit this to my sister, or even to Dom, but there was such a sadness in his eyes at times that it wouldn't surprise me if he had decided not to continue on his own path. I try not to think of his daughter, the shock and then the desperation on her face as her mother tries to break the news to her.

Sadie comes out of the classroom, first in the line, with Bruno further down the pecking order, dragging his bag in that way of his. Perhaps it is true that they don't spend any time together at school. My niece walks to me, aware that it won't be her mother collecting her today. She barely says 'hi' before Bruno catches my eye and begins to run in our direction. I decide against talking to them about the dead birds right now. It can wait until we get home from the school.

'Mum, the new kids are so nice. They gave me all their marbles at playtime.'

It is Bruno, excited. He loves to meet new children. I guess he's talking about the kids from the other field.

Sadie doesn't ask why her mum doesn't come to the school anymore. Ros will have explained it to her. She doesn't mention her father either, and I am thankful. Sometimes it feels as though I am walking with another woman – a beautiful, knowledgeable woman. It's difficult to believe that she is only just eleven, although in some moments she seems much younger. I notice she is hardly speaking and grab at her hand, which she doesn't pull away. I want to wrap her up in my bodily warmth, in the enormous jacket that I steal from Dom.

Bruno is babbling about the new kids, *Marie and Kenny.* 'And they live right near us, Mum! I've seen them in the other field. There are six of them, actually. They've invited me to play after school. Can I?' He doesn't stop for breath, and I feel tired already, wondering how I am eventually going to break the news about Ellis being the man the police are searching for.

At my side, I feel Sadie turn to look at him. She shakes her head a little, moves away from us. 'I'm going to look at the tern's nest,' she says. It seems a bold notion, and I don't want her going over there.

My reaction is to keep hold of her hand, pull her towards me by the wrist. I'm a little rougher than I had meant to be, and she pulls her hand away, looks down at the red mark beginning to swell around her wrist. The way she glances at me is a mirror image of how Dom looked, when I had pulled at his arm that day of the bonfire.

'That hurt!'

It sounds like she's about to cry.

'I'm sorry!' I hadn't meant to hurt her. I just wanted to keep her close. She doesn't know that the Romany man, Tad, suspects her, perhaps, of the bird-killings around the village. I don't think she did it. I just know, as her aunt, that she can't have.

'I just want to see the birds, Auntie Fran. Please.'

Bruno is quick to back her up. 'The terns? Mum, they're for anyone to look at.'

'The men at the camp like to look at them too.' Sadie is still rubbing her wrist. It's becoming a burning hue of scarlet, and I try to swallow down the bolt of guilt in my throat.

We've stopped walking, my feet not wanting to take me on any further. My son is looking up at me. Sadie stares at the pair of us, not blinking. I step aside as a group of parents and children try to overtake us.

'What?' There wasn't meant to be any shaking in my voice.

'I said the men from the camp like to look at the tern's eggs.'

I am jogging, slowly at first, away from the children. I overtake the group of kids and mothers further up the path, aware of their eyes on the crazy middle-aged woman who is stomping her way ahead. I'm not even sure Bruno will follow me. I run until I reach the end of the path, where it twists left instead of right towards our home, and I keep going until I am in sight of the reeds, the marshland.

The tern is there, sitting on her eggs, secure in her nest. She cocks her head to one side, eyeing me, her black head tilting. I'm sure she's asking why I'm so concerned.

# TAD

I saw the red-headed man today, walking around the caravan park next door. He looked kind of agitated, kept trying the doors of some of the caravans, was having a wander inside a couple that had been left unlocked. He didn't see me, but I wanted to approach him, see if I could help. I made my way through the fence that separates the two fields from each other, a quick check over my shoulder to see if Jade was watching me go.

'Hey,' I had called, hoping to sound as friendly as I could. He was just exiting one of the vans at the front of the park, near where the *Fran's Holiday Vans* sign is erected. For a moment, he stopped, and I noticed there was sweat dribbling down his forehead, sticking to the curls that hang there. It wasn't that warm, but clearly he was in a bit of a mess.

'I'm just looking for something,' he muttered, as I got closer to him. I could hear him breathing fast, panting, almost.

'We've met briefly before,' I said, remembering the anger of the man at my bonfire, as well as that time on the path.

He narrowed his eyes, so much that his red eyebrows pushed against each other, forming one. 'We have?' But then he stopped looking so confused, and his face fell into embarrassment.

'Sorry, I do remember you now.' He looked down at his feet, kicked at a stone in the dust. 'You know a teacher has gone missing at the local school?' he continued, perhaps trying to divert the conversation elsewhere. 'It's been all over the news.'

I nodded, said nothing.

'And my brother-in-law is missing too. Well, nearly-brother-in-

150

law.' He took the sweater that was tied around his waist, used the sleeve to mop his brow. Then he was looking straight at me. *Brother-in-law*.

'So, you're looking for him in the caravans?'

He shifted from one foot to the other, as if pins and needles were taking hold. 'Something like that. I thought I could perhaps find his phone. It doesn't sound like he even took it with him.'

I waited for him to say a little more, but he remained quiet, covered the sun from his eyes, looked towards the shore. 'Perhaps I'll try the path in the woods.'

'Yes, good idea,' I heard myself say. I didn't really want to keep on walking, but it felt impolite to turn back, to leave him.

He had partially smiled at me, nodded, curls still stuck to his face. I hadn't known if he wanted me to join him or not, perhaps he was too polite to say. We walked at a leisurely pace, down the path from the fields to the pebbly shore that leads on to the wooded area. I stopped to watch a pair of gulls fighting over some already torn-up rodent, its limbs pulled away from the rest of its body. Some of its entrails were dragging on the stones. A feeling of sickness came over me, my feet itching to turn back. The man stood next to me as I watched the gulls fight. After a minute or two, he told me his name was Dom. I asked if little Bruno was still not enjoying school so much these days, and his father turned to look at me as we walked. 'Not enjoying school?'

'Sorry, I should have said,' I was tripping over my words, as well as my feet. 'Bruno sometimes comes to chat to me, over at my van, and with some of my family there. The girl comes often too. Sadie.'

Dom was barely walking at this point, his eyes fixed on me. He didn't say a word, just stared, as if waiting for me to come out with more details. I wonder now if that would have been a good time to turn away and head back home, to take myself away.

I felt obliged to carry on speaking, him leading the way through the woodland as if he had been there a million times. 'They both just come to have a chat, really. Doesn't mean anything. Maybe it's more exciting for them to go somewhere they think they're not allowed!'

Still, the man didn't say anything, but I could see the outline of his clenched jaw, the almost-furrowed brow again. I swear I could hear his teeth grinding. He reached the hide ahead of me, and I offered to stay outside, a good distance back. My body was turning away already; I felt the sudden need to get home. I half watched as Dom tried the door handle first, pushing with more force than was necessary. The door flew open, he stepped inside. I don't know if he said a single word when he staggered out, think perhaps his hands just flew into his hair. I could see from where I was standing, beyond the hide, that she was lying on her back, eyes to the ceiling, mouth slightly ajar. The pallor of her skin was something akin to a solid block of paper. She'd been there a few days, you could just tell. The blanket that had been lain to try and cover her up had clearly been blown away by the wind that carried into the structure through the glassless hole in the wall. Dom raced past me. I remember the sound as well as the smell of my own vomiting. When I glanced up, I could see Dom was just standing there, hand frozen to his chest, eyes nowhere. Then he was sobbing.

# FRAN

## 17 March

Dom didn't come home until late last night. I had been in a great mood in the evening, was thinking of cooking something special for dinner and perhaps getting us some wine to enjoy. The relief at the sight of the tern in her nest and the knowledge that her young will hatch any day soon temporarily superseded any worries for my sister and her missing partner, I'm afraid to admit. Just for an evening.

I waited until 8 pm for Dom, then decided to just make some cheese-on-toast for myself, smashing the plates around as I removed them from the dishwasher, my disappointment obvious. Bruno had already eaten; pasta and salad at Sadie's place, apparently. I had walked over there at 6 pm to bring him home. The pair of them had run to Sadie's caravan from the path home from school once they had realised I was making my way to the marsh.

I hugged my sister upon seeing her, *was she OK, did she need anything?* Immediately, I felt the stabs of culpability for not spending the past couple of days with her. She had been crying, her eyes globby and swollen, her red nose snuffling. I asked her if the police were hunting for Ellis themselves.

'I don't even know,' she replied. 'They just keep saying they want to talk to him. I know he didn't do anything to that woman, Fran.'

I wanted to stay, to comfort her; it took all my effort to put an arm around Bruno and steer him down the steps and towards home. He was asking to go to look at some of the birds on the marshland, but I managed to distract him by saying I would watch him play football against the wall of the house when we got home.

At nearly 10 pm, the front door opened quietly, and I heard my husband's feet stepping into the hallway. He seemed to take forever. I don't know how he got home, unless on foot, as his car had remained on the driveway all day since he went out.

'Hi, Fran.' His voice was sheepish, clipped.

I didn't even turn to look at him, kept my eyes on the television. It seemed to be a trailer for the *Eurovision Song Contest*; men in tight black leather trousers, women singing in fluorescent clothing. Their voices were terrible, like high-pitched, screeching gulls.

He didn't sit, didn't make his way to the kitchen for food. I knew he was waiting for me to look at him.

When I turned my head, I could tell he'd been crying. He was holding papers in his hand. Police papers. An iciness began to trickle its way up my spine, I moved in my chair to try to ward it off. I didn't want to know what he was going to say.

'The teacher, she's called Eve. She's dead. I found her body.'

# TAD

The bloke I saw leaving the caravan park with the crumpled carrier bag, that was Ellis. I've worked it out; that was Sadie's dad, the one the coppers are looking for. Nobody told me, I just eventually figured it out for myself. He must have been leaving for good, his few belongings in that bag of his. I might have to tell them I saw him.

After we found the body, I needed to take a little time out. That Dom bloke, he went into some kind of shock. I'm surprised I didn't, really. I think we both sat down for a while outside the shed building, gathering our thoughts. The sea was loud, the birds louder. Some of them were swooping down and gathering at the edge of the little wooden hut, screaming, demanding answers. I think they could smell her. I slammed the door shut on three of them, but the others were insistent, some of them flapping their way into the open window of the hide. It didn't take me long to work out that some of the birds had already started on the body, and perhaps some other animals had too, but I didn't want to look for long. Dom was pulling at the skin on his wrist – it was so red-raw at one point I nearly pulled his arm away. I remember that, even before we found Eve, he wasn't saying much. I've forgotten what we were talking about anyway. I was the one who called the cops. I don't have a mobile phone, but I gestured to Dom that I was going to use his, seeing as it had slipped out of the pocket of his jeans and onto the ground. He didn't even nod *OK* at me.

They arrived in about fifteen minutes, along with an ambulance, although at that point I couldn't really have told you how much time had passed. All I know is that they went in there, matter-of-fact, and came out with her covered up by a black body bag, on some type of stretcher. They'd managed to get the ambulance onto the beach, along with the copper cars. I couldn't help but notice how the shingle had all been pulled one way by the tyres, the speeding vehicles not caring for the beauty of the beach as they pulled up. They must have driven down the pedestrian paths, as there's simply no room for cars anywhere else. There was an arm around my shoulder, I think it was one of the women, Mandi, from our camp. She's only mid-twenties but she has the air of a middle-aged mother about her. I think I remember her leading me home, but I don't remember most of the walk. I didn't want to stay in my trailer, but I knew I had to be there for Jade. All I wanted to do was find Charlie, my little brother Charlie. In all the commotion, I had forgotten about my daughter, and a dagger of shame had pierced me through my ribs when I saw her pacing back and forth, back and forth outside the door of our trailer. 'Dad dad dad,' she said when she saw me, as if by rote. It must have only been around 10 pm by then, but it felt more like 5 am, like the start of the next day. I hugged her, told her to get inside the van. She was reluctant to let go of me, wanted to sleep in my bed. I don't know yet if the others had told her what happened, where I was. I didn't even want to ask. I watched her slide out of her shoes, climb into my bed fully clothed, and I decided that I would take the sofa. Her hair, I remember, was a mess – twigs, leaves, crumblings of soil. I remember thinking I'd change the sheets in the morning. Her nails, they were disgusting, deeply embedded soils under them – brown, burgundy, black.

# FRAN

## 19 March

I don't know how to speak to Dom. I've never discovered a dead body myself before. He's not going to work, and probably shouldn't for the next few days. He was sharp with Bruno, told him he still had to go to school. We haven't told him what's happened; I guess we were both hoping the school would do it for us. Ros phoned as soon as she heard, although I could barely make out what she was saying. It's not looking good for Ellis now. I've offered to stop at her caravan to collect Sadie, take them both to school. She said no, it would be fine, Sadie could walk up to ours seeing as we live nearer the school. Bruno knows something is up. He can see his father staring out to the back garden, seemingly looking at nothing. Neither Dom nor I slept, nor have we spoken. He's gone into some kind of trance.

'Why's Dad funny?' The words are innocent. I don't want to tell him.

We are relieved by a rapping at the front door: Sadie. She looks as if she hasn't slept either.

I glance towards Bruno to check he's got his shoes on and has located his bookbag. We leave the house, not bothering to lock it, begin to walk. Nobody speaks for a while, then I decide to ask my niece how she is.

'Not bad, thanks, although I'm quite sad today.'

Bruno looks over to her immediately.

She tries to explain. 'Ms McConnell. Our teacher. Mum told me.'

I am expecting Bruno to ask what she is talking about, but he doesn't. He has pulled a feather from his bag, has it positioned in his fingers like a plane once again, is dancing on his tiptoes, ready to fly.

'Auntie Fran, Bruno does know, doesn't he?'

I bite down on my tongue, taste coins, metal, don't answer her question. My son is ahead of us now, twirling on the tips of his feet, plane noises coming from him. He throws the feather; we all watch it waft down to the ground in slow motion. We are at the part of the path that splits in two, one leg heading towards the marshlands, the other leading to the school. My feet are itching to walk to the shore, to leave the kids again, to sit with the birds and pretend none of this has happened. I am in such a trance that I don't hear what Bruno is saying as he flies back towards me.

'What, Bruno?'

'I said, the other mums and children are turning around.'

I look up the path towards the school, see the parents I vaguely know walking back towards us. One of them is shaking her head as she looks in my direction. It's like when you're in a huge traffic jam and the cars coming towards you are flashing their lights, telling you to turn around, that there is no point continuing.

'School's closed,' says one of the kids approaching us.

Bruno looks at me.

I notice Sadie stops dead in her tracks. 'I thought it might be.'

I'm debating whether to keep walking towards the school, to ignore what the others are saying. My feet have stopped, though, and my eyes fall to Bruno, whom I know is waiting for my attention.

'Why is it closed, Mum?'

I am grateful that Sadie begins to walk away from us, back along the path we have just walked. She is taking tiny pigeon steps.

'What's happened?' His voice is so innocent, already I can see tears pooling in his eyes. 'Mum?'

I can't tell him here, not on the path with the other families beginning to bundle together as they make their way home. I hold his hand, and we walk down the other leg of the path, towards the marshland. He keeps looking up at me, but all at once, I take his bookbag from his other hand and I run ahead. I know he will follow. When we get to the broadest part of the marsh, I let myself crumple to the ground, into a sort of seated position, gesture for him to follow suit. He almost tiptoes towards me, as if afraid to make a single noise on the sand. I am already crying. He puts his hand out to my cheek, tries to wipe the tear away, but it's trailing off my chin. There are gulls sneaking closer to us, their heads creeping forward, waiting for food. Perhaps they can smell the crab-paste sandwiches in Bruno's lunch bag, safely wrapped in their protective layer of foil. Bruno stamps in the sand close to them, shooing them away. They cry, flap a little, then land again, even closer to where we are sitting.

'Ms McConnell. She's been found in a bad way, Bruno.'

I can't tell if he is looking at me, I'm staring straight ahead. We are a good fifty feet from where the tern's nest is located. I can't see it properly from here. The wind bites at us suddenly, and I pull the thin cardigan I'm wearing tightly around my chest. At least Bruno is wearing his little blue coat, more of a winter coat, really. He wasn't even going to bother to bring it, when we left the house earlier.

'What sort of a bad way?' His hand is resting on my lap, I can feel he is shaking. 'She's dead, isn't she?'

I can't think of any response other than to nod. He stands, doesn't speak, then I feel a slight rush of cold air as he begins to run towards the sea. I'm not going to chase him. I try to take in the moment, notice what my senses are telling me. The air is so sharp, and I remember that it is only about 8:30 am; there is nobody else on the beach. It would be so relaxing, just me and him here right now, if not for what we are both trying to absorb.

\*

We have been here an hour now, and my strongest feeling of sadness has been eclipsed by the chattering of my teeth and the icy chill that I can't escape. I call to Bruno, who is still wandering along the shoreline, head down. He looks up, slowly starts to step towards where I am sitting. I think he's stopped crying now. His face looks like it's been bitten by the sharp sea wind; no swollen eyes, just mottled, raw skin on his cheeks.

Suddenly, a practical thought kicks my senses back to normality. Today my caravan park is to welcome its first holidaymakers of the year. I need to be home, need to be available to give the keys to the first groups of guests as they bundle enthusiastically to our door.

'Let's go home,' I say.

# TAD

The mood round here continues to be flat. Nobody feels like doing anything. Charlie is staying in his trailer, alone. I don't go to him. Some of the others stay put too. There have been no police around recently to talk to any of us.

I told Jade what happened, that I was one of the men to find the body. She didn't ask me any questions, just sat, stared out of the window. I wonder if her interest in the girl has waned. At first, I suppose, I had found Sadie kind of mysterious. I had wanted to know more, to spend time in her company. She was almost like a woman – an arresting, confident woman, casting her spell on everyone around her. At the same time, though, she was just a child, a child needing some love, some time spent on her.

Jade stood up after about half an hour, wandered to the door of the caravan. It was drizzling outside, a relentless grey rain that found its way in once my daughter had slipped on her shoes and pulled the front door open. Charlie calls it *mizzle*.

'Where are you going?' I tried.

'Beach,' she said, not signing back.

'In the rain? In this?' I was pointing outside.

She didn't care, didn't acknowledge my comment, jumped down onto the step, walked away.

# FRAN

## 26 March

It's been just over a week since Dom found the teacher's body. Sometimes, I will wander into one of the upstairs bedrooms, looking for somewhere warm to dry the laundry, or looking for a shirt that I know needs ironing, and he will be sitting there on the bed, staring into space. If he wasn't talking a lot to me before, he certainly isn't now. I've called his work, told them what happened, that Dom won't be in for the time being. They're issuing him with compassionate leave, so that will be a help. Thankfully, it's Easter time now; the caravans are being booked out more, and there are people walking around the site, taking in the views and wandering down to the shore. It becomes a complete contrast to the winter months, but I love those too – the grey skies, the darkness of the woodland even before the late afternoon has arrived. I feel slightly torn at the beginning of the season, having to share my beaches, my woodland, with strangers. It feels like I am having to give up something that is only mine. Nobody has ventured into the hide since the incident. As far as I know, it's still covered in blue-and-white police tape. I believe there was some blood on the ground of the hide too. The post-mortem is yet to happen, but the police are saying it was an intentional death. *This was no accident.* They are starting to search actively for Ellis too, now. I don't know why they have taken so long to do so, but I am grateful that they have held back until now. I know Ellis has an unshakeable protective streak for his daughter and all who may stand up to her, but he would never do this. Well, I don't think he would. Leaving at the same time as the teacher's disappearance isn't helping him, though. It wouldn't help anybody.

Since the morning on the beach, Bruno hasn't mentioned Ms McConnell. I don't know what there is to say to him. I realise, as a mother, a modern-day parent, I am meant to encourage him to talk through whatever he is feeling, but I don't feel ready to. I don't yet want to encourage his sadness. We have been through enough of that with his dad, and the melancholy will no doubt run through the corridors of the school when the children return. I am trying to keep things in this house upbeat, create a sense of normality. I don't know if Bruno knows the police are trying to track down his Uncle Ellis, though I'm sure Sadie has been told by now.

*

Dom is crying, big gulping sobs as he sits in front of the television. He's not even watching whatever is on the screen. He has his head in his hands. I can't take it for much longer, plonk myself next to him on the sofa. He doesn't look up, doesn't acknowledge the hand I am placing around his shoulders.

'It's OK,' I say.

'It's not,' he snuffles. For a moment, I think he is going to push my hand off him. 'She was only thirty-four. What a complete and utter waste. All that personality... that brain... and beauty... gone.'

Something jolts in my stomach. *Beauty*. I pause for a moment before deciding not to say anything at all. I don't think I've heard him speak like this about someone before. A death makes you look back at someone with rose-tinted glasses, even if it's a person who hasn't played a big part in your life. Your brain makes that person seem perfect.

'We... we didn't really know her, Dom. She was a teacher at the school, not our friend.'

He lifts his chin up slightly, looks at me through his red-and-blue eyes. 'Is that the point?'

I hang my head a little. I've come across as cold-hearted, I know.

'Fran,' he says, beginning to stare at me a little. 'Have you ever been the one to discover a dead body?'

I gulp slightly.

'Have you been the one to stare into that ghastly face, see the blood surrounding her? Have you ever experienced shock? No, you haven't. And until you have, you don't really know what you're talking about. No wonder I used to go to chat to Ellis and Ros for the occasional evening. At least *they* know how to listen.'

Another jolt to my stomach; I stand up, let my hand drop from his back. *Those evenings he spent there. Because he feels he can't talk to me.*

'Are you going to walk out of the room now? Leave me here?' He is spitting the words out.

My mouth opens as if to speak, but I all manage to say is a weary 'no'.

I stand there for a moment, then let myself drop down into the armchair opposite the sofa. Being in this chair makes me think of the time Ellis was here, planning his move into our home. He had seemed sheepish, embarrassed almost, but not angry, not agitated. Not like he was about to go and finish off the teacher that had suspended his little girl from school. My mind wanders as I keep an eye on Dom, his eyes seemingly staring through the walls at things I cannot see.

# TAD

I've heard the police have now issued a warrant for that guy, Ellis, for his arrest. His partner must be beside herself. I see her sometimes, going in and out of her van. It's funny how you notice people more once you know who they are. I notice Sadie coming and going, too, although she never seems as tearful and sombre as her mother. I sound like some kind of a spy. I'm not. I'm just the sort of person who is aware of things happening around me. I'm aware of the morose feelings of my brother, of the family around us, who are all feeling more than unsettled about the incident. The apparent murder. I hope for that Ellis's sake that he chooses to return soon, to show his innocence. If he *is* innocent.

I am walking to the hide, I don't know why. It's warm, the sun peeping out periodically behind white clouds. There are other people strolling around. Must be holidaymakers from Fran's park. I don't know why I am choosing to retrace my steps from the last time I went down there, the time I went with that Dom fella. *That* time. I haven't seen nor heard from him since, but then why would I? I remember one of the police escorting him back to his front door after it had all happened. The bloke was in a right state.

I am almost tiptoeing down the path to the woodland, keeping my head down. I'm not sure why, I haven't done anything wrong. When I reach the edge of the woods, I keep my eye on the sea. A couple are sitting down near the shore's edge, basking in the newly appeared sun. The water pulls forward, lurching near their feet, then pulls away again. I watch the gulls floating on the surface, see the fingers of the waves reach out to them. If I pause, I can imagine that none of this has happened, that there isn't the dead body of a thirty-something professional teacher lying in the local morgue, cold as stone. Eve. I try to picture her face. She was so pale, her skin as delicate as paper. I'm no poet, but there was something ethereal about how peaceful she looked. Like all her difficulties had upped and vanished. Already I am walking towards the hide, and I feel my heart quicken. The memories from the last time I walked there spark up again, a reliving of the horror. The police tape has gone, just a flap of it left around one of the trees, fluttering in the breeze as a reminder. There are still the signs of my vomit, dried up on the ground outside the structure, some other stains that I pray aren't blood. The door is slightly ajar, and I need only to push it gingerly with two of my fingers. I stay standing outside, don't want the claustrophobia of the place. She is sitting on the bench there, her hood up over her head even though it is nearly twenty degrees today, or something similar.

'I used to come in here with Bruno occasionally,' is all Fran says. She has a notebook in her right hand, a blunt-looking pencil in her left. I stand on my tiptoes at the doorway, try to sneak a look at what she is doodling. She snaps the book shut. 'Just sketches.'

I find myself wondering if she likes to be here as a way of escaping other people. Her husband, perhaps, or that sister of hers. 'So, you come and draw here a lot?' It sounds like a ridiculous chat-up line. *Do you come here often?*

She laughs, looks across at me for the first time. 'Not a lot. I've kind of given up on my drawing skills, and anyway, I built this hide in the wrong bloody place. Won't you come in?'

I shake my head *no*, and for a moment, the cogs of my mind pause. *She had this built here herself? How can you build a hide in the wrong place?* There are birds everywhere around here, even on the damned roof.

'For the rare birds,' she adds, as if sensing my thoughts. 'Listen, thanks for coming to my place to tell me about what's been happening to the birds around here.'

I watch as she stretches her gaze out of the glassless window in front of her. There's an unrivalled view to the shore here, through a spot in the trees, a clearing of sorts. There are only gulls, hopping around some smaller birds, fighting over the remains of a crab or some other shelled creature. I don't know my sealife, don't pretend to.

'So, did one of the kids admit to it?'

She glances at me again, the notebook still resting on her lap. 'Nope.'

'You chatted it through with them?'

'Well, it wasn't Bruno. And I don't think it was Sadie, either.'

I nod, to appease her, not sure how she would know this for sure.

She pulls her hood down, shakes her hair about. She could be quite attractive, on a good day.

'So, who else is likely to have done something like that?'

Fran smiles, a wry smile. 'Your guess is as good as mine, Tad.'

I shrug. 'Well, I don't know that many people around here. Not like you.'

There's a couple of minutes of silence. I change position in the doorway, lean against the other side of the frame. It's not that comfy, but I'm not stepping inside.

'May I ask, how is your husband doing?' I pause. 'Since we discovered Eve?'

'Eve?' She is looking at me again. Her feet are swinging, not reaching the floor. She seems almost like a toddler. Perhaps they built the bench a little too high. 'Oh, yes, that was her name. We knew her as Ms McConnell.' But then her face folds a little, like she's trying not to frown. 'But when Dom came back from here the other night, he called her *Eve*. We always just knew her as Ms McConnell,' she repeats. 'Anyway, Sadie, yes, she's not been getting on well at school. Her behaviour is less than perfect. She got excluded.'

'Yes, she did tell me this.' I can feel her eyeing me, waiting for an explanation. 'She comes to see us sometimes. Her and Bruno. I think they like our camp.'

She turns her head back to the view out of the window and watches the birds, flapping about above the sea, not landing on the water, instead letting themselves land with grace on the shingle. There's a fawny-coloured bird, large like a magpie, a hint of turquoise under its wing.

'The jay! It's back.'

'It's a good one to spot, yes?'

She's frowning again now. The bird disappears from view as quickly as it arrived. 'Not especially. They're shy, not rare.'

She must see disappointment on my face, as she adds, 'They are really pretty, though. Bit sneaky. Like magpies... They're from the same family, did you know?'

I admit that I didn't. I want to talk to her about who she thinks could have killed those little birds, I'm not sure how to bring it up again.

Fran stands, pulls her substantial-looking coat around her despite the warmth of the day. 'See you later.'

She passes me, leaves through the door that my body has been holding open. I step backwards, letting it close softly behind us. Sometimes, when I try to picture the floor of the hide, there are still red speckles, near where Eve's head would have lain. I don't even let myself think about the huge blotches of burgundy, swallow down the threat of the contents of my stomach lurching up again.

There is nothing to show that the jay was once in front of us on the shore, its muted rainbow colours bobbing around among the stones; only the other, more coarse-looking seabirds remain scrabbling about. It's like it was never here.

# FRAN

## 1 April

The post-mortem results came back. We went to the newsagent in the middle of the village to buy the paper, before any were delivered to the houses. It was Dom's idea to get it before everyone else had a look. I wasn't sure what he was hoping to achieve by finding out exactly how she died, but I wanted to support him anyway. I'll do anything to help him back to normal. The press are saying she was married. I couldn't picture it somehow, was trying to focus on being in the moment.

We had sat parked at the side of the road for some time, not wanting to get out of the car, the sun barely up. I had been looking at my reflection in the flip-down mirror of the driver's side, noticing the fine lines beginning to develop around my top lip, around my eyes. Perhaps he's been struggling to find me attractive lately. It felt slightly strange to be driving my husband about; I don't always drive when it's the two of us going out together, but something told me he wouldn't be up to it today. The article was just a short summary of the results; the real report no doubt already grabbed by the national press, but Dom wanted to see it before anyone else in the village could.

He saw a counsellor a few days ago. I told him to. She said that he needed to grieve, and then to find *closure*. I felt like telling her that this teacher was virtually a stranger to the pair of us, but I wasn't even allowed to speak to her in the end. It was Dom's thing, I wasn't allowed to enter the counselling room. She said he could be on the brink of suffering from Post-Traumatic Stress Disorder, finding the body like that. He had just mumbled, 'PTSD,' when he had left the building, I had to look it up when we arrived home. This is all he's said to me for days.

It felt strangely intimate, being in the car with him, alone, just before we read the results in the newspaper. It was just us two, no Bruno or Ros craving my attention, no telephone ringing, no new punters at the door of the house wanting to sign into a caravan. For a moment, when I had looked at him, he had just been my straight old Dom, always worrying about something, and I had felt a pang of real affection. It quickly disappeared, though, as I made to grab his hand, to try to comfort him, and he pulled it away.

It took a while to understand what the results were telling us, but reading the few lines of content several times, we came up with the main picture. She died from being hit on the back of the head with a *heavy instrument*. Dom and I have not discussed this at any length since. We both read the words at the same time. I could feel him peering over my shoulder in the car, felt his breath on my cheek. When he reached the few words of detail, I heard him kind of gulp, sit back in his seat. He got out of the car again, started pacing around the car park. I didn't dare look at his face. We have barely glanced at each other since the body was found. I never knew someone could be so affected by finding a body, but then what do I know? As the car echoed with a new silence, I was left with only my thoughts, my stomach turning at the idea of someone bashing the teacher over the head with something monstrous in their hands, something full of weight. My mind was trying to picture what it could have been… *a lamp, a doorstop, a vase.*

*

My husband is crying as I hover on the landing. My hand is poised on our bedroom door, not knowing whether to push it open and go in to see how he is. For some reason, my brain is halting me from going to him. I can't quite understand his reaction. I am startled by a sudden hand on my shoulder – Bruno.

'Mum, why are you just standing here?'

I want to tell him to *shush*, that his father will know I've been lingering on the landing, wondering what to do about the crying. I raise a finger to my lips but let it drop, knowing that my little boy won't understand. He pushes the door into our bedroom and finds his father sitting on the floor, his back against the bed. Dom doesn't even lift his face.

'Dad,' Bruno says in a whisper. 'Daddy, it's OK.'

He drops to the floor too, lifts his right arm up unnaturally high to place it around his father's neck. Dom glances up at him, tears dampening his lashes. His face nearly matches the colour of his hair. 'Bruno.' It seems to be all he can manage.

Bruno glances at me, then back at his father.

Dom pulls himself free from his son's grip and stands, a little wobbly. I can see there are four or five empty beer bottles by the side of the bed and hear myself let out a lengthy sigh. He's never really been one to drink. *Why do these events lead people to the bottle?* He avoids eye contact with me, lurches past my body on the landing, and Bruno follows. They both head down the stairs, and I hear the front door lock being battled with, and then there is the slam of heavy wood. From where I am standing, I raise myself onto my tiptoes to see out of the little window above the front door. I see Dom stomping ahead, slowing, turning to talk to Bruno. He's still crying. They stop walking for a moment, then Bruno steps forward and they continue walking together towards the path to the beach.

# TAD

Sadie sticks out like a sore thumb, clearly not one of the holidaymakers, that girl. Sometimes she stands with a steely glare, hand over her eyes, seemingly inspecting the cars that enter the field, heading for their designated caravans. They have to go to Fran's cottage first for the keys, I presume, to sign in. Today, perhaps in her boredom, Sadie is eyeing down a Volvo, a silver one, until her mum comes out of the caravan, tells her to stop staring.

She seems to be by herself a lot these days, less time spent with the boy. Perhaps Bruno's mum prefers it that way. I still can't get used to calling her Fran; I don't know why. The sister, *Ros*, she spends most of her time inside her home. I can't say if that's normal for her or not, since her partner left. The papers have been issuing photos of him, and his image has appeared on the news. I don't watch the box much, but I've been looking out for him especially. The picture they used of him is old, I would say. He has shorter hair, but still so black, and dark blue eyes that I hadn't noticed from the distance I saw him from that one time. He looks as innocent as a man could be, but it just goes to show. There isn't a one-size E-FIT face for what a murderer looks like.

Today I watch Sadie go back and forth to the caravan, holding things in her hands. I can't tell what they are. She is going into the small copse maybe fifty feet from her van, bending, picking up things and returning them to the outside of her caravan. Her dress is white, almost matching her hair, and I realise it is a Sunday, no school. She looks as though she could be attending church in that outfit. Her shoes are muddy – could be trainers. I've heard the others talking about the school holidays, and I realise for the first time that the kids in my camp have been playing out longer, their parents not calling them in for tea as early as they usually would. The camp is slightly more relaxed this week; Charlie is seemingly less morose, and the younger men are not keeping as much distance from him. They talk to him as they usually would.

I fling on some clothes and my old waxed coat, make my way over to the fence that separates the girl's world from mine. She sees me eventually, stops in her tracks, stares down at whatever she's holding in her hands. Birds. Headless birds, all different types. I pause, my heart beating faster. I can't quite believe I've caught her in the act, step closer to see what she's been doing with their little bodies along the underside of her caravan. Each bird, six or seven of them, is propped up against a rock or a brick that she has found. She has balanced their heads back on top of their bodies.

'I was fixing them,' she says, eyes on her day's work. Then she disappears, hopping up the concrete steps to her caravan, wiping her dirty hands on the sides of her white dress, her plumage tarnished.

# FRAN

## 4 April

Even though we're well into the school holidays and I should still be tucked up in bed at this early hour, I am making my way down to the beach, on my way to the tern's nest. Only a few days and her eggs will be hatching. I cannot afford to miss this, the only highlight of my life now. Bruno is at home, unaware of my leaving, and his dad will still be lying in our bed, sleeplessly. The sea is unusually calm, the wind barely pressing against my hair, my cheeks. Behind the grey cloud, I can feel the sun threatening to show its face, and I find myself willing it to stay covered. I slow my walking speed to take in my surroundings and the peacefulness of everything laid out in front of me, a landscape painting. My being here, my being human, is taking away from the naturalness of the place, and a slight feeling of self-loathing murmurs in my stomach as I am treading my path towards the marshes. I'm so tired of everything that's happening in my life. So tired, so worried for my sister, calling me in a state of desperation because the police are at her door again, this time wanting to bug her van in case Ellis should get in touch with her on a different phone. I'm sick of my husband dealing with his shock, his *post-traumatic stress* in such a silent way that it makes me feel as though I don't exist. Tad, from the Romany site, came to speak to me again last night. About the birds. He said he'd seen Sadie. That she'd been holding headless birds, lining them up, trying to balance their heads back on top of their bodies. At first, I couldn't find air to breathe, hearing this. It was hard to draw oxygen from anywhere. She had told him *she was trying to fix them*. I believe her.

There is something red that catches my eye, a flash of colour from among the reeds in front of me. My breath catches in my throat as I see the man I had talked to the other time, bending and staring to his right, at the tern's nest. His name: *Charlie*. He's wearing the same red top as the first time I saw him. I clear my throat, and he turns to look at me, says nothing. I want to ask him if he's been watching her as closely as I have, but I refrain. It would be too disturbing to the animals here. I pick my way over the reeds and kneel right next to him. I can almost smell whatever body spray he has adorned himself with, he is so close.

'How's she doing?'

He grins, his head tipping slightly to one side. 'Pretty well, I would say.'

'Yep.' I can only agree.

'I come every day,' he declares. 'You just a fair-weather watcher, then? Only seen you here a couple of times.'

I know he is only mocking me, trying to be friendly, but the comment irks me. But the man on the path, the one who was standing there that time, the darkness of the trees concealing him as he walked away – it was him. I almost laugh with the relief.

'Every morning, at six, I'm here. More like five, actually, now. I leave the dogs behind, of course.'

I don't speak, am racking my brains, trying to think of the last time I was here at daybreak. The sunrise is getting earlier and earlier now that summer is nearly here. There is a heat that is threatening to spill onto my cheeks, a feeling that I have been caught out, that he is the more committed birdwatcher than I am.

'You don't have a family?' is all I can come up with. 'I've just been so busy with mine.'

He pauses briefly, looks sad, almost, then shakes his head *no*, proceeds to tell me about all the kids on his site that he helps to take care of. He tells me, not for the first time, that he is from a Romany travelling family. That they are different from Travellers,

Irish Travellers. I am interested, want to ask more questions, but don't want to seem too keen.

'You planning on nicking the eggs?' He says it as bold as brass, but there is a glint in his eye. I shake my head vehemently again, even though I know he is joking with me.

'I was just messing with you there.' He stands slowly, walks away without saying another word, and then I am alone. I watch him pick his way over the reeds, his long shorts not quite fitting with his red top.

\*

It's van-cleaning day again. Funny how it seems to come around so quickly; well, it's more like every other day now we have some of the caravans full with holidaymakers. The money is much needed. Without this spring flurry of punters, I wouldn't have much of an income. The vacuum cleaner feels hotter than ever as it vents out its angry steam of air, brushing against my legs as I run the hose along the sides of the beds, the corners of the rooms. It's the van a couple along from Ros and Ellis's home, been empty for the most part of the year. I still need to clean them regularly. The hoover stutters and chokes, something caught up in the main tube. I curse, beads of perspiration dripping their way down my forehead, and kick out at the damned appliance. Always sucking up things I hadn't noticed. I swear I spend more time pulling out things that have become stuck in the hose than sucking up the stuff that needs to get in. I insert a couple of fingers into the tubing, can touch the edge of something, like leather strings. Forcing my hand with a little more conviction, I manage to pincer-grip the tassel-like strands, pull out what seems to resemble a bracelet. My mind takes a little time to get a grip of itself. Dom's leather bracelet. I bought it for him a couple of years ago. I sit down on the edge of the unmade bed, mind spinning as the *whoosh* of a sudden wind tries to batter down the door of the caravan.

# TAD

Charlie's been spending a little more time with us recently, and it seems to have cheered Jade up a little. She's been affected by the things around here, I don't doubt. Even though she may find it hard to tell us, I can tell when my girl ain't herself. Today Charlie is playing cards with her at a table we've set up outside with a few chairs. I can see Fran's caravan park from this side of my van, but all I want to do is watch Jade play cards. Some of the holidaymakers on the other field are doing the same with their families, under the fancy red-and-white striped awnings they have attached to the caravans over there. Charlie always picks a game Jade knows well, and one that she has a chance of winning. I watch her giggle and whoop when she knows she's got a good hand, her poker face non-existent. This keeps Charlie in a good mood today, knowing that he has brought a smile to my daughter's face. He slams down his hand on the wooden table, eyes on Jade, and whoops loudly himself. She knows he has won, but she doesn't become upset. There is always the next game. And the next.

After another hour of playing, Charlie stands and makes his way into my caravan, no doubt looking for a drink. He sees the chicken I have prepared by the stove, goes to say something, stops.

'What?' I ask him. He's not normally short of words.

'You seen that girl who's always wandering around?'

'Sadie?'

'She was called something else. Like a country or a river or something.'

I remember that she had asked me to call her Sahara for a while. And that I had chosen to stop calling her that.

'Sahara, yeah. She's actually called Sadie. Why do you ask?'

He sits on the bench at my table, the one where she sits when she pays me a visit.

'Saw her with dead bird bodies or something the other day. Bit odd.'

I nod. He saw her too.

'There's still that woman down at the beach who's fun to wind up a little. She came to look at that little rare bird's nest again. Is she something to do with Bruno and the girl?'

He means Fran, obviously doesn't know her name. I think of the last time I saw her.

'That's Bruno's mum. Fran. She runs the caravan place next door.' I nod over in the direction of Fran's Holiday Vans.

Charlie doesn't say anything for a while, doesn't look in the direction I've nodded. He's playing with a bit of skin on the end of his thumb. I wonder if Bruno has ever said anything about his mum, the times he's been with Charlie.

'Should we tell her about the girl? And the dead birds? Does she know the girl?'

'She's her aunt. I don't know if Fran and her sister get on, mind.' I'm thinking of the time Sadie said something... *My mum is always pissed off at my aunt...* or words to that effect. 'I've already told her.'

He runs a hand through his short hair, drinks from the beer he has helped himself to.

*

Charlie is out more and more lately, his previous dark mood lifting. I'm glad for him. He's been through a lot. It's the birds, he tells me. They give him a bit of a purpose in life, watching out for them. He comes back from his walks sometimes with Jade in tow, sometimes without. He'll always knock at my window as he returns to his trailer, just to let me know he's back. It's a cheerful kind of *rap-tap-tap*. I'm never expected to answer. I just like knowing that he's there. Jade has picked up too. She's leaving my side more frequently, not just daily trips to the woodland or the beach, but bus trips into town. The first few times my sisters took her, and I looked after their kids for a bit, a right handful. They're my godkids as well as my nieces and nephews. Anyway, I digress; now my daughter can venture there alone, best clothes on, bought on such trips, mostly with money from Charlie. Apparently, she's talking a bit more when she's out too. My brother and my daughter are flourishing, and it warms my heart to see. It's been so dark around here for so many weeks, yet I don't want to move away; there is a safety in these fields by the shore.

# FRAN

## 11 April

I've been visiting the shoreline every morning at sunrise, much to the amusement of that Charlie man. I just like to see how my tern is doing, warming up those eggs of hers. I wonder if I've lost track of time again, perhaps they should have hatched by now. Anyway, today I'm not wandering around the marshlands, I've decided to make the most of the hide. The serenity that eases its way through me is a welcome rush to my mind as I sit down on the wooden bench, the sound of the breeze in my ears. The trees seemed to have moved a little since I last sat here, the weight of recent rains making them bow and reach to the east. With the branches leaning a little out of kilter, I can see more of the beach now, through the gap that has been created. There are gulls, of course, a lot of them, but I am seeing other birds now, perhaps a marsh harrier, a lapwing. I find myself wishing I had come back here more often. That would have been a way to avoid that grieving husband of mine.

We haven't had a proper conversation since before he found the body. He avoids eye contact, but manages to speak to Bruno, albeit in an absent-father-visiting-for-the-weekend kind of way. I don't know how we are going to resolve this. I do agree that he's in shock. He only attended the one counselling session, but now I think I'm going to have to force him to do more. The PTSD is affecting our family life. As I sit here, in the room where the teacher was discovered by Dom, I try to picture myself walking in and discovering the woman on the floor. I wonder if the smell of sawdust and homeware stores would have hit my senses first, as it always does in this place. Or I wonder if I would have spotted the woman immediately. I would have been scared, horrified, of course, but I think my practical ways of thinking would have kicked in. That's why I think I might have made a great nurse. I would have bent down by her side, listened to her chest, felt for a pulse as I held her wrist. From what I've heard, they didn't do these things. They must have been in such shock. Perhaps they had already seen the bash to her head, the blood that had spilled out of her. They may not have been able to tell that anything had happened, if the blood had stopped. Perhaps they were paralysed with fear.

A glance at my watch tells me it's nearly 8 am, and I should have been back at the house half an hour ago. I am hoping that Dom is helping Bruno to get ready for school, now that it is open again. A part of me doesn't want to rush back home. Let him take care of Bruno. Perhaps the need to do something for his child will kick him back into action, make him realise that life goes on. I resist the urge to rise from the bench, even though my heart is speeding slightly with the anxiety that our son will not have the initiative to get himself dressed and fed for the day. I make myself stay on the bench for at least another ten minutes, watching the different-sized birds fight over whatever it is they have discovered in the sand. The gulls are so obvious in their approach; they rush, peck at their rivals. The smaller ones wait, hover in the air, biding their time before they go in for the kill.

At first, I am impressed that there is another man in this village with the same hair as my husband – all red curls – and a certain lope to their walk. I only wish that Dom would demonstrate as much affection towards his partner as this man is doing now. The couple don't face each other, or even glance at one another. I notice they are both looking straight ahead. All at once self-conscious, I pull my head back a little, but there is no way they can catch me watching them from where I sit. They are not smiling, particularly, certainly not laughing, but perhaps there doesn't always have to be such obvious joy in order to be happy. I can't even tell if they are speaking to one another, they are such a distance away. I find

I am squinting, my eyes focused on the beach before the man and the woman disappear from my limited view. Branches, waving in the gusts of wind that are beginning to start up for the day, are obscuring my view, and I swear out loud with annoyance as I rise to my feet to get a better look. The couple are gone. I realise with a start, once I cannot see them any longer, that the man was wearing the same hoodie as my husband often sports. The woman his arm was wrapped around was tall, wispy, wrapped in black Lycra. Despite my brain telling my feet to run, to rush through the door of the hide and towards the shore, I am grounded to the spot, adrenaline making my heart pound in my ears. Perhaps this is what paralysing fear feels like. Perhaps this is shock.

# TAD

The kids haven't been here for a few days, so I'm surprised to find them hammering at my door. It's not early – perhaps mid-afternoon – but still, I'm happy that they have chosen to come to me. As I open the door, the girl pushes her way through first, the boy lingering behind her, waiting for permission to be invited in.

'Bruno, come inside. Look, your little friend has already made herself at home!' I nod towards Sadie, who is sitting upright at my table, glaring towards him. She doesn't respond to my passive-aggressive comment.

Bruno scuffles in, eyes watering a little, but it's hard to tell if he's crying.

'The eggs have gone.'

It's the girl's voice, almost unflinching. I glance again at Bruno, who is delicately placing himself onto the bench at my table. His sniff is undeniably loud.

'The eggs?' It takes me a couple of moments to register what Sadie has said.

Bruno looks up at me for the first time, eyes spilling over. 'Mum is going to be so upset.'

Sadie frowns. 'Yeah. The eggs, the rare ones. They've gone.'

For a moment, nobody speaks. I can't think what to say. I think of Fran, of my brother Charlie, and resist the urge to run over to his caravan, to tell him that I know what has happened.

'Well.'

'You've got to tell the police,' says Bruno, the tears not yet materialising. 'Please,' he adds.

'Bruno is too scared to tell his mum. My auntie. Can you do it?'

I don't say anything for a moment.

'Please,' says Bruno again.

I am struck, not for the first time, by his politeness. The police, though? I can't approach them. It was terrifying enough before, at the Common, when they were looking for my brother. Calling them when we had found the body in the hide had been a necessity.

'Sorry, Bruno, I can't. It's not really my business. And besides, the police will be too busy with other things.'

'More important things?' Sadie is staring straight into my eyes now. I find myself looking away. 'More important than rare eggs being stolen?'

I find myself snapping at her, shouting something about her being too young to speak to me in this way, that it's *disrespectful*. My voice was much louder than I think I had intended it to be. It scared little Bruno too. Still, I'm too tired, too old, to be dealing with these things, for visitors who turn up all the time, unannounced.

She doesn't take long to disappear. I see her scuttling towards her aunt's caravan park, hair flicking over her shoulders. Her body gets smaller and disappears into her shadow on the ground.

The boy's stare makes me uncomfortable, makes me step back from my standing position in the kitchen area. Forehead pressed to the nearest window by the door, I watch as the younger men play around on the green outside, one of them waving a cricket bat around, another chucking a ball up into the air. We love a bit of cricket, our family.

'Why did you shout at her?'

I think it is quite brave of little Bruno to ask, turn to face him. He deserves an answer.

'I don't know. I just lost it. Completely lost it. I'm sorry. Something about the calmness of your little friend. I don't know.'

His eyes are huge, they trail their gaze to the floor. 'Do you think she's the bird-killer? Is that why you don't like her?'

Again, I have to stop for a minute to think. The dead birds. 'No, no. I do like her! Like I said, her calmness just unsettles me.'

It seems to be enough to satisfy him. 'Sadie's always been like that. But she just wants people to like her. She has a bad time at home.'

I lean my face back against the windowpane, the coolness of it making the skin on my forehead slightly numb. I wonder if I can numb my whole being this way. Perhaps that's why people take drugs. To become numb all over. 'I don't know if I think she killed those birds.'

The boy is behind me, but I can't hear him move from his seat. 'I don't know either.'

It strikes me that he's no longer protecting his best friend. Perhaps he truly doesn't know whether she's capable of such a feat.

'You know, I saw her laying their little bodies out by her caravan the other day. Very carefully. Charlie saw her too.'

'So, she did kill them.' There doesn't seem to be any shock on his face, though the muscles are pulled taut around his mouth. *Surely he would know if his friend had done this?*

I walk over to the table where he is sitting, let myself fold next to him on the soft bench.

'So, who do you think took the eggs?' His voice is strong, confident, almost.

I am shaking my head so hard it's uncomfortable. 'I have no idea,' I tell him.

# FRAN

## 12 April

I think I must be starting to get bedsores, I've been lying in this bed for so long. Ros has been trying to call me; there are two missed calls on my phone, but two doesn't mean urgent. She's probably just calling to tell me she's got an inkling of where Ellis might be. Or that she's thought of a different reason for his disappearance. As for Dom, he's been keeping his distance so much that he's not even returned home since I saw the pair of them at the beach. I dread to think where he is now, and I don't let my mind wander.

It occurs to me when I hear the front door creak open that it must now be about 6 pm, and I never made it to the school to meet Bruno. I can hear his footsteps as he walks down the hall, forgetting to take his shoes off, heading straight to the fridge to devour some fruit juice that he can't be bothered to pour into a glass.

'Mum?'

I am tempted not to reply, to cast aside any responsibility, like his father seems to have done of late.

'Mum?!'

His little voice. There *is* still feeling in me. 'Bruno! Up here! Take your shoes off first!'

He runs up the staircase with no attempt to be quiet or delicate with his movements; I can feel the floor vibrating under the bed. 'Hi, love.'

I can tell immediately that something is wrong, that he's been crying.

'I didn't come home straightaway,' he splutters, out of breath. I

186

was hoping all the football was going to have made him more fit, but it doesn't seem that way just yet.

'I know, I realise. Sorry I didn't come to meet you. I was… I was caught up in something.'

He's not even listening. 'Mum, I don't want to tell you. I don't want to. But the eggs, the tern's eggs, all of them, they're gone.'

He's only just got here, but I don't want to hear any more. I eye the tablets by the side of my bed. I only took a few an hour ago, but how could a couple more do any harm? He is saying something, but the sound is beginning to blur in my ears. It's like when you're a kid falling asleep in the back of the car with the radio on in the front – the sound becoming further and further away as your mind begins to close.

'Mum?'

'Go and play football, my love. I'll get your dinner on in a moment.' I pull myself up in the bed so I can lean against the headboard. Clouds are shifting in my brain, as if the wind is pushing them along; my mind is slow to catch up with what my eyes are seeing. I remember that I drank a little vodka, neat, to help the pills down. I was hoping that Dom would return to see me in this state. Perhaps the sight would knock him back into the land of reality, and he would realise he has a decent wife here for him, someone who cares about him. For a moment, I am tempted to grab at my phone on the bedside table, to fire off an accusatory, toxic text to the pair of them, telling them how they have successfully broken up two families. Or maybe something cryptic, like simply the words *I know*.

'The eggs, mum!'

'The eggs, the eggs, the eggs!' I find myself replying without taking a breath. My mind is whirring; I picture the tern, the gulls, the wagtails, all of them, sitting on giant ostrich eggs, unable to keep their balance.

Tears burst out of my little boy's eyes, but he doesn't move.

'Hey, Bruno,' I say, suddenly thinking of the parents' evening at his school. I never did have the chance to ask him about his drawings. 'Why didn't you tell me about those bird sketches? At school?'

His blue eyes stare straight into me. 'Huh? Mum?'

'You know. You did the most beautiful drawings of some birds in your artbook at school.'

I see his already-glowing cheeks redden slightly more. His speckly skin looks like the mould that sometimes gathered on our bedsheets when I used to use the broken washing machine.

'You saw them? My drawings?'

I am nodding, and he doesn't say anything else. In the back of my mind, I am waiting for the front door to open again, for my husband to return with flowers or something similar, telling me that he is so sorry for how he has been acting, that it has all been so *unnecessary*. But all the time I am talking to my son, I don't hear the sound of the door opening. 'I particularly liked the bird's nest one.'

His mouth is hanging open slightly.

'Did you not want me to see that drawing?'

There's a reason I don't drink, and this is it. I become volatile. Even with my own child. Chuck down a few pills, and the situation is made ten times worse.

'I just… I was just embarrassed. I don't really do drawings at home.'

'Why would you be embarrassed?'

He has been standing at the end of my bed this whole time, and now he makes a move to sit on it, near my feet. At any minute now, the tears will come again. I watch his face. No tears appear.

'I don't know. It's just weird. I thought it might make me seem…' He hunts around in his head for the right word. 'Girly… or something.'

'You mean you didn't want Sadie to see them, your drawings? You thought that she might laugh at you?'

He is nodding, his head bowed, chin touching his chest. I can see a tear drop from the end of his little snub nose.

'Love, it's alright.' I want to reach out to touch him, but some part of my brain is stopping me. 'I just wondered why you had decided to draw the tern's nest in particular.'

'I just liked it, Mum. I liked how special it was.'

'Liked it enough to draw? So, you think you know who took the eggs?' I don't even pause. 'It was you, wasn't it, Bruno?'

I can't believe the words that are coming out of me but seem unable to stop my tongue. I know that a part of me is liking this, being a different person from the boring middle-aged woman that I usually am. Boring old Fran. Fran, who runs the caravan site, does everybody's laundry, hoovers the vans. Fran, who is taken for granted.

His face is crumpled now, and little sobs escape despite his closed mouth. 'No, no, Mum! You're scaring me!'

'Scaring you? You don't like the questions I'm asking?'

He is shaking his head *no*. Of course, I know he didn't take the eggs. For a moment, I thought I was experiencing more clarity in my mind, but now the second dose of pills is causing my vision to sway. I won't be standing up to go and prepare his dinner at this rate. He is wiping away his tears as the bedroom door is violently pushed open, and Dom is there, at the bottom of the bed. After all that waiting, I didn't even hear the front door.

'What is all this?'

I stare at him through my glazed eyes, point to our son.

'Bruno, what's wrong?'

My husband's eyes turn back to me, take me in. His eyes cast over the top of my bedside table, the drink, the bottles of tablets. 'What the hell, Fran?'

I can feel my eyes rolling. I try to pretend it's deliberate.

'Fran! For God's sake! What's wrong with you?'

I don't know where to begin, to be honest, and I'm not sure if I'm physically capable of starting on him. It's the first time he's addressed me in weeks.

I watch Dom sit down on the bed next to Bruno, put an arm around him. A flashback from earlier dances goadingly in front of my eyes: his arm around my sister as they walked along the shore.

'Lost your leather bracelet?' The words have burst out of nowhere.

He doesn't flinch, doesn't look away from our child. I can't see either of their faces properly anymore.

'I said, where's the bracelet that I bought you, Dom?'

He stands, pulling on Bruno's arm, encouraging him up from his seated position.

I am aware of the pair of them leaving the room, imagine my child telling his father that his mum was *freaking him out*. Nobody is answering anyone's questions today.

# TAD

I was awoken by a right screeching match this morning. At first, I assumed it was foxes, as I drifted in and out of sleep, but when I came to, I realised it was women's voices. The shrieking was coming from the other caravan park and did little to relieve the hangover I seemed to have woken with. I shared a few beers with my brother last night, smoked a couple of cigarettes too, seeing as he needed telling about what the kids told me. At first, I was worried about his reaction, thought he might lash out at me, but no. He was as concerned as the kids were when they came to me yesterday. I didn't even have to ask him if he was involved, I could tell by the sheer desperation on his face that he had nothing to do with the eggs' disappearance. He hung his head when I first told him. It was like someone had died again. I wonder if he will take off. I know he had started to spend a lot of his mornings over there by the marsh, but it was like a light had gone out when he heard the news. For a second, I thought he was going to crumple, to cry. I reassured him that the mother tern would be fine, and that at least she wasn't taken too. He didn't say much, just opened his second beer and began to down it, not really looking at anything. I assured him that perhaps it wasn't even a person who took them, perhaps it was another animal – a fox, most likely, or someone's bastard dog, let off the lead.

Anyway, back to the women ruining my last moments of sleep. I sat up and knew I was dazed for a while, recalling last night's news about the eggs and my brother's reaction to it, my brain trying to figure out what the women were shouting about at the same time. Before I even had a chance to look through my window,

I had worked out that it was coming from Fran's sister's trailer, or its doorsteps. I pulled myself up onto my elbows and managed to then hoist myself onto my knees, despite the pain that rang out. I wondered if the other members of my camp could hear the squabbling too, if it was disturbing them. Through the dirty pane, I could make out Fran herself standing on the bottom step, arms gesticulating everywhere. That's a good word, *gesticulating*; I learnt it from my dad. He used to use it about Mum when she was in one of her rages. *It's no good gesticulating like that, my love, your arms will drop off eventually.*

The sister was equally angry, I could almost see sparks coming off her. All I could hear from her, over and over, were the words, 'Do you really think I would do that?' Seemed like she was getting no real response, the way she kept saying it. Seems Sadie was right, about her mum being angry at her sister. Sure did come across that way. After what felt like forever, and something that sounded like a slap, Sadie herself emerged from the van, pushed her way out of the door, through the warring women. I felt a bit sorry for her again. I couldn't see her face from my distance away, but I wondered if she looked sad, rather than feeling the need to display her usual poker face. For a moment, I thought she was going to run towards our camp, but she just disappeared into the woods for a bit.

She must have seen and heard some things growing up to seem so cross at everyone half the time, and to go around putting birdshit in other kids' bags. Poor kid. I guess we need to be more sympathetic towards her. It's not her fault.

# FRAN

## 13 April

I saw them, I'm not doubting that part. I just can't believe either of them would have done this to me. How am I supposed to believe they *just bumped into each other near the beach*? *Both in an awful state*, apparently. I didn't tell her that I had my binoculars to hand, could practically see the stitching of her black Nike running outfit, the interior sheep's wool of the FatFace hoodie that I bought him three Christmases ago. She doesn't deny being out on the beach with him that morning. She can't, because she knows I was there, but she doesn't know I was watching the pair of them like a true twitcher, standing on my tiptoes, eyes desperate for a better view. Why didn't she come to me? I'm a bad person. I must be, and the thought makes me want to double over and sob. He has admitted walking along with her too, says he was on a *dawn stroll* when he *saw her crying on the shoreline*. Yes, my husband has been leaving the house early some mornings, occasionally, before I have risen. I had assumed he was trying to clear his mind, or perhaps that he was wanting to see something of the tern that I've been talking about.

I decide to go to see Ros again, straighten this whole thing out. A knock at the door of her caravan proves fruitless, and standing on my tiptoes at the window beside the door, I can't see any faces. I leap up the steps, try the handle, pull it down, and the door swings open with ease. My heart is ticking with anticipation. 'Ros?' No answer. I call her name again. There's no sound, no movement, not in the living area, anyway. Something in me tells me not to leave just yet, even though there is a ringing in my ears, my own blood pounding. I remember being a kid, Mum telling us to hold the large curled-up shell we had discovered on the beach of a Cornwall holiday to our ears. 'It's the sea you can hear,' she informed us. I believed her for a long time, we both did. I walk towards the smaller of the bedrooms, see Sadie's bed, half made. There's a distinct lack of toys, books, anything in her room, and I try to ignore the sensation that's biting in my throat. I step over to the other bedroom, Ros and Ellis's room, push the door open with the tips of my fingers. The bed has been made, at least. On the side, there are a couple of mugs, one still half full of coffee. A pen with a silver glitter inside it lies on top of a navy-blue book. I pick up the pen, heart still firing hard, look at the book. I know what it is. I know I shouldn't pick it up, but I am compelled. It opens naturally at an entry from March, a month back.

*

*So, I don't know what to do now. I'm kind of trapped here — no job, no money. I don't feel like I have a partner, not now. Everything's changed. I wanted to scream, tell everyone what's happened, leave, but where would that get us? Our daughter can barely function. No wonder she's going off the rails. Everyone feels sorry for her recently, I can see it. I do too. Nobody wants a parent who has done such a thing. Sadie is misbehaving at school, going off on her own all the time. I just want her to spend more time with her family, more time with Bruno, even. She's upset that she's not seeing him so much anymore; I don't know if Fran is deliberately keeping him away… Perhaps I'm being paranoid. I suppose I should be worried about her too; the birdwatching, the sheer obsession of it, and those bloody terns she talks about. I don't know if she's OK, but what I do know is that I don't care. Besides, I've got too much to think about right now. My little girl needs my support, and food in her belly. I can barely afford food, there's no money left.*

*

I hear noises outside, jump, put the diary back under the pen on the side, make my way out of the van. Cats, fighting. I shake my arm at them, kick out my left leg to scare them away, find myself creeping back home.

*

I am painting. It started with wanting to do a little pencil sketch of the church, has now progressed into an image of a raging fire taking over the building. It is quite satisfying to create. The little flames came first, flitting around under the main doors of the structure I have drawn, followed by the spitting black and orange plumes that have seemingly burst through the church's glass panes. It must be the anger coming through. All day, I have been wondering about Ellis. I know now what he's capable of. I don't know whether to tell Ros that I know. *Is it my job to alert the police?*

I think about Dom, whether to leave him, or if I should stay. I've done nothing wrong. I curse myself for not flicking forward in my sister's diary, looking for information about her liaison with Dom. Maybe I can go back soon and look again. My mind keeps returning to what she wrote about Ellis. I'm hoping she is just mistaken, got the wrong end of the stick, somehow. He can't be the one who did it, my brain decides. I momentarily try to ignore the things she's written about him as well as me. Nobody understands my love of the birds.

When I get to the school, the first time in a couple of weeks, Bruno is looking at another boy, they are doing a thumb war in the line as they idle out of the classroom. I note he does not look around for me, just turns with the boy and begins to head towards the path. I notice, also, the greenness of the new trees surrounding the area – shoots, fresh leaves that weren't there the last time. The birds are more voracious in their song, their calling high and warbly. I feel like a new guest, being here at the school. My son must have got used to his mother not coming to collect him. I see Sadie, alone, a few steps behind Bruno for once, feel a great pang of sympathy for her since reading what crime Ros thinks her father has committed. Sadie's reading some letter from her bag. I always wonder how her uniform can look so halfway decent when I know what a mess of a home she has come from. At least Ros tries, you can tell that. At least Ros doesn't neck vodka and a series of pills to block out her troubles, her responsibilities. My face still smarts from the slap she gave me early this morning. It seemed to come out of nowhere. I just remember the sting, the suddenness of the sound, and then Sadie forcing her way out between the pair of us. For a moment, here, I feel like approaching Sadie, leaving Bruno to make his own way home with the boy he's chatting to. It's been a while since I've had a conversation with my niece, and my heart breaks a little seeing her try to cope alone.

She sees me coming long before I've decided what I'm going to say, her eyebrow raised, her hands lowering the school letter back into her bag without her eyes needing to look. 'Oh, hi, Auntie Fran.'

I am still thinking of something to say, but it's not coming easily. Perhaps I should mention the eggs, that I know Bruno didn't take them. Perhaps he hasn't mentioned this to her. The eggs seem so trivial now, with everything that is going on. 'How are you, Sadie?'

She doesn't stop walking but does slow down a little. 'I'm fine, thanks. You?'

She's just a child. I'm ashamed of her witnessing my shouting at her mother in the early hours of the morning, on the doorstep of her home, so I don't say anything. I curse myself for thinking it, but there is *something* about her that I can't quite put my finger on. I can see she's about to speak again.

'I'm sorry my mum slapped you. Sorry about how she is with you.'

I hold my hand to my face, then let my arm drop. 'Well, that's what I wanted to speak to you about, Sadie. I'm sorry you had to see that. I'm sorry I came to your home and shouted at your mum like that. I shouldn't have done.'

We walk along for a while in silence, my eyes keeping on my dark-haired son, who is only a few feet in front. I see him say goodbye to the other boy, a childish wave, watch him continue walking along the path alone. I resist the urge to call out to him, to tell him that I'm sorry, that I will only be his normal mum from now on.

'They're not having an affair, anyway,' Sadie announces.

I take my eyes off Bruno, snake them across sideways to my niece. 'Huh?'

'Uncle Dom comes over sometimes. He's not interested in my mum, though. He's married to you!'

I find myself smiling at her, weakly, want to hug her. She's the messenger today, the bearer of good news. It's been a while since I felt any joy. All at once, I notice the clearness of the blue sky, the freshness of the air I am breathing, sharp in my lungs.

'Thank you, Sadie.'

She pushes back some imaginary hair from her face, adjusts the strap of her bag. 'You might want to run along after Bruno. I think he misses you.'

# TAD

Things are beginning to calm down around here. There are no more arguments between anyone, and no upset kids coming calling with news of missing things from a nest. I use my time carefully now that the sun is getting hotter, the days longer. I don't want to be outside in the heat for too long, not with my pale skin. The others are often out there in their deckchairs, feet up, flip flops on. It's my birthday in a couple of days, not that I like a fuss. Charlie is usually the only one to remember, and even then, that can be pushing it. I'm not going to say exactly how old I am, just that I am enjoying the slower pace of life these past couple of weeks. There's been very little news on Eve. The police, I suspect, will still be keen to get a hold of that Ellis man and interview him. There don't seem to be any other leads, not that I've heard of. Jade is still out and about most evenings; the new days stretching out ahead of us all make us want to spend more time outdoors. Her speech has come on a lot recently. She's gone from using singular words to putting together whole sentences, mostly brought on by a new flare of confidence, and spending time with her cousins and the other kids here. I try not to feel guilty, that she has not established this with me back along in her childhood. It's OK.

I wake up on my birthday to a knock at my door and balloons being foisted upon me as I lie in bed: silver, blue, all too shiny and bright. Charlie, both of my sisters and their kids stand at the door, cheering. It's all I can do to try to sit up. They hand me a phone, a brand-new-looking mobile phone. They try to show me how to use it. I've used the others' before, can just about assemble a text or two.

They're making me more modern. We spend the rest of the day outside in the sunshine, Charlie standing at the barbeque he's put together for the coming summer months, turning meats on a stick that glimmer in the sunlight. Some of the others sit on wooden chairs or the stripy deckchairs. There's always a radio on, a phone in their hands. I wonder how they survived without them. The trees surrounding this field have become thick and lush, there are hedges bordering the field like arms reaching out, protecting our land from the rest of the world. I know I sound like a sap. There are dozens of holidaymakers around now, from Fran's site, but you can only hear the vague tinkling of their voices, a child complaining, laughing, nothing disturbing. I like it, like seeing the families on the beaches around here, some still wearing their coats to protect them from the sea wind. I never expected everything to flourish like this. These days are the best I have known since moving over to this part of the land, even with the sea and the birds and everything that has given me joy over the past few months.

I must have been dozing in one of the deckchairs, as I found myself brutally awoken by one of the younger boys throwing cold water over me from a bucket. I was angry, but I tried to hide it, tried to laugh along. There's an itch of a memory creeping up my spine of the last time I lost my temper. It makes me feel shame, although I swallow down this feeling as quickly as I can. It wasn't very long ago at all.

# FRAN

## 17 April

I suppose our whole scenario would have been even stranger had Ellis come to live with us in the end. One man in each of the spare rooms, both there under clouds of disgrace. It amuses me to think of them politely offering the bathroom to the other in the morning, until weeks had passed, and they became sick of bumping into each other at the crack of dawn on the landing, their politeness dropping by the wayside. I don't see my husband in the kitchen in the mornings anymore, not even to be ignored. I'm wondering why he can't just talk to me, come clean. He's returned to work, must have called his office to tell them that he's fine. I don't really know how all of this will end. He swears there was nothing in it, as does Ros, yet it's only Sadie's take on things that sometimes makes me doubt the conclusion I have come to. I long for someone to confide in, to tell what I know about Ellis. There is no one. It's a secret I must keep to myself.

*

I leave the house in the afternoon for a stroll to the marshlands; perhaps I can come across something worth seeing that is almost as breathtaking as the tern's nest. I'm hoping I might see my niece on the way, wonder if I can surreptitiously leave a twenty in her pocket, help her out without Ros knowing. I don't see her, though – she must be back in her caravan.

I try not to think of the nest, brush the thought away into the back corners of my mind. Instead, as I make my way over the bedraggled reeds and coarse wetland, I think of the pictures I used to paint: the birds, the wildlife. I think of why I stopped drawing and accidentally bite down hard on my own tongue, a copper taste materialising, just as I find myself tripping over substantial tree branches in the sand. I realise within moments that they are not boughs of some fallen tree, but a man's legs, placed at slightly awkward angles.

'Afternoon!' It's that Charlie. Again. He hitches his legs up towards his body, contorts his face with faux pain. 'She's just foraging for fish!'

His accent seems stronger than I remember it. 'Sorry, I was miles away.'

I realise he is still down here at the beach even though the eggs and the nest are no longer present.

'You know the tern's eggs aren't around anymore?' I almost hear my voice cracking.

Of course he would know. The nest no longer rests in the flat part of the marsh where it used to lie. Its absence chills me. Charlie is nodding, and I notice he drops eye contact like a hot stone, just lets his gaze wander out onto the horizon, under the expanse of darkened clouds that hover above us. He's done that before with me, let his eyes disappear elsewhere. There is no sun today, unlike the other days just gone. It's easier to spot breeds when it's cloudy, less blinding from the light and fewer birds hiding in the shade of whatever they can find. Sometimes, on the brightest days, they disappear altogether, choosing to migrate to a different, more woody area of the beach.

'Yeah, my brother told me.'

'Your brother?'

'Yeah, Tad, you know. Your kids came to tell him that the eggs had been taken.'

My back is beginning to ache from standing, and I allow myself the luxury of squatting down on the sand. At least it's not as freezing to the touch as it is in the winter months. My mind is whirring, cogs turning very slowly as I absorb his words. 'I don't know that the kids would have told him. I don't think they knew 'til very recently.'

He is smiling, and I have no reason to believe it's not a genuine smile. He pulls out a cigarette from one of his pockets, a lighter from another. I watch him inhale as he lights the cigarette. I find myself craving one as the smell hits me. It's been years since I've had a smoke. Nineteen years. Ever since I met Dom. I decided to start the relationship with a clean slate, clean lungs. I hadn't looked back until today.

As he exhales again, I notice his delicate features, his high cheekbones. 'Don't be underestimating the power of those kids. They know more about the world than we ever can.'

I know I am pulling a face, and I try to stop, but I can't make much sense of his words. He sounds like some old rip-off fortune-teller. To avoid further confrontation, I stand to move away, but Charlie stomps over from where he was crouching, grabs my hand, startling me, and I let out a pathetic squeak. I can smell the smoke on him, taste it in between my teeth. My cravings don't leave.

'You don't need to be scared of us. Or my cigarette.' He laughs.

I manage to shake his hand off, despite its warmth, turn my shoulder towards him.

'Fran? You don't have to feel threatened by us, Fran. We're not here to scare away your business. Is that what you think we're doing?'

I don't answer, just begin to tap my hands against my side, the need to get away suddenly strong. I can feel my heart picking up speed, a shiver coming over the tops of my arms. Anything could happen here, and there would be nobody to help. 'I think I'm going to head back now.'

He is relentless, still smiling in that way of his, flicking ash from his cigarette onto the sand below us. It disintegrates, ash into sand, so much so that you can barely tell what it was. I notice he's almost handsome in this light.

He sees me looking at his cigarette. 'Want one?'

I find myself nodding, reaching for one from the packet he is holding out. I put it to my mouth, he leans forward to light it. I inhale the first mouthful of nicotine I have had in years, the feeling sending my legs a little shaky. At first, I think I am enjoying the feeling, but soon a firing of heat powers its way through me, and I realise I might be sick.

'Whoa, hold on, take it slowly.' He sounds genuinely concerned.

I realise I must make it back to my home, to lie down. I haven't felt this awful in a long time.

'I'm going home, I feel terrible. Thanks for the cigarette.' My words are whipped away at once by the wind, a low, blustering gale, delivered straight from the sea. It makes the sand sprinkle in circles dramatically between us. I wonder how much of it is ash. I'm not even sure he caught any of my words as I trip my way over the tangles of reeds, turning to see him start to follow.

I won't run, but he is on my tail. The smile has dropped from his lips – concern? He is not speeding up, which I am thankful for. A quick glance at my watch tells me that, once again, I have missed pick-up time for my son, that he will have made his way home by now. Staring over my right shoulder, I can again smell the smoke that emanates from Charlie's clothes, or perhaps my own body, as he continues to pursue me, catching me up with each several feet that he covers. 'Fran, take it slowly!'

I hear his boots behind me, getting closer. He must have dropped his own cigarette. Perhaps next to where I abandoned mine, in the rushes. Still, I won't speed up. I've got to keep to this pace, otherwise he will know I'm afraid. And you can't ever show that you're afraid. I keep my eyes to the ground, I can concentrate better this way. What I would give to see my sister or even my husband right now, standing in front of me, wearing a smile, coming to save me from my sickness. The smell of the smoke on his clothes is getting stronger, and it's beginning to cause friction at the back of my throat. I can hear him calling my name, over and over. *FRAN, FRAN, FRAAAAAN.* He's saying something else, but my ears aren't able to catch the words, the wind from the shore lashing at my face, obscuring the sound. It has started to rain, there is moisture prickling at my face, my eyelids. It will be refreshing, in this heat that is building up around, a much-needed shower. I don't know why he is following me, why the smell is getting stronger. I can't keep up the pretence of being unafraid any longer, let myself break into a run. I need to be sick. I can feel the contents of my stomach shaking around, a surge of adrenaline hitting my muscles. His footsteps are immediately behind me, heavier and louder on the little stones as he draws closer. It's all I can do not to cough, not to stop to splutter the filth from my lungs. As I eventually reach the path that leads to my driveway, I halt, letting myself breathe hard, my body wanting to double over. I look up to the cottage, different from normal, its new blackened form against the oppressive grey sky.

It wasn't the smell of his smoke-stained clothes that was making it so hard to breathe, nor the nausea from my own cigarette.

# TAD

One of the younger men raised the alarm first at our camp; my nephew, running, hurdling over the fence that separates our land from the rest of the world. It wasn't even me who heard him first, but one of my sisters, as she was hosing down a couple of the dogs who had been in the sea. She said he looked like a crazed man, or like someone haunted. He apparently was heard screaming, *Cottage is up in flames!* I'd just been having a wash by Charlie's tap, having fallen into one of my afternoon naps. Wasn't quite ready for the drama, the rushing around that followed. Women and men all raced there in the quickest time I've ever seen people cover land. I guess it pays to be fit. Both of my sisters went too, leaving the littlest of the children with me. I let them toddle around my caravan, watched them picking bits out of the bin that they should never have been allowed to touch. My eyes were on the view over the *Fran's Holiday Vans* sign, the black gulf of smoke that was reaching up into the clouds. I remember thinking it was difficult to tell where the clouds started and the smoke stopped, they were so immersed in each other, a blackened snake curling its way guiltily towards the sea. The smell was tickling my throat even from that distance, and I worried about the toddlers a little, closed my windows. I couldn't see any people from where I was standing, at the back of my home, but I could hear the voices being carried on the wind. I saw Fran's sister, standing on the steps of her own caravan, on her tiptoes, obviously concerned about what was going on in that direction. She must not have realised it was her sister's house caught up in the blaze.

# FRAN

## 17 April (continued)

I think I must have stood there in total shock for a good hour, but I doubt very much it was that long. Charlie, he was right behind me, of course he was; he was the first one to run into the flames. We didn't know if Bruno was in there. I just didn't have a clue. All I remember is the sweat – my clothes drenched, the grinding of my jaw. I remember my throat being red raw from what must have been the screaming, remember the soreness of the smoke already in my lungs by the time we had arrived at the cottage. Minutes later, I found Bruno, further along the path that leads towards the school. He was white, like paper, limbs floppy – like a dog under anaesthetic. I had to carry him to the car, not an easy task. His eyes were on the multiple fire engines, the police car, but he couldn't speak. I hadn't known the pain of the noise of a siren before, the blinding of the blue lights in the middle of the day. We left them to tackle it. Tad drove us to the hospital to get us checked over. He said he was nervous, hadn't driven for a long time. Not that we cared. He was talking about how he'd had to hand the kids he was watching back to their parents, how he felt guilty about it. I clung to my boy, both of us shaking, our chins jittering with the movement of my car over bumps in the road. No real smoke inhalation for me, I was fine. Tad waited for us in the car. We must have been in there a couple of hours, but he didn't seem to mind. Bruno was treated for mild burns on the palms of his hands; he had stupidly touched a couple of burnt timber joists as they lay on the ground by the front of the house, before he had run to the path.

Now I look at our home, and thankfully, most of it was salvaged. It's just the back bedroom that's been destroyed – my room. Mine and Dom's. They say that's where the fire started. They found the metal casing of one of my church-style candles. I can't think about it right now. Dom got home from work around the usual time: 6.30 pm, he said. At least he spoke to me on my return with Bruno. By then, the fire was out, the men gone; just the remains of the skeletal frame of our back bedroom to tell him that anything much was different. Well, if not for the charred waste in the front garden, the astringent sting of burnt wood and the jumble of plaster all around. We weren't back from the hospital at that point, he must have stumbled across the sight on his own.

Nobody in my world is innocent right now, save for my child. Dom and I make our way to the little shed that houses the keys to the caravans, help ourselves. We're lucky to have these vans at a time like this, otherwise we could be holed up together, in some B&B. I take the key to caravan number two, not yet occupied, and I think the most recently cleaned. I don't even look to see which key my husband has taken. He reaches forward to ruffle our son's hair, tries to get a smile out of him, fails. Bruno cannot take in what has happened. His eyes are everywhere and nowhere. I think of my sister, wonder if anyone has informed her of what has happened, but then I stop. She probably doesn't need informing. There's a stabbing pain in my chest when I think of how I hate being at odds with her. We were always with each other as kids, every moment of the day. When Mum passed.

As I help Bruno get ready for bed, I can see he is starting to come back to life, touching things in the caravan. He runs his hands over the table, traces his fingers over the salt and pepper shakers. I lean past him, pull the pleated curtains shut over the dining table area and the other window in the kitchenette, try to imagine that this is what it's like for my sister every night: barely any room to move or get out of each other's way. I realise neither of us has eaten, scroll through the contacts on my phone to find a half-decent takeaway that might deliver to us in the next hour. I have purposely chosen to spend tonight in a caravan that isn't close enough to Ros's van to be able to see each other, one that faces outwards and not towards any of the other vans. I saw the eyes of the other vans watching us as we trod our way to our own one, those judging rectangular eyes watching our every step.

'Are you OK, my lovely?' It must be the fourth time I'm asking him.

He nods, changing into a pair of shorts that I salvaged from our lost property cupboard in the shed that houses the keys. A bit small, a little dusty, but they'll do. Must have come from last year's guests. Then, a moment later, I experience a little surge of nausea, the thought of my child in filthy clothes, someone else's filthy clothes at that. If I was better prepared for such things, I would have had a spare outfit for him. In case of fire. I think of myself last; I'll just have to sleep in the same clothes tonight. I'll be calling the insurance company first thing in the morning, that's for sure. Bruno snuggles into the small double bed with me, occasionally pulling the netted curtains to one side for a glimpse of something, anything. 'Will Sadie know what's happened?' His words are coated with innocence, white and smooth, like the one star we can just about see in the sky outside the window. I forget sometimes he is such a young child.

'I expect so. Her mum will have told her.'

'But how will her mum know? It won't be on the news yet, will it?'

'It might not be on the news at all, my love. Just a house fire. Sadly, they happen all the time.'

His eyes seem bigger in the light from the caravan outside. I think he is going to ask how Ros will know, then, but he doesn't, just settles his head back onto the foreign pillow, his arm grasped around my middle. 'Dad will be OK in his own caravan, won't he?'

I am nodding. I try to close my eyes, noting that the cheap

curtains in the bedroom let in a host of light, the brightness searing through the glass panes. It's like a policeman shining a torch in my eyes.

# TAD

What pandemonium. I knew I shouldn't have tempted fate by commenting on the calmness of this place. I was terrified, driving those two to the hospital, didn't have a clue how to get there, let alone how to operate her *automatic* car. All the others were preoccupied with helping the fire crew as best they could, despite being told not to. Charlie risked his own life running into that house. I didn't even know if he would come out again, the time I left for the hospital. I didn't know if my little brother would make it out. You may not know what that feels like. Fran found Bruno on the path that leads to the school, wouldn't let me run in to find Charlie, to let him know the boy was safe. She's crazily strong, that woman. I couldn't break past her. She didn't notice my shakes in the car, I guess she was so shocked herself. They both sat on the back seat, all huddled together, don't even think they had seatbelts on. You don't think of stuff like that in the middle of a crisis. The boy, he was a ghost, white, coughing, coughing. I wonder if he saw his father there at any point, or his aunt. I know that's who his mother will be blaming. We don't even know for sure if it was arson. Could've been an accident. We have accidents all the time. One of the little kids got burnt touching a damned iron his dad had left out to 'cool down'.

As it turns out, Charlie came out of that cottage just fine. A lot of wheezing – hacking away, he was – but no trip to the hospital. He didn't want any fuss. Just wanted to go back to his van, to rest. I tried to invite him round for dinner that night, but he wouldn't hear of it. Said he'd been spending time at the beach with Fran before they found the fire together. He said he'd given her a cigarette, that she'd felt sick and that he'd followed her home to make sure she would be OK.

We try to continue as normal, make the most of the beautiful weather, but we are still so shaken. We don't talk about it, but there is something in the air that means we cannot relax, not yet. It's not enough for me to sit around in the shade of the trees that cover the one side of our field, watch the kids playing with their buckets of water and cricket bats. Jade is becoming restless anyhow. She didn't leave the camp for several days after the fire. I think we all sense it was perhaps deliberately started, despite my telling Jade and the rest of the kids it was an accident. They wanted to try out how easy it was to knock a candle over, some of the kids were begging their parents to light some candles in their trailers, then asking if they could do it out on the grass. Kids are funny, aren't they? I see Fran, head down, walking to her new home, the caravan at the edge of the park, sometimes with Bruno, sometimes not. She couldn't have picked a van further from her sister's if she tried. I guess that was the point. I have yet to see them wander near each other, let alone engage in any form of conversation. I haven't spoken to her husband since the day we found the body. I forget his name, it's my age. Begins with a 'D'. I used to be so good with names, certainly with faces. He sure was messed up that day. I've seen him around, it's hard to miss that red head, but he appears to be in his own caravan now, as far from Fran as possible. Strange, I notice that it's only a door or two down from her sister's van, though. There must have been no other vans free.

# FRAN

## 22 April

There's going to be a whole police investigation into the cause of the fire before the insurance company will consider paying out. Thankfully, it's nearly May now, and we have enough guests here to ensure a decent income, and the caravans aren't too chilly for Bruno and me. I still have a joint account with Dom, can still access 'his' earnings, anyway. He came to speak to me this morning. Seemed concerned about relations, wanted to talk about *us*. We sat down in my caravan, had a bit of a talk. He still vehemently denied doing anything with Ros. I'm *almost* beginning to believe him. I didn't tell him I've been crying myself to sleep every night, that I feel so abandoned by both him and my sister. He sat a little too close to me, but it wasn't unpleasant. It was almost welcome. I wondered if he was going to put his arm around me, like he used to when he knew I was down. He reiterated the point that he was only trying to calm my sister down, that he had caught her having a bit of a meltdown on the beach. The more he talked, the more I felt like believing him. But I shouldn't, I can't. I cannot trust anybody here. He seemed OK for a while, and we were almost like old times, but I mentioned something about Bruno seeming lonely and he just broke down. I haven't seen him cry like *that* before. I don't know what it really was that set him off. He was crying that he *just loves the boy so much*. I told him that we would continue to parent Bruno as we had done before, show him lots of love, but discipline too. The comings and goings of life recently in this village shouldn't be enough to get to him. Yes, he lost his teacher, but children bounce back. He's a great kid, and we are great parents. I told Dom this.

There was snot running from his nose, his eyes bulged up and so red. I nearly told him that he could move back into our home, once our room has been rebuilt, but I realised I needed to put myself first, be on guard. It was a nice, albeit very temporary feeling, knowing that one day there could perhaps be a chance for us, that perhaps I had blown the whole thing with Ros out of proportion. Minutes later, though, after he had gone, the doubts were creeping back. I decided to make it my duty not to listen to any more of my family's tales.

I visited the house after Dom came to see me, to grab some of my clothes that had been stored in a wardrobe in one of the spare rooms, the smaller one. I grabbed some of Bruno's clothes while I was there, too, noting the tidiness of his room compared to the black charred remains of my own. The police working in there barely looked my way. Half of the floor was missing, a blackened chasm melted down into the room below. I choked back the lump that was threatening to rise in my throat, I remember that.

I keep meaning to find Charlie. I should probably walk over to his camp, find him, thank him, but I just haven't got around to it. I do need to thank him; then I tell myself he didn't do a lot, just ran into the cottage to look for Bruno. As it turns out, he hadn't needed to. His heroics went to waste. I'm sure the others would have said thank you to him anyway. Tad would have. My heart is breaking now for my son, I just need to focus on getting him back.

I feel empty, hearing nothing from my sister. It's a feeling of belonging to nobody. There's only so much time that can pass before one of us goes to find the other; I hope, anyway. And I did try once. She just wasn't in. A couple of times, I've found myself walking towards her caravan, with the hope of bumping into her on the path, perhaps on a walk somewhere with Sadie. It hasn't happened yet. And I just can't bring myself to go and try her door again.

When a sudden knock on the door of our caravan vibrates all four walls, I expect it to be one of the policewomen who are working on the case. I wonder, in this village, if it is the same police team who have been working on finding out who killed the teacher. The case remains open, and nobody has managed to track down Ellis, if that's who they still think did it. I don't forget it, nobody around here does – that a woman was killed in a bird hide, just a couple of hundred feet from where we all live. It makes me want to hold my child all the closer to me. I open the door, and my facial expression must have got stuck, as my niece is staring at me with what looks like concern etched across her face. 'Fran, are you OK? Auntie Fran?'

I don't want to saddle her with my worries. 'Yes, Sadie, fine, thanks. You?'

She blinks at me, looks over my shoulder. She seems younger than her eleven years today.

'Bruno isn't coming out today.'

Her face drops, and immediately I feel awful.

I can hear Bruno walk over on the cheap lino flooring of the kitchenette behind me, feel him peer around my body. 'Hi, Sadie.'

'Please, Auntie Fran, please let Bruno come out with me, just for two minutes. There's something I need to tell him.'

I turn to look at my son, still pale, his eyes bluer against the pureness of his white skin. He looks ethereal, almost. 'Mum, can I?' I waft my hand, give a quick nod of the head. I don't really want to keep the pair apart. And now I don't need to, with Dom being gone. There's a slight warmth buzzing inside me as I let Bruno past me and towards his cousin.

I watch the pair of them disappear into the nearby copse, not concerned, as the trees aren't particularly dense; you can still see whoever is standing among them. I watch her now from a distance, her face sombre with whatever news she is passing to my son. He doesn't appear to be saying a word, not even nodding; he is more of a blur. From where I am standing, as the light catches her white hair, she is an angel, conversing with a human. Her yellow dress only adds to the image. Within ten minutes, they are back, Bruno's eyes sadder than before, his dark hair covering half his face. His mouth is hanging slightly open. Sadie doesn't really smile, pushes imaginary strands of hair back in that way of hers and gives me a quick look. 'Thanks, Auntie Fran,' she mutters.

Bruno goes straight to his room, if you can call it that, hovers near the bed. I follow him in without permission.

'I know who took the eggs,' he says, and throws himself down on the narrow single mattress.

# TAD

Charlie is being questioned by the police right now, just in his trailer. I know that my brother will be bricking it. There is a feeling in my stomach that I can only describe as sludge. Sludge wanting to erupt; I feel as though I might be sick at any moment, can't take my eyes off his trailer. Can't stop wondering why they have chosen to talk to him, and him only, not any of the rest of us. Perhaps that will come. My brain won't stop churning, my palms are wet, can't even manage to hold onto my knife and fork to eat breakfast. Not that I have any appetite. I don't even know what they are asking him about – the fire, those bloody eggs? Please, God, don't let it be about the murder of the teacher. None of us attended her council-paid-for funeral. I wonder if anyone in the village knew her well enough to attend. You would think the police might have interviewed him before she was laid to rest, but who knows. Until they've got their man, anyone could find themselves under scrutiny. At last, his caravan door opens, and two policewomen leave. I sit down with a jolt at my table, lest they should see me spying. Shortly after, Charlie himself shows, running a hand through his getting-too-long hair. It's another warm day. The warmest April I can remember. He walks to the outside tap, runs it a while until the women are exiting from the only gate in the field, walking towards their white-and-black car. Then he bends over, cups his hands so they're collecting the water, pours it all over himself. When he stands back up, his T-shirt is drenched. It's hard to know if it's the water or the sweat.

Couple of hours later, and I knock at his trailer. No answer. I walk around the other vans, looking for a hint of his presence, but most of the folk are out of their homes now, enjoying the unexpected warmth of this time of year, the strongest of the sunrays reaching out to us through the trees. I am calling his name, just a couple of times, nothing desperate, but two women, and one of the younger men, shake their heads *no*. Nobody's seen him. Knees already sore from my trudge around the camp, I pause, deciding whether to head for the beach or the woods. I am able to walk only short distances these days, but perhaps today I can walk slowly, savour the sunshine. I eventually find him on the stretch of beach where it's all marshy; I've never really travelled over that way before, apart from to the church. He sees me, doesn't stand, but smiles. It takes me a while to hobble over to him, and once again I am reminded of the age difference between us. Two sisters in the middle, each girl six years apart, then us at opposite ends of the order. It's always made me so protective of him, my brother.

'Thought you might come looking.'

I pause, unsure whether to try and let myself sit on the ground, knowing that, most probably, I won't be able to get up again.

'Wait,' he says. He fumbles around with that huge rucksack of his on the ground, yanks out a fishing chair. He pulls at the legs, makes it stand. I lower my body slowly into the seat, nodding my thanks at him.

'It wasn't what you think.'

I turn to look at him. He's caught the sun, that's for sure. His forehead is speckled red, the skin on his nose beginning to peel. It's not just from today's heat, I shouldn't wonder; it's an accumulation of being out in the open these past few days.

'Do you know,' he continues, 'I have been out here on these marshes for four weeks straight? Even when you thought I had vanished. Every morning.' He clears his throat a little, pulls at the neck of his shirt. 'There were two nests. I don't think anyone even realised that, that there were two. The first lot got taken by the tide, I saw it. Those eggs had been there two weeks, the mother watching over them. There was nothing I could do, I got there a moment too late. The second lot, they were just so close to hatching. They were *this close*.' He gestures with his fingers, to show a size of less than an inch. 'And now they've been taken, for cryin' out loud.'

I watch my brother for a while, only once before ever seeing this sensitivity in him, and never having known him to lament the loss of birds or such creatures. For a moment, I think he is going to cry, and there would be no shame in it if he did.

'I didn't know you were coming out here so often, no.'

He glances at me, in my wobbly fishing chair, looks like he's going to laugh, instead turns his face back to the shoreline. I wonder if he's spotted another type of bird to look at. Me, I'd like to learn even more about the birds they have here, the seabirds in particular.

'She was coming and going around here, then she seemed to stop for a little while. She missed the terns being taken by the tide. Probably didn't know that when she returned it was a brand-new nest altogether, different mother.'

I take it he means Fran. He had mentioned seeing her a couple of times.

'She made out she was really interested in the terns.' He takes a cigarette from his pocket, fumbles around for a lighter, sparks up. 'It was a bit of a shitty job for me, running into that burning building for Bruno!' He gives a little laugh.

My mind jumps back to the police visit of this morning. 'What did they want to know, the coppers? You know you can tell me.'

He is fiddling with a reed that he's holding onto with his left hand, attempting to pull it from the ground. I know he doesn't want to talk.

'Charlie?'

Now he's looking the other way, I can see his throat moving, gulping, his lower lip jutting out like a child's. He gives up on the cigarette, throws it under his right boot, grinds down on it in the sand. From my chair, I am sitting above him. Feels like I'm judging the man.

'Charlie, was it about the fire?'

He stands up, doesn't face me, wipes the sand off the back of his shorts with his hands. I get another whiff of his newly-put-out cigarette. For a moment, I think he is just going to not respond.

'They said they were just waiting on some fingerprints that had been taking ages. They asked me if I killed her, Tad. That's what they bloody asked me. And I'm not talking about that woman from back on the Common.'

# FRAN

## 27 April

So now Bruno has decided he would like to spend most of his time in his father's caravan. To me, it's the very last straw. I feel like a broken doll. My nights are completely empty, and it's only been two so far. He packed up the few belongings and clothes I salvaged from the cottage these past few days, shoved them all into his canvas bag, asked for a *big towel*. I got him to pack his new little phone too. He can stay in contact with me that way. His dad will be taking him away tomorrow for the weekend, somewhere with a swimming pool. We had thought about getting one put in for our holidaymakers, but after seeing the cost, decided against it.

I'm making my way over to Dom's caravan, need to talk to him about the police, as well as find out where exactly he is taking our son away to. I toy with telling him about Ros's diary entry, decide against it. I just need to see Bruno. It's the first time I think I've ever spent away from him. I don't think I can do it for more than a few nights. I miss his voice, his innocent questions.

I walk past Ros's van, try not to peer into her windows, keep my face turned the other way as I go by, but the action makes a lump form in my throat. For a moment, I feel as though Sadie is going to come bounding out, notice a stab of joy that I might get to see her, speak to her. She doesn't materialise. When Dom answers, he looks dishevelled – ginger stubble, bleary eyes. He could have been crying again. Bruno is there too, I see his eyes peer through one of the windows. I swallow down the urge to run to my child, to grab at him, take him in my arms. 'What is it, Fran?'

I take a step back, down one of the concrete steps. Thank God there's a handrail; these days, I seem to be less aware of how to balance myself. 'I've just come to say goodbye to Bruno. And to check where you will be taking him away to.'

He rubs his eyes with his thumb and forefinger. I haven't seen him without his glasses for so long, he looks so much older, the skin wrinkling around his narrowed eyes.

I sense my husband look over towards Ros's van, crush down the urge to ask if she will be joining them on their trip too.

'Bruno, your mum is here to see you!'

His red eyebrows close up together, and again I am fighting against emotions, the feeling that I am losing my child as well as my husband. I can see movement behind him, Bruno, gathering things together. I wonder if Dom will ask if we can get back together.

'Hey, Bruno!' I call. He doesn't come to the door. I try to think of something to say to Dom. 'Have the police been in touch with you?'

'The police, yes. They don't need to speak to me again. I was at work all day, that day of the fire.'

I feel my shoulders sink a little. Nobody official has updated me on who the police have and have not ruled out.

'Right.'

I can see my husband is trying to close the door on me a little, he is turning, muttering something to Bruno, who is still moving around behind him, collecting things. It's almost like he doesn't want to share him with me.

'Bruno, come say goodbye to me!'

My son doesn't show his face.

'Try later?' suggests my husband.

There's nothing else for me to do but wander back to my own caravan, tail between my legs. I let the tears fall as I walk.

\*

As I turn towards my caravan, trying to wipe away most of the evidence of my crying, my attention is caught by someone leaving from the direction of what would be Tad's van, in the other field. It's a tallish girl, large build, walking with a slightly uneven gait, mousey hair. I haven't seen her before. I step towards the fence that separates their field from ours, trying to get a look at whatever she's carrying in her hands. She doesn't seem to notice me, I brush the hair from the sides of my face, can just about pick up the sound of humming emanating from where the girl is wandering. My hand filtering the sun from my eyes, I see she is holding what look like little bird bodies, is kissing them one by one, laying them down on the ground. I don't have the capacity or the energy to think about it, so enter my own caravan, burst into more tears at the emptiness of the space.

# TAD

I've been with her since the moment she was born, that girl of mine. You could say I know her better than any parent knows his child, the number of hours we've spent in each other's company. She barely even went to school when she was little. I mean, I know we moved around a lot, but Jade, she doesn't deal with new faces so well. The kids at the schools didn't seem to get her silent ways, the teachers less so. Then there was the bullying. So, we let her stay home. A lot. The authorities would knock at our door, of course they would, but they couldn't prosecute us or anything. We would just move on again. I've been so happy that she's been carving out her own way of late, finding her independence at last. Her mum would have been so proud, so it's killing me, what I've heard.

They were lined up in a row, just along a stretch of trees, the birds were. I remember Sadie was the one doing this just the other week, balancing their heads back on their little bodies. Ping pong balls, they were. Ping pong balls with little eyes that didn't close. I found six of them just this morning. Disgusting things, half rotted. I decided enough was enough. I didn't know if Sadie herself was responsible for killing them, but I found myself hobbling over to her trailer just the same. Her mother answered the door, I forget her name now. She always looks like she's in a right state. Hair everywhere, black stuff around her eyes. Well, of course she's in a state. As I get older, I find it harder and harder to put myself in other people's shoes. Well, it's not that I struggle with that. I just forget stuff, what they're going through. I ask to see Sadie, she says *sure*, doesn't seem at all concerned about an old man asking for her child. Maybe she knows who I am, *the friendly old man from the Romany site*, or something like that. The kid appears at the door, it must be around 8 am, and she's fully dressed. Dirty white jeans and a pink top, her blue eyes staring at me. 'Yes?'

'Hi, Sadie.' I suddenly feel a little fearful, her mother still on the step, listening. 'OK if we go for a little stroll, so we can talk?' The question was aimed more at her mother, but the woman wanders off into the dimness of her caravan, after shoving the door closed as the girl and I stand out together on the top step.

'Fine,' says Sadie. Her expression doesn't change as we step down from the van, me leading the way. 'What did you want to talk about?'

I begin to stroll ahead, not saying anything, hoping she will keep up with me. She takes longer strides, stays by my side.

'Just, well, you know there have been some strange things happening around here of late, don't you?'

'Well, yes.'

I concentrate on the view ahead of me, the beauty of the white clouds, the sharp blue sky, birdless.

'Want to go to the hide?' Her boldness bubbles up, the boldness I haven't seen for a while.

'What about the beach?' I glance back at her caravan, wondering if I should go to check with her mum, but Sadie waves her hand noncommittally. 'Don't worry about her. She won't mind.'

We stroll together down the path that leads to the shore, that twists its way alongside the woodland. It strikes me as odd that one of the few times I have walked this path with another person was the time I found myself walking with Fran's husband. *Dom*. The name suddenly comes to me.

'So, what would you like to talk about?'

We find the only bench on the shore. The girl isn't looking at me as she settles herself on it, is wiping away some leaves from the surface of the seat. 'Because if it's the fire, I don't know anything about that. Did you want to talk about how my teacher might have died?'

'Huh?' My brain is struggling to keep up with her words, trying to shut out the image of the dead woman on the floor, the blood underneath her.

Her feet don't quite reach the ground, she is swinging her legs in a way that makes her seem all of her eleven years. Reminds me of the other day, Fran swinging her legs on the bench in the hide. 'Bruno and me, we know nothing about the fire. But we do know other stuff.'

'Like what?' I suddenly find myself doubting that this child, as endearing as she is, would know anything.

She tilts her head to one side, purses her lips for a moment. 'The bird deaths.'

We both focus on a dog of some kind, a terrier perhaps, bouncing in the surf, something caught up in its mouth. A woman, presumably the owner, calls its name from a distance away. The view here is better than just sitting in that hide. I don't like the feeling of the place, how dark and hidden away it is.

'So? Who do you think was responsible?'

A pause, then she speaks: 'It was me.' And now she won't look directly at me. I find myself pulling my body further away on the bench, trying not to picture what she did to kill them. A wind pulls at us, sucks us sideways, pushes me towards her. She continues to stare out at the waves, eyes not moving. 'And Jade.'

I stand up, the wind strong, don't know what to do with myself, sit down again. 'Jade?'

Sadie is nodding. 'She took a liking to me, you know. We became friends. It was her. I don't even think she meant to. It looked more accidental to me. I was the one who got upset, swore I would put them back together. But that was the second lot of birds she killed. She only killed *this third* bunch a couple of days ago.'

She knows I am looking at her. I don't care that I'm swallowing down an obvious lump that's appeared in my throat. 'Accidental?'

'Yeah. She would pick them up early in the morning, when they were looking for food. She wanted to cuddle them. We both did. She just cuddled them too tight. Her hands were massive around their necks.' I can see the girl is fighting back tears.

I don't know if it's relief that is chewing at my bones, or compassion for my daughter, or just sadness.

'So, you were involved? But you didn't kill them?'

'I told you, I was the one trying to put them back together. I should have started sooner.'

I put an arm around her; she rests her head on my shoulder, crying silently. Any doubts I had about the girl are immediately washed away. She was the reason Jade had been leaving the caravan so frequently. So confidently.

'You're her friend? Jade's?'

'I already said that.'

'Well, then, all I can really say to you is, thank you. It doesn't matter about the birds. Thank you.'

The girl looks up, smiles, continues to stare out to sea.

# FRAN

## 29 April

I can barely rise this morning. When this weekend finishes, Bruno will return, not that he seems to be keen to. I have received one solitary text from him since Friday. But I need to be positive. Life can begin again. I will have tried to work things out with Ros, too. I'm just waiting, waiting for the bitterness of the pain to disappear.

Most of the caravans are full now, save for one or two. I'm getting the money sent to my private bank account from now on, not the shared one I have with Dom. I really do need to start carving the way for just Bruno and me now. I can't imagine getting back together with Dom, I just can't bring myself to believe him about his not having an affair with my sister.

Sadie's been at the door of the caravan I'm staying in. I told her Bruno isn't around this weekend, saw her eyes staring beyond me, a little red-rimmed. The second time she came, she wasn't searching for him in earnest, just asked if she could come in, said she was sad. I let the door swing wide open, gestured for her to come inside. It felt weird, me letting her into a tiny caravan when usually it had been the other way around. I pretended I wasn't watching her, made my way to the back of the caravan where I'd piled a lot of our washing, began to fold it.

'Do you get lonely?' I heard her voice from where she was seated by the table.

'I do now.'

There wasn't a response for a while, so I remember stepping back from the chair I was standing at, crooking my neck around to

227

get a view of her. Her head was slumped in her hands, eyes out of the window.

'Sadie, are *you* lonely?'

Again, she didn't speak, but her head dropped even lower in her hands.

'Sadie?' I remember walking over to her, some sheets doubled up over my arm.

'Everyone thinks I'm bad. They do, don't they?'

I stopped, don't think I was breathing for a second or two. I wasn't sure how to react to that one. 'No, of course they don't. Where did you get that idea?'

I remember she turned to look at me. 'They think I'm bad at school.'

'Maybe you only did that thing to that girl's bag because you were feeling sad. Or scared.'

She just kept her head dropped low in her hands. I still don't know if Ros has accepted that her daughter did commit the bird-shit crime. Perhaps she is still in denial.

Sadie's here again this afternoon. I guess she doesn't have any real friends to spend her weekend with, now Bruno is away. I gave up on keeping the two of them apart, anyway. It hurt to do it. I push away the thought that I left my only two friends back in Surrey, have heard little from them since we moved this way. Sadie has begun to chat more to me, and not for the first time, I feel a slight ache in my stomach. She's not addressing me as *Auntie* anything, she's only calling me *Fran* right now. I wonder if she knows I'm still not on talking terms with her mother and decide against asking how my sister is. After a while, her conversation turns to Ros, anyway. 'Mum is always so sad. Barely remembers to buy us food anymore. If you weren't doing our washing, we would always be in dirty clothes.'

My heart sinks a little at this, guilt beginning to gnaw its way through my limbs, a rodent nibbling. I haven't done any washing for my sister in well over a week now. 'Sadie, would you like to go to your van and collect up all the sheets and clothes that need laundering?'

'A bit later, if that's OK. I like chatting right now.'

I nod. *I like chatting right now.* 'Would it help if I did a food shop for you and your mum?'

*Perhaps it's a way for me to contact Ros, an offering.*

There's a slight pause, and then she is nodding enthusiastically. I remember all at once she is only eleven.

'Are you hungry right now?'

'I'm always hungry.'

I feel another stab of shame at failing to remember that my niece was perhaps not being cared for in the way she should have been.

'Let's get in the car now. We can go shopping together. You can choose whatever you like.'

Her expression is one of elation. You would think I had offered her a trip to Disney. *Perhaps she's too old for that.* New York, then. She stands up with a jump, and I abandon the washing I was sorting on the bench where she'd been sitting, grab my purse and keys. We make our way out of Fran's Holiday Vans together.

\*

At the supermarket, her eyes are on stalks. She reaches out to touch bottles, packets, forgets to steer the trolley she was so keen to push.

'You'll have someone's foot off in a minute.'

She laughs at my comment, and I try hard not to keep eyeing her, this child, my niece. Today she is dressed in jeans, pale blue but dirtied, plus flip flops and a blue T-shirt that have seen better days. I've only ever thought of her in dresses, white and yellow, floaty.

'Can we have doughnuts? The salted caramel ones with yellow custard inside?'

'Are they your favourite?'

She shakes her head, both hands returning to the trolley. 'I've never had an iced doughnut. Just seen them on TV.'

I let her grab the packet, six of them inside, and I see her stare at them as we continue to push the trolley around the shop. After another twenty minutes or so of my niece loading up with the most multicoloured food you can imagine, she looks at me, just as we are standing in the queue.

'Thanks,' she says.

There's heat threatening to flood my face, my cheeks. I don't want her to be so grateful. 'You don't need to say that, Sadie. We only went shopping.'

'Dad used to do most of the shopping. If I don't go to school, I don't get lunch.'

We reach the front of the queue, and I hand my card to the checkout boy, turning my face to the car park outside, wiping away the sudden trace of hot moisture on my cheek.

'It's OK, Fran. Don't be upset. My mum tries. And I've always got you.'

I smile thinly, feel almost worse that she thinks she only has me to depend on.

# TAD

That Ellis guy is back. I heard commotion in the middle of the night – well, I say *middle of the night*, but it was around 11.30 pm or so. I tend to go to bed early, so does Jade, when she's not on one of her wanders. I haven't spoken to her yet, about what Sadie told me. Instead, I just feel a certain warmth that she has a friend, a person to look out for her. And I'm not so sad about the dead birds anymore.

I heard people shouting; I opened the window in my bedroom, stuck my head out as far as I could without trying to be spotted. Fran's sister was on the steps of her caravan, yelling. There is a light on the front porch of the van. It illuminates anyone who stands directly under it, like a spotlight on a stage. They could have been in a little midnight play. I could see the form of a man in front of her. One moment she was hugging him as if she would never see him again, the next she was shouting and crying uncontrollably. Sadie was there. It became hard to see what was going on, it was so dark, and the porch light began to flicker on the figures. Within minutes, a police car arrived, no siren, and after a brief stand-off, they took the guy away. He didn't even fight, but the woman did. I remember scrunching my eyes up, trying to absorb some detail about what was happening. Could see her hands pummelling against the copper's chest without any real conviction, just like something she thought she should do. The other copper just stared at the ground, said something to Sadie. I watched her disappear back into the trailer. The car crept away into the darkness, making no sound, and I watched the woman, slim as a reed, becoming less and less distinct on the top step as the car's headlights drained away around the corner.

# FRAN

## 30 April

It's on the local TV news today. They've got Ellis. I haven't heard from my sister to confirm, to hear when Ellis did return, or when they arrested him. I'm dying to run to her van, to ask her, to comfort her. I'm just trying to pluck up the courage. I think I'm still using the excuse of waiting for her to contact me first. I can't ask Dom for confirmation as he's away with Bruno still, even though it's now Monday, a school day. I haven't heard from either of them, apart from a short text from Dom saying simply: *Back tonight. Got a flat tyre.* My days are fractured without my child, shards of glass puncturing pain repeatedly into my organs. Most of the time now, everything just feels so pointless.

Maybe the police will realise, after questioning Ellis, that he's not the guilty party. Perhaps they will begin to look for someone else. Maybe some more evidence will crop up. I'm guessing they found no fingerprints on the woman's body, her clothes. Or perhaps they did. Perhaps that's what they are holding Ellis for. I then remember the comments in my sister's diary about her partner, and my stomach drops. My heart goes out to little Sadie. I think of offering to let her sleep in my van from now on, but perhaps my sister needs the support of having her daughter with her.

The police are finally finished with our house, the verdict being that they can't be certain if it was arson or not. There were the metal remains of my candle-holder involved, yes, with my fingerprints, but I can't give them a clear answer as to whether I left the candle lit or not. I just cannot remember. I do like to have a candle or two burning when I get ready in the mornings, especially if I take a bath, but I just can't commit to saying it was me who lit one, left it burning. They are letting the investigation go on hold for a while. I told them about my suspicions, that my husband could be to blame. They wrote it all down, he was interviewed. Like Dom said, he's now free from any suspicion.

*

I'm a real mother again, sitting here in this caravan, cradling the eggs. The nest is wedged in the corner of the shed, between a couple of filing cabinets that nobody ever notices. I've just recently put up a lamp, directly over where the eggs have been lying. The lamp will keep them warm, keep them safe until it's time for them to hatch. Then I will care for the little fledglings. They need a mother like me. I have stopped anyone else taking them for themselves.

Sadie knows it was me. That was what she told Bruno that day in the copse. She would have found her way into the shed, where I keep the keys to all the caravans. She would have seen the nest. I must have forgotten to lock the shed at one point.

# TAD

We've taken longer than usual to decide to move on. We sometimes go at the start of the long spring, a time before the trees are glorious with green. I guess we were just too settled; well, I was. I can't always speak for the others. There was more than enough work for everyone here – the phone shops, the computer work. One of them worked in a surf shop, not that I've ever seen anyone surfing around this shoreline. Seems it's drying up now; they've worked in most of the stores around here, and it will be time for us to go again. Charlie's keen to leave, and once they have all decided it's time, they don't sit around. The police are happy to let him go, seems the interview with them came to nothing, though they are still waiting for matches to the fingerprints they found on the body. I suggest to the others that they start cleaning up their homes a little. Nobody is keen. They seem to be spending whatever time they have down at the beach, with the kids. I can hear them whooping with joy, jumping the waves, competing over who can go the furthest into the sea.

Just as I am shoving some more crap into our bins, considering whether to go and say goodbye to Fran, I am aware of a presence, the sound of cars, their engines cutting out next to where I stand. There are no sirens. They ask who I am. Another copper asks for Charlie, and I pause, momentarily seeing the future flash before me like a black flag. I could lie. Say I'm someone else. Say Charlie's gone away. Eventually, I point my finger in the direction of his trailer, where I can see him clearing stuff out of the front door. He doesn't see us. He's a dog, betrayed by a bullet to the back of the head. The first copper grabs my arms, forces them behind my back, wrenches and twists my wrists into a mulch of metal. The kids who were running around stop, stand on their tiptoes, look at their parents for reassurance. I ask the police why they want us, but they won't give an answer. I see two police people, a man and a woman, stride over to Charlie, ask him to confirm his name. They tell him they are arresting him for the murder of his wife, Eve McConnell.

They tell me I am arrested too, for partaking in a murder. They had our fingerprints, you see, not only on her body, but in bloodstains found under the back shelf of the cupboard in the classroom. And I thought we had cleaned up all the blood with the towels we took along with us. The ones we burnt to smithereens afterwards.

# FRAN

## 4 May

I am running with a speed I don't think I have mastered before. It must look like desperation. The weight around my stomach and breasts is swinging as I take off my shoes and run barefoot, flip flops dangling from my right hand. I can hear the police talking, taste the petrol of their cars on my tongue. I can see they are leading Tad and Charlie away from their caravans. They're handcuffed.

I see one of the other men, younger, catch his eye, ask, 'What's happening?'

He remains tight-lipped, shakes his head. They are all gathered in a group by the pair of police cars. I try some of the women. They don't answer me either, just pretend they haven't heard. Little children pick their way across their parents' shoes, a makeshift bridge.

The younger man grabs me by the arm, almost hisses, urging me to be silent. 'They've arrested them for the murder of Charlie's wife. Eve. They're saying it's murder.'

I can feel my eyes widening, tearing up, my hand flies to my mouth. 'Eve? What? His *wife*?'

We watch the policemen march Tad and Charlie to the passenger seats of the car, push Charlie's head down like they do in films and TV series, to fit him into the vehicle. He is looking up at family, tears prickling in his eyes. His face is red, blotchy, but he doesn't try to fight. 'You know me,' is all he shouts. Tad, tall, almost weedy, is forced down into the car at the same time.

As the policewoman gets in, the last door slams and the car trails away. The family begin to make their way back to their own vans, most of them in tears. I can hear the little children asking again and again *what is happening*, pulling at the hands of their parents, their siblings. The whining drowns out any other conversations within earshot.

I am standing alone, alongside the only man left – the man whom I had gone to speak to that very first night, the man with the wife with the baby on her hip.

'She was Charlie's wife. Not much different from the rest of us, a nice girl. Educated. Charlie loved the bones of her. The police have his fingerprints on her body, apparently. In the bloodstains in the classroom cupboard, too. And some of Tad's.' He pauses, adds, 'They've only just recovered them. We can't believe it.'

'But they did it, then?' I have a million questions on the tip of my tongue, waiting to fire like bullets.

He shakes his head. 'We were all desperately worried when she disappeared. And then it was just inconceivable when Tad told me what they had done. He only said last week. In case the police came, he wanted us all to be aware. He had to see her body all over again, that time he was walking with your husband.'

I stare, not sure what to say now. My limbs are shaking as if with cold. The realisation that perhaps Ellis was innocent was beginning to prick its way through my skin as I made my way over here just minutes ago. Now it's teasing my senses with flutters of relief. Ros, she needs to know. For some reason, I had needed to see Charlie and Tad being taken away. 'I didn't know she was married to a Traveller. Eve,' I manage.

'*She* was a Traveller, too. Romany. Same as us.'

I realise I am cold as well as shaking with fear, and that we are just standing there on the field, in the void the police cars left behind. I think back to my memories of the teacher, her pink-and-green stripy tights, the pink pineapple hair, the black platform shoes. I don't know how I had expected a Romany woman to look, but she hadn't been my expectation. None of these people had been.

'Why would they kill her?'

The man, whose name I still don't know, gestures for me to walk back towards the caravans, leads me towards his own. 'They didn't.'

I know I am frowning, can't be bothered to stop it. He sighs, loudly, stares at me. 'They helped shift her body, after Charlie was called to the school by the person who did it. They waited until dark, in that tiny room, with the body. Tad and Charlie had to shift her, to the hide, from the back of the classroom. It's a long bloody distance. Luckily, it was pitch black by then. They just moved her body. They didn't kill her. That's why there are their fingerprints on her. All their clothes would have been burnt, to hide the evidence, I guess. Us lot are often having fires.' He gives a sad little laugh, that turns into a cough.

We arrive at his van, door hanging open. He steps up, ushers me in. We sit on the bench of his dining table. I wrap my arms around myself.

'Ok…' I say, awaiting more information. 'So, it wasn't Ellis? Or was it? Did they all work together?' I am wondering what I can tell my son.

He shakes his head. I watch him twisting the cords of the blinds, backwards, forwards, between his thumb and forefinger. He's quite young, perhaps mid-twenties. 'It wasn't that bloke Ellis. He wasn't involved at all. Charlie and Tad have taken the blame here. They're going to be put inside to protect the future of a child.'

'Huh?' He's lost me now. Completely.

'Eve… She was killed by a child.'

'A *Romany* child?'

Already he is shaking his head in a slow, sad way. Doesn't seem offended that I've accused one of his family, although I am immediately embarrassed that I have.

The man reaches towards a bureau, littered with pens, standing at the edge of the kitchen area. I wonder if he writes letters to people. Pen friends. Your mind suggests strange things when it's in shock. He opens a little drawer at the side, pulls out a folded piece of paper, hands it to me.

'Destroy this once you've read it.'

I prise the paper apart – it's a little stuck together at one of the edges, makes it tear slightly. All it shows is a couple of lines in squiggles. I can see it's been signed in large, scrawly handwriting, by Tad.

I look up at the man. He seems so similar to Charlie, in a way. I don't ask how they're related. Cousins, perhaps.

'Have you read it?'

I shake my head *no*, not wanting to look back at the piece of paper in my hand.

'You need to.'

I stare past the man, out of the window of his van. You can see a lot from where I am sitting. You can see the trees that border the edge of the field. They're so green right now.

He gently takes the piece of paper from my hand, clears his throat.

My stomach is leaping. I don't want him to read the words.

*'Fran. We had to do it, to take the blame. It was Bruno, you know. We couldn't let the boy go down. Tad.'*

Already I am standing, making my way down the steps of the man's van, running towards my own. I stop to throw up in a hedge, wipe my mouth, continue walking home.

# TAD

Two of the hardest things I've ever had to do, rolled into one afternoon. You never know when the moment will come that you have to send your own brother down, for something he was barely involved in. Something he did to help a kid in distress. He loved his wife, he did. But he couldn't bear to see the shock on that little boy's face once he realised what he'd done to Eve, when he realised he'd probably spend the rest of his life in an institution. But that's my brother for you, selfless to the core. And I think he believed that he deserved life in prison, for that woman he accidentally killed back on the Common. The one that was in self-defence. She went for him in the middle of the night. It was a one-night stand, after all, a spurned woman. And she didn't know he had a wife. What chance did he have? I just came along for the ride, to help not only Bruno, but Charlie too. He couldn't go down alone. Besides, hers was a heavy body to drag all that way. I don't know why we chose the hide, of all places. I think we were in shock. All that mattered at the time was that Bruno was back home safe, in his bed.

When that Dom guy saw the teacher's body, he knew. Bruno had been telling his dad all along about how much he hated his teacher, how she treated Sadie. He'd been telling me too, afterwards. Along with other stuff. He'd told his dad he was feeling so angry lately, that he was worried he was going to end up hurting someone. Dom can't have imagined this. Ten years old. Well, you know what they say about the quiet ones.

Charlie had promised from day one that he'd go down, spend

the rest of his days in prison, to save little Bruno. They had become quite close, you know. I couldn't let him do that alone.

The other thing: letting a mother know that her brilliant, beautiful only child is a killer. In a letter. A note. Telling her that he had been saved by my brother Charlie. That I barely came into it.

Didn't even bother letting her know that the police think she started her own fire herself. *Accident*, of course. They think maybe she is starting to lose the plot.

# FRAN

## 5 May

I just don't know what the hell to believe. All I know is I've got to look after these eggs, my babies. Sadie said, 'Auntie Fran, they're not gonna survive now!' That they won't hatch without their mum, but I'm sure they will. Bruno – well, he's come back from Felixstowe now, I saw him and his dad return. I don't know how to look at him. I find myself wondering if they were lying, Tad and Charlie. It could have been Charlie the whole time, the one who killed her, alone. Maybe it wasn't my son at all, or Tad, although Dom called me and told me Bruno has admitted everything. Says he hit the teacher over the head with a brick, late after school, when everyone else had left. Said it was easy. Then he just called Charlie on that bloody mobile phone I got him, asked him to come and help with what he'd done. Said he had wanted to 'make Ms McConnell better right away', for Christ's sake. According to Dom, he also admitted to smashing the window of Ros and Ellis's caravan back at the beginning of all of this. Dom said he realised our son had killed the teacher as soon as he found her body. Said he suspected Bruno would do something sooner or later, but never expected it would be this.

I guess I feel a little of the guilt someone is meant to feel when they falsely accuse someone of having an affair. I'm packing up. I can't face Ros. She has done nothing wrong; it's me who has. I will miss the birds, so terribly, but the eggs are safely cocooned in my rucksack, wrapped in old T-shirts and such. An advert for the sale of the caravan park is coming out at the estate agents in the next few days. Makes me feel a little mournful, the thought of the *Fran's Holiday Vans* sign being pulled down, replaced with another name, another face. I wonder if they will love the birds too, if they will use my hide. I guess I want it to go to some use.

The Romany are on the move at the same time; I'm not sure if the police told them to leave or not. I heard them in the middle of the night, heard the engines starting, stuck my head out of the window to get a good look. I've seen Tad do that enough times, to stare at my conversations with Ros. I notice now that the field is spotless, only some marks left where the wheels had rested these past few months. Imagine living somewhere for such a time, where so much has happened, only to leave barely a trace.

My door raps with a sudden noise, the sound making me jump out of my skin. When I pull the door open, wearing only my nightgown over my jeans, half dressed, it is Ellis. His hair is longer, the front still swept across his eyes. I can see his navy irises, just about. His long lashes, the look of smudged eyeliner. A *New Romantic* from the eighties. I am fumbling for something to say.

'Hi, Fran. Long time no see. Can we have a chat?'

I am gulping down the sudden excess of saliva, but waft my hand to my side, offering him entrance to the caravan. It's a bit of a mess, clothes strewn on different piles on either side. The cigarettes I've started smoking lie abandoned in a makeshift ashtray – a china saucer.

'I know you're putting the park up for sale, so I'll be moving on too. I guess Ros will need to find somewhere for her and Sadie to live at the same time. Wanted to say thanks for letting us stay for so long. And for paying for my rehab course. I'm actually not drinking again, you know. Not since I've been gone.'

I nod, smile, lean against one of the kitchen cabinets. 'Where the hell had you been all that time?' It's worth me trying to steer the conversation in the other direction. 'Ros had been worried bloody sick.'

He runs a hand through his hair, his habitual trait, and leans against the fridge opposite me. I see it tilt a little under his weight. 'I had to get away. I'm sorry. I guess I was freaked out by the thought of being looked after by you and Dom. I know you were being kind with the offer of letting me stay.'

I am nodding again. I understand, of course I do. It would have been too close. I want to ask why he chose now to return.

As if reading my thoughts, he says, 'I couldn't keep away much longer. I needed to see Sadie. Missed her like crazy. And, well… you know… I saw the papers. I wanted to clear my name, I suppose.'

There's a pause where neither of us speaks.

'I've nothing against you.'

'I know,' I am saying, lightly. I wonder when the police released him. Must have been as soon as they got the DNA results of Tad and Charlie's fingerprints.

'It's just too difficult. And I know I should have stayed with Ros and Sadie, but they are so… It's all so emotionally draining.'

I turn, open the bottle of wine on the counter, pull two glasses out of the skinny dishwasher. At first, he shakes his head, but seconds later, he is accepting the glass from my hand.

I know I should tell him what Bruno has done. The words don't sit right in my head. I want to get them out. I haven't spoken to my son since it came to light, since I accepted it. I'm going to have to tell Ellis. But not now. Please, not now.

The wine is sloshing into my empty stomach; it will be only moments until my legs begin to grow heavier.

'We're going to have to tell Dom,' he suggests.

I know he can't be talking about the murder. Not looking up at him, I just stare into my glass. I can feel the wine puddling in my stomach, try to focus on that, pretend to be clueless as to what he's talking about.

'Fran, it's time to tell Dom. Plus, me and your sister, we are over.'

I walk over to the window in the kitchen, push it open. I rethink the words I found in that diary. About what I thought Ellis had done, how *she* apparently could never look at him in the same way. *But now he's been proven innocent of the murder.* The heat today has been unbearable, it just adds to my mental confusion. From where I'm standing, I can see the rucksack I've prepared, ready on the floor near the doorway of my bedroom. All my belongings in one bag, minus the clothes I haven't yet packed. But the most important things are in there, nestled between two small towels, old T-shirts. My almost-children, the sacred tern eggs.

'You know the reason Sadie's been funny?'

It's a question I wasn't expecting; I am rudely startled from my thoughts of the eggs in the bag, the words from the diary. 'What?'

He is rubbing at his dark stubble, swilling the wine around in his glass, staring hard at it. It's left a slight red stain around the rim where he's been drinking. 'Come on. She told me you were nice to her recently, took her to the supermarket to get her food. She knows you were feeling extra protective of her.'

'I felt so sad for her; I have done for a while now. They had no food in the van. I wanted to take her shopping.'

'She said she just couldn't keep pretending that she didn't know.'

I decide to sit down at the table, my legs are losing feeling slightly, they're leaden, weighted. 'What are you on about?'

'She knows, Sadie knows.' There's a pause as I let my tongue root around, poking every tooth in my mouth. One of them has a crack in it; I can force my tongue into the slight gap.

'She told Bruno. And she told the bloody teacher. I guess she just needed to confide in someone.'

I feel sober, but I'm shaking. It's all trying to pull together, piece by piece, in my foggy brain. A jigsaw puzzle that I've been reluctant to complete. Bruno, my child, killing the teacher. I'm still struggling to find a motive.

'If you're leaving, Fran, I want you to leave Bruno here.'

I stand, dump my glass on the side, make my way towards the rucksack. I glance at the key dangling in the lock. I could grab it, go fetch my son from Dom's caravan, leave right now. But I don't. I don't know how to talk to the boy now.

Ellis has seen me look at the key, shifts his body in front of the door. 'You're not going anywhere.'

Instead of feeling threatened, I feel attracted. Like years ago. I try to swallow down the feelings, look down, anywhere that isn't into his face.

'Fran, you need to leave, and you need to leave on your own, not with Bruno. Leave my son with me.'

The world stops for a little bit, seconds not turning into minutes, the stars in the sky static. He guides me by the shoulder back to the padded bench, supports me as I try to sit down.

'The teacher knew that Sadie and Bruno were half-brother and half-sister,' he says, in a soft voice, but deep, so deep that again I can barely make out the words. 'I wonder if she was planning on spreading that information around.'

I am gulping at my wine; he pulls the glass away, back onto the table. 'Leave the drink,' he says, in an authoritative voice I don't think I've heard before.

A silence sits between us for a minute, perhaps two. My mind wanders to Bruno, his intentions with the teacher, the reason that he killed her. He wouldn't have wanted that news to get out, that his cousin was really his sister. My mind casts itself back to before, Sadie's statement that she and Ms McConnell had been so *close* for the first few days of school starting. Close enough to talk about big things.

I sit up a little, cough. 'What about Dom? He'll go spare.'

'We can't leave Dom not knowing about you and me for the rest of his days. It isn't fair. I can tell him, if you prefer.'

I nod, somewhat gratefully. He hasn't said anything about Ros. Ros, my sister.

'And does she know? Ros?'

His turn to nod.

'She does?'

'She found out a while ago. Well, a few months back.'

'What? How?' I drop my head onto the table in front of me.

'She just felt indebted to you,' he continues, not answering my question. 'What with you paying for my rehab and giving us a free home. Like she couldn't say anything.'

I note the coolness of the table under my cheek, allow myself to think of Ros's indifference towards me in recent weeks, the smile that had disappeared from her face. She hadn't seemed like my sister anymore. And I had just assumed it had been from the struggle of having no money and a drinking, disappearing man for a partner.

'How did Sadie even find out? Was she OK with you?'

He answers my second question straightaway. 'She was horrid to me when she did discover it. That's really the reason I went away, in the end. I guess it's difficult to find out that your cousin is actually your brother. Half-brother, anyway.'

I lift my head slightly from the table, feel his arm around my shoulders. I am still not crying. I'm dried out, all emotion having left me hours ago. I can't believe that my sister had tried so hard to treat me almost normally since finding out. I am not worthy of her love. 'It's affected all of us, you know. Eleven, twelve years of lying. I couldn't even let myself draw, paint. The guilt at feeling joy.' I stare at my wine glass, waves of nausea taking over. 'Tell me how Sadie knew. And Ros.'

His mouth twists into a bit of a smirk, and for a moment I think he is laughing at me. 'Bet you never thought a man would keep a diary, right? Rookie bloody mistake.'

I try to remain poker-faced, think again suddenly of the words I read that day in his caravan. 'They both read the diary you kept?'

'No. Only Sadie. I guess she then told her mum.'

My weak laugh of disbelief turns into a groan, and then my stomach is heaving, the wine trying to come back up.

'Why don't you just stay here in your van tonight, leave in the morning?' He seems to have gained authority since he entered my caravan tonight.

'But… we don't know that Bruno will want to be with you! He might want to stay with Dom.'

Ellis shrugs, and I notice his wide shoulders, want him to wrap his giant arms around me.

'That's the risk I take,' he says.

248

He stands and stretches, elbows nearly touching the ceiling of the caravan. We don't say goodbye, I just watch him make his way out of the door, see it close and then I take myself to bed. On the floor of my room, by the bin, is a pair of Bruno's screwed-up pyjama bottoms. I lift them up, cram them to the bottom of the bin. As I climb into bed, I listen to the gulls swooping and windmilling in the sky, the clatter of their feet as they land on nearby caravans. The sea is loud tonight, pulling towards land with more angst than usual, crashing onto the shore. I picture the little tern, looking for her nest, cocking her head to one side, wondering who would take her babies.

# TAD

They've probably been on the move three, maybe four days now. I don't know where they'll end up, but a couple of weeks ago one of my sisters got a tipoff that there's land over in Essex. It's not that far from here, and they've settled there before. I still don't know if it was worth it, moving the whole family of ours to the coast so Eve could take up that bloody teaching job of hers. I know she was worried that she wouldn't have found a job so close to our last place, not with the police sniffing around Charlie. I suppose I'm glad she got to live her dream of teaching, if only for a little while. I know Charlie was so proud.

*

I spend most of my days in my cell. Sometimes I cry. I won't live to see another day out of this place. I do know that Jade will visit me every Sunday, and to be honest, that is all that is keeping me going. I find myself wondering who will look out for her, now that I'm gone. I'm hoping it'll be Mandy, or one of the other women from the camp. None of the other men are like my brother; they wouldn't know how to treat her, give her the things she needs.

Things aren't quite the same without Charlie. I thought we would have been put in the same prison, the same block. I had wanted to be with him. But we're separated. Different towns. I find I am almost wishing my days away; I won't see him again now. Sometimes my eyes are just on the clock, watching the seconds ticking by. I often wonder how many days I have left. Should probably stop the smoking, but don't care enough to try.

There's a little window in this room, barred, but I can strain my neck from my bed, or I can try to stand on the chair, and sometimes I'll catch sight of a tiny little sparrow or a robin, making its way past. I think there must be a nest nearby, perhaps tucked into a ledge or a chimney, if there is such a thing on these buildings. If one should fly past, I will be able to tell a herring gull from a tern. Charlie taught me those birds. Well, some of them. I suppose Fran told me about some of the others – that a jay is shy yet still a menace, not unlike its cousin, the magpie. I will always know my pied wagtail, its presence signalling where there's good luck to be found. I won't need the people here, their interrogations, their interfering. I think I will only need the little finches, the gulls that still swoop by overhead, screeching out in earnest for their next meal.

You've always got to listen to the birds.

# Acknowledgements

I would like to thank my family: Jimbo and my kids – Tilly, Felix and Raffy. I wouldn't have been able to write the first draft (or make the subsequent revisions) if Jimbo hadn't towed Raffy over to Wales every school holiday so I could do so.

Next, I would like to thank my editor Jenna at VERVE Books, and the rest of the team there, for the support and ideas, for helping so much with the edits and for loving *Bird Spotting* in the first place! I'm so glad that you took on me and my book.

I would also like to thank my agent, Bill Goodall, for his patience and guidance, and for his support over the period of bringing *Bird Spotting* to publication.

Credit must be given to Damian Le Bas' book, *The Stopping Places*, where I gleaned the information about the Romany community presented in my novel (all things animal and relating to wagtails).

Thank you to Sophie Hannah, Midge Gillies and everyone on the master's degree at Cambridge University. This includes my friend Tracey Morton, as well as Eliza, Relly, Tera, Jonathan, Susan, Andrew, Phoenix, Sarah, Anne, Kate, Pam, Kim, Marcia and Jo, for listening to my early pieces in the workshops. Thanks to my tutor, Jane Robins, too.

Thanks Lisa, Charlotte, Kemi, Yvonne, Carol, Alyson, Felicity and Matt W, and my in-laws for the enthusiasm. Special thanks to Stewart McDowell for almost-daily listening and for being my sounding board.

Mel, thank you for the cider and chips at our semi-regular meet-ups and for taking my mind off The Book.

And thanks to my mum for buying me all the Enid Blyton and Point Horror books when I was younger (and a copy of *Rebecca*), which basically served as my inspiration, as well as the *Spotting Birds* handbook from my dad

# About the Author

Author Photo: Matilda Meredith

Sophie Morton-Thomas was born in West Sussex and has always loved reading and writing – she had about ten penfriends as a child. She is now an English teacher as well as a mum to three (two grown-up!) children and two cats. Her first novel, *Travel by Night*, was published by darkstroke, an imprint of Crooked Cat Books, and was a #1 Bestseller across multiple Amazon Kindle categories. She is a graduate of the University of Cambridge's Crime and Thriller Writing master's degree and recently moved to the coast for work – but also for inspiration for her stories!

**vervebooks.co.uk/sophie-morton-thomas**
**sophiemortonthomas.com**
**@sophiemorton_thomas**

# Book Club Questions

1) Why does Fran take so much pleasure in bird spotting? Why are the tern's eggs so important to her? Do they represent something else?

2) How reliable do you think Fran's narrative is – particularly her portrayal of Dom, but also Ros and Ellis? To what extent do you think she projects her own feelings onto Dom? Do you think she has a strong sense of self and a solid grasp on her reality?

3) There are several different parent-child relationship models within the book. Discuss their similarities and differences. Do any work well?

4) Is Sadie a bad influence on Bruno? Or is this just Fran and Dom's perception of what's happening?

5) What is it about Ms McConnell that bothers the playground parents so much? Do you think the rumours about her are true? Or is there another reason for the parents' discomfort?

6) Is Tad's narrative just as unreliable as Fran's? Think about his storytelling style and the way he characterises himself.

7) Do you think Fran and her family display prejudice, consciously or unconsciously, towards the Romany community? How does the depiction of Romany characters in this novel compare to other representations in literature?

8) What does Sadie's friendship with Jade tell us about each girl's character?

9) How much of the intrigue and tension within this novel is due to the coastal small-town setting?

10) Do you think Tad and Charlie do the right thing in the end? How do you think what they have done will impact Bruno and his family? And their own community? Do you think this is the final outcome, or will the truth come out?

# VERVE BOOKS

Launched in 2018, VERVE Books is an independent publisher of page-turning, diverse and original fiction from fresh and impactful voices.

Our books are connected by rich storytelling, vividly imagined settings and unforgettable characters. The list is tightly curated by a small team of passionate booklovers whose hope is that if you love one VERVE book, you'll love them all!

## WANT TO JOIN THE CONVERSATION AND FIND OUT MORE ABOUT WHAT WE DO?

Catch us on social media or sign up to our newsletter for all the latest news from VERVE HQ.

**vervebooks.co.uk/signup**

📷 f 𝕏 ♪ **@VERVE_Books**